Dear Jen,
I hope you
to the tt
Best Wishes,
Tina-Marie
xoxx!

Everything Happens
for a Reason

TINA-MARIE MILLER

MUM AND DAD

Love is eternal xxx

CONTENTS

ACKNOWLEDGMENTS

I have received so much support whilst writing this debut novel, particularly from my family who have been super amazing.

I give my thanks to my beautiful daughter Alexandra who is such an inspiration to me. Her unending support and encouragement has been immeasurable as well as being my forever sounding board.

I give my thanks also to Chris and Maximilian for their patience and support and for helping me to create and build an online presence.

I have been overwhelmed by the remarkable warm welcome I have received from the writing community on Twitter and Facebook who are incredible and generous in their support.

I would like to give my thanks to Nico J. Genes who, despite knowing for just a short time has been a great source of encouragement and help, particularly with this cover revision.

Finally, I give my thanks to you, the reader. I hope you enjoy my debut novel and I welcome your valuable feedback either directly on Amazon or through social media as detailed below.

I would also like to acknowledge the amazing help and support of the following:

Edited by:

Jessica Grace Coleman www.colemanediting.co.uk

Cover Art by:

Shari Ryan www.madhatcovers.com

Connect with me:

Facebook www.facebook.com/tinseymiller/

Twitter @tinseymiller

ONE

Poppy was running late. She really shouldn't have shared that second bottle of red with Orla last night, she reflected as she got ready. Still, if she skipped breakfast she was certain she'd make the office in time, and having to swing by the printers beforehand had now turned out to be a blessing in disguise.

After checking her appearance in the fading antique mirror propped against her bedroom door, she called out a quick 'bye' to Orla before rushing off to the tube station, eager to reach the office before Greg. She certainly did *not* want to be late for Greg Sable.

Greg Sable was the CEO (as well as being the major shareholder) of Hawkins, Monroe and Sable investment stockbrokers, and as Poppy entered the station, she recalled with amusement his story of how he'd first met the other partners, Dom Hawkins and Alfie Monroe.

Having just flown to the UK from Canada, Greg had arrived at his aunt's house in the middle of Oxford late at night, ready to start his first year at university. Clambering out of a taxi, feeling rather crumpled and exhausted, his attention was drawn towards two men who were struggling to fit a rather large television into the back of a waiting van. Greg being Greg was only too happy to assist the struggling duo, who thanked him profusely before fleeing the scene at an alarming rate. Feeling extremely satisfied with his good deed as he watched the van disappear into the night, Greg was suddenly alerted to a succession of shouts.

Greg stood transfixed as two figures ran towards him along the now deserted streets, frantically waving their arms and not looking very impressed at all. Greg was later to realise — to his absolute horror — that the two men he'd been helping had in fact just stolen the television from Dom and Alfie's apartment! No wonder they hadn't looked impressed.

Fortune seemed to be favouring Poppy as she discovered an empty seat on the tube; quite a rarity for this time of the morning. She sank down into the firm yet welcoming rich, moquette seating, ignoring the envious glares of the standing travellers as the carriage trundled through the maze of underground tunnels towards Russell Square, gently rocking her from side to side. She'd been in the city barely three months and she'd never been happier. She had a great job, a great boss, and her very own flat... well, not *quite* her own just yet.

She'd done a lot of growing up these past few years; she'd had to. Staring at the floor of the carriage, tears pricked her eyes as she recalled that fateful Saturday when her life had changed forever.

The day had started out so well too, with her mother Grace cooking her and her best friend Sally a hearty breakfast before waving them both off for their fun-filled spa weekend in the Cotswolds. They'd only been at the hotel a couple of hours when her father had called, the devastation in his voice lingering in her memory even now, drifting around her mind like a fallen butterfly. Losing her mother so suddenly...

Poppy shook her head, trying not to let her mind wander too far in that devastating direction. If it hadn't been for Sally's guidance and support back then, she certainly wouldn't be where she was now. Sally was, undoubtedly, *the* best friend *ever*.

Her thoughts were abruptly torn from her mind as she noticed the carriage approaching her destination, and jumping up, she prepared to do battle with the other commuters. The moment she arose she was swamped with passengers wanting to secure the prized vacancy, which was swiftly won by a slender, statuesque woman who slinked into position like a mature cat that had unashamedly got the fresh cream. She also had the self-satisfied smirk to boot.

Rush hour. What fun.

Poppy made her way from the tube station to the printers as quickly as possible. She had to collect the mock-ups for the new company brochure that Greg had ordered for the forthcoming Hawkins, Monroe and Sable annual conference. Taking a quick glance to ensure everything was in order, she decided that if she took a cab she could just about arrive at the office by 9 a.m.

Stepping outside she waved her arm, relief sweeping through her as a black taxi came to a halt right beside her. She was just about to open the door, however, when she was jolted sideways – like a child knocked over by bracing sea waves – and all she could do was watch with her mouth open as, quick as a flash, some ignorant fool cheekily pushed her aside and jumped into the now stationary cab, leaving her stranded on the pavement. *Honestly!*

Rather than wasting time scowling after *Mr. Rude*, she set about finding another cab and was – thankfully – soon on her way. But hey, this was life in the city, after all: fast, competitive, ruthless, and... *fun.*

TWO

Poppy settled back into the soft, leather upholstery of the car, very much appreciative of Greg's offer to drive them both rather than having to battle with the train. They were on their way to a conference, and hosting it was her opportunity to shine – she was determined to grab it with both hands.

They discussed the two-day itinerary, with Greg making slight tweaks to the plan every now and then. For one thing, there was to be a Gala dinner that evening, which he'd asked her to attend, even placing her at his distinguished table. She was rather apprehensive about this; after all, there was going to be a number of blue-chip clients there whom she'd have to try and impress.

And, on top of everything else, she knew that the conference (and thus her organisational skills) would be compared to last year's event, which had been organised by Dom's PA, Amanda, and which everyone had noted to be a resounding success. Poppy, on the other hand, still had a lot to learn; getting to grips with the ins and outs of the business was a complex and demanding task, and she silently prayed that nothing would happen to make her seem like a frivolous idiot.

Already, some of her friends were asking her for investment advice just because she now worked for one of the largest stockbroking firms in London. She was a PA, for God's sake, not Head of Global Equities!

From the driver's seat Greg glanced at her knowingly, as if he were reading her thoughts. 'Are you looking forward to the dinner?' he asked, raising his eyebrows.

She bit the edge of her lip. 'I'm a bit nervous, in all honesty. There's a lot more interaction at a dinner compared to greeting someone at the office.'

He smiled reassuringly. 'No need to worry. You've met most of the major players already – and they've nothing but compliments for you. These guys just expect you to be professional, and you always are.'

'I just hope no one asks my advice on what to invest in,' Poppy replied, only half-joking.

'Oh, just say gold. That's what I always tell 'em,' Greg quipped back, his smile turning into a laugh.

Poppy laughed too, his light-heartedness helping her relax. Perhaps it wouldn't be so bad after all.

*

'I see you've got your hands full!'

Poppy had been so focused on making up the press packs that she hadn't even noticed anyone approach, and when she looked up, she was momentarily taken aback to find herself gazing into the bluest eyes she'd ever seen – eyes that seemed to be twinkling at her. Who was this guy?

As Poppy soaked up the image of the handsome stranger standing in front of her, however, her face fell as recognition set in, and she could feel her cheeks begin to burn with raging horror, something she feared didn't go unnoticed by the arrogant man looking down at her.

Well, well, if it isn't Mr. Rude.

Clearly oblivious to their previous altercation, he offered his hand to her in introduction, smiling teasingly. 'Oliver Sullivan. Very pleased to meet you.'

Poppy politely accepted the outstretched hand, sensing a tiny tingle of excitement as their hands touched. His grip was firm and he held on for just a second or two longer than was necessary.

'Are you part of the Hawkins, Monroe and Sable team?' he asked, that teasing smile still lingering on his lips.

'I work as PA to Greg, actually,' Poppy explained.

'Ah! So you're the new *hotshot* PA, eh? I've heard great things about you – all decent, I promise.' He held his hands up in mock surrender, and despite what had happened earlier, she couldn't help but laugh a little. 'I'm here for the conference. Am I too late for the next seminar?'

'Not at all,' Poppy replied, smiling back at him. 'I'll show you where the meeting room is.'

He followed behind as she led him towards the meeting room, watching patiently as she discreetly opened the door. After peering into the room, Poppy swiftly stepped aside, allowing him to enter – all whilst trying her best not to disturb the seminar that was in full swing inside.

'Hope to see you later,' he whispered as he passed by, causing her to blush again; she could feel her face turning red.

After gently closing the door behind him, Poppy took a deep breath. *What a cheeky so-and-so!* But secretly she'd quite enjoyed the attention – and who wouldn't? After all, he was certainly more than easy on the eye, and even though he seemed a bit of a charmer – *and* even though he'd previously stolen her cab – he'd certainly ruffled her feathers. And it had been a long time since anyone had done that. A long time indeed.

You'd better watch yourself, Poppy Jackson. She giggled to herself before thinking, *I should be so lucky.*

Rather reluctantly, she returned her focus to the press packs.

*

Later that afternoon, Poppy re-joined the seminar and couldn't resist sneaking little glances in Oliver Sullivan's direction, taking in his tall, slim build and his strong, chiselled jaw. He certainly was very handsome, and his short dark hair – which was cut into a French crop – suited him perfectly. As she stood there, she also admired his suit – bespoke, she guessed. And therefore expensive. Navy, coordinated with a lavender-coloured shirt and matching tie.

She was still quietly commending and analysing his appearance when he unexpectedly turned and looked at her – straight in the eye. A grin momentarily played on his lips before impertinently winking at her again.

Horrified to have been caught out so obviously, Poppy blushed again, this time turning redder than a beetroot. What was even worse, however, was the thought that Greg might have seen it too. How unprofessional.

What ARE you doing? Get a grip, Poppy Jackson.

She pinched herself several times on her inner wrist in an attempt to bring her concentration back to the seminar, and it seemed to work. For now.

It was no surprise, however, that as the meeting drew to a close, she started to grow increasingly anxious – particularly when Greg sought her out. She was expecting the worst, but to her unending relief, he appeared oblivious to the fact that his PA had suddenly become a man-hungry predator.

'Great meeting, Poppy. We've certainly generated a lot of interest!'

Poppy nodded, smiling politely. This had been the last seminar of the day, and quite a lengthy one too; some of the delegates looked exhausted, and were now making their way to the bar.

'I like how you arranged for the room to be set out; it brought everyone together.'

'Thanks, Greg,' Poppy replied, 'I got the idea from Amanda.'

'Really? It's good to hear that you PA's get together and share tips.'

She laughed; he made them sound like a knitting circle, which honestly couldn't be further from the truth.

Greg had just started discussing the evening's dinner arrangements when he stopped mid-sentence, his eyes widening in surprise. 'Good heavens, it's Oliver Sullivan!'

Oliver stepped forward – seemingly out of nowhere – to grasp Greg's outstretched hand. 'Hi Greg, great to see you,' he said in that low, charming voice of his.

It appeared, much to Poppy's absolute surprise – and discomfort – that these two knew each other. When he'd mentioned Poppy being the 'hotshot PA' before, she'd just assumed he knew Greg in a business capacity, but they actually seemed to be friends.

She waited politely whilst the two men exchanged pleasantries, and then Greg turned to introduce her. 'Oliver, you must meet Poppy, my PA.'

'Oh, I've had that pleasure already,' he exclaimed, grinning.

Poppy cringed, inwardly apoplectic at what he might say next. She just hoped it wouldn't be along the lines of: *'actually, I caught her checking me out several times during the meeting, with a somewhat hungry look on her face. Haven't you fed her lately, Greg?'*

No, that wouldn't do at all. She looked at Oliver, almost

squawking with anticipation.

'Poppy kindly directed me to the correct meeting room earlier,' he explained. 'I got held up, so I'm afraid I was a little late arriving.'

Greg nodded before asking, 'I take it you're joining us for dinner?'

Please say no. Please say no.

'Dinner?'

'Didn't you receive an invitation?' Greg asked, eyebrows raised.

Poppy and Greg exchanged quizzical looks. She certainly didn't recall an Oliver Sullivan being on the guest list, now she came to think of it.

'Er... well, you've got me there, Greg,' Oliver replied sheepishly. 'The invitation was actually addressed to Ed, but as he's away, I requisitioned it. Hope you don't mind?'

Greg laughed at his artfulness. 'Not at all. It's good to have you here, and besides, there's still time to join the dinner, isn't there, Poppy?'

'Absolutely,' she replied, while thinking to herself, *He can take my place.*

'It would be great for us to have a catch up first,' Greg thought out loud. 'How about we meet in the bar in what, 30 minutes?'

'Perfect,' said Oliver, holding his hand out again to Greg. 'I shall let Poppy organise me.'

Greg excused himself, eager to go in search of Alfie. He was particularly interested in this potential business opportunity and he needed more background information.

THREE

'Ah. Poppy.'

Greg approached, walking over from the dining room's side entrance. He'd chosen to wear a white tuxedo for the event, which drew attention to his muscular physique, as he well knew. At just over 6 feet tall and with neatly sleeked back, obsidian hair, his good looks turned many a head wherever he went – and tonight was no exception. Poppy, however, certainly had no designs where that was concerned. Besides, he only had eyes for one lady anyway, and that was his beloved wife, Marnie, whom Poppy had struck up quite a friendship with.

'You're looking very smart, Greg.'

'Thanks, you scrub up pretty well yourself.' He gave her a devilish wink. 'If you're not careful, someone might just sweep you off your feet tonight – looking like that.'

She grinned, certain that he was being more polite than anything else with his remarks – he always was. She'd chosen to wear the regulatory but elegant 'LBD', which clung exquisitely to her slim curves. Sophisticated, but not over the top. Eye-catching, but not *too* eye-catching.

'I really do want Oliver to sit at our table,' Greg blurted out as they looked over the seating plans again.

Attempting to appear unfazed upon hearing those words, Poppy cleared her throat and began searching for suitable options. 'I'm sure we can accommodate him,' she started, as an idea sprang to mind. 'The simplest option is for me to move to table seven, as that's now one short after Jonathan Bryant cancelled. Then we can just move Oliver into my seat.' She stepped back, pleased with her quick but simple resolution. Relieved, too.

'No, that's not ideal,' said Greg, frowning. 'I need you to get to know these clients better. You need to stay at my table.'

Poppy's heart sank. *So much for that idea.* 'Let's have another look then.' She perused the plan again. 'How about we move Harry Smithson to table six, place him next to Ian, and move Sarah Lambert to table seven? Then we can move Oliver to table one.'

'Now that makes better sense,' replied Greg, staring at the plan himself. 'Although, can we switch Ellie Bailey to where Harry would have been sitting? Then Oliver can sit next to me. I've got a good feeling about him and I want to keep our earlier discussions going.'

Realising that this also meant he would be sitting next to her, Poppy changed the seating plan rather apprehensively. For some reason, Oliver Sullivan seemed to bring down her defences and she was concerned that the good feeling Greg had about Oliver was different to the good feeling *she* was getting. At least, she hoped it was!

At that moment she found herself innocently wishing that some desperately urgent situation would arise which demanded her immediate attention, forcing her to rush off, her face etched with dramatic concern for all to see.

Sighing, she gave herself a reality check, sadness filling her heart as she recalled a time when she *had* received a desperately urgent call whilst staying at a hotel, one which had delivered the devastating news of her mother's passing. Feeling her eyes begin to smart with tears, she quickly blinked them back, with a cloud of remorse for her ignorant thoughts.

There wasn't a single day that went by when she didn't think of her dear mother. What on earth was she thinking of? She really didn't want to receive news like that *ever* again.

Glancing at her watch, she realised it was almost 7 p.m. Guests would start arriving promptly for pre-dinner drinks at any moment, so she went to join the waiting staff in the adjoining room, ready to hand out Champagne aperitifs. As she entered, Greg walked over and handed her a glass.

'Knowing you as I do...' He paused, giving her a look. 'I daresay you were just on your way to help hand out drinks rather than take one for yourself?'

She laughed, shrugging. 'You got me.'

'Tonight, I'd like *you* to be one of the guests for a change. You've worked damn hard since joining the company; it won't do you any harm to relax a little.' He smiled. 'You deserve it, Poppy.'

She accepted the proffered beverage with an appreciative smile, understanding exactly what he meant: relax, yes, but don't drop your guard completely. She knew better than to let that happen, though. *Didn't she?*

By now the room was beginning to fill up, everyone milling around and talking animatedly to each other. Most of the delegates tended to already know each other reasonably well at events like this. In fact, it was a measure of success as to how many of the big players actually turned up. Time was money, after all, and these people were ruthless with both. Naturally, they had an obligation to be, given the huge financial responsibilities placed upon them. Therefore, unless it was certain there was something worthwhile to be gained, most didn't bother attending. However, Poppy had quietly yet proudly noted that there was a significant turn out to this conference, more so than she'd seen at any others. *No doubt the recently reported half-year earnings had something to do with it.*

This lingering thought reminded her that both Alfie and Dom were joining the dinner, so she headed off to reception to check that their rooms were ready. No matter what Greg said, she couldn't just stand around drinking champagne all night.

Incidentally, she encountered Alfie on the way, and he greeted her warmly. 'Hello Poppy. You look gorgeous, as always.'

Poppy was fond of Alfie – he was such a gentleman, and he was always impeccably dressed, no matter what the occasion. She admired his immaculate black dinner suit and crisp, white shirt, complete with a faultlessly placed bow-tie. At only 5 feet tall, he might not have been the tallest of men, but he was certainly amongst the smartest and he didn't suffer fools gladly.

'Hello Alfie, it's good to see you. How was your journey?' she asked politely.

'Not too bad actually. Has Dom arrived yet?'

'I haven't seen him, but I was just on my way to reception to check that your rooms are all in order.'

'Oh, you're a star. You do look after us all so well.' He patted her on the shoulder. 'I've checked in already, thanks, and I must compliment you on the choice of venue; it's a most impressive hotel and I've been given quite a stunning room, too. In fact, it's quite a shame there isn't anyone here to enjoy it with me; I think they'd love the four-poster bed.'

He gave her a knowing wink, making her almost baulk with surprise. Usually, Alfie was quite a closed book, and seeing him out of the office environment and in such a relaxed manner stunned her immensely. It was strange, but nice.

'Come on *you*,' she chided, playfully. 'Follow me – I'll show you where the drinks are being served.'

As they walked towards St. Benedict Refectory – where the dinner was being held – Poppy was able to appreciate exactly what Alfie had meant about the hotel. *Friars Retreat* wasn't a venue she'd used before, but she was glad she'd used it this time. It was elegant and opulent – a stunning converted monastery that claimed to have been *'welcoming travellers to Worcester since the 16th Century'*. The hotel had undergone an element of refurbishment, but it still retained most of its unique period features, and it invited the image of long-suffering romanticists scribbling into the night, huddled under a flickering candle flame. The rich, dark wood panelling throughout the hotel further added to its ambience and mystery. Poppy loved it.

She just hoped everyone else would too.

A moment after they'd joined the other guests, Poppy saw one of the hotel managers approach Greg, speaking to him discreetly. The manager then hastily rushed off, and excusing herself, Poppy ran after him.

'Everything alright, Angus?'

'There's an urgent call for Mr. Sable,' he explained.

'Oh? Do you know who it is?'

'No, 'fraid not – reception just asked me to pass the message on.'

She thanked him before heading towards reception, mentally noting how odd it was that they hadn't put the call through to the meeting room.

When she got to reception, it took her a while to find Greg – quite a few people were milling about, and he was in the corner, using one of the heavy-looking guest telephones.

Watching him, Poppy hesitated, unsure as to whether she should approach him or not. A moment later he placed his hand on his head, as though in disbelief. Clearly, something wasn't right. When he ended the call, he stood there for a brief moment – deep in thought –

and then he looked up sharply, immediately catching her eye.

'Poppy, thank goodness. I need to leave right away; there's been an accident.'

For a split second she was taken aback, thinking yet again of that fateful day when she'd got the call about her mother. What was he saying? A flickering thought ran through her mind. *Oh, no. Not my father... surely not...*

'Poppy!' Greg's voice cut into her thoughts, claiming her attention. 'It's Marnie and the children; they've been involved in an accident. I need to get to the hospital *now*.'

'Oh my God,' she said, before she even realised she was going to say it. Her thoughts were flying all over the place. 'Are they okay? Is anyone badly injured?'

'I don't have much to go on at the moment, which is why I need to get there *quickly*.'

'Yes, yes of course – I'll organise a car right away. Which hospital are they in?' She was back in PA mode, trying to focus on what she needed to do and not *why* she needed to do it.

'The Royal Surrey.' He ran his hand through his hair, making it stick up awkwardly. 'I need to grab a few things from my room; can you arrange for the rest of my belongings to be packed up for me?'

'It's fine, don't worry about it; let's just get you on your way.'

Thankfully, due to past experiences, she often placed a car on standby for such events, and she had one waiting right now. There were always the late arrivals, the slightly inebriated and, as today proved, the utterly unexpected.

She made a quick call, the car arriving at the front entrance just minutes later. Poppy hurried out to brief the driver, and soon after, Greg appeared.

'Listen Poppy, you need to tell Alfie and Dom what's going on, but only brief them – no one else, okay? After today's success we don't want anyone thinking that we're losing control.'

She nodded her acknowledgement.

Halfway into the car he stopped abruptly, attempting to gather his thoughts together. 'Damn. I forgot about Oliver.'

Even just the mention of Oliver's name made her shiver, but she just nodded politely.

'Might you explain that I've had an urgent family matter come up and that I'll call him when I can?'

She nodded again, before babbling earnestly, 'I really do hope everyone is alright, Greg. Please give all of them my love.'

He patted her shoulder fondly, appreciating her sincerity. Marnie and the kids were truly fond of Poppy, he knew. 'As soon as I know anything, I'll call you, okay?'

With that he got into the car, shutting the door with a strained effort. And then he was gone.

She stood there for a few moments, utterly stupefied at how everything had developed so quickly. Her thoughts went out to Marnie and the children as she silently prayed they would all be okay. Having met up with them on several occasions now, Poppy adored them all – especially little Louisa. In fact, just a fortnight ago they'd had a wonderful time playing games when she'd been invited to join them for dinner at their Surrey home. Later in the evening, when the children were safely in bed and she and Marnie were chatting away like old friends, Poppy realised just how much she'd missed having a girlfriend around.

Of course there was Sally, but they hardly saw each other now that Poppy lived in London, and then there was Orla – her flatmate – but as much as she loved her gentle ways and sing-song Irish voice, Orla was far more interested in her boyfriend, Frank, than spending any quality time with Poppy. She sighed.

Then, suddenly, Poppy recalled her thoughts from earlier in the day, making her gasp. Hadn't she'd wished for an urgent drama to appear, enabling her to escape tonight's dinner? Completely horrified at having harboured such thoughts – which had now become reality – her hand flew to her mouth in an effort to stifle the sob that was currently rising in her throat. Of course, she knew it wasn't her fault really, but that didn't stop the small feeling of guilt from blossoming deep in her gut.

Ironically, she'd only had those thoughts because she'd wished to avoid Oliver Sullivan, and now it looked like she was going to have to spend the evening entertaining him anyway – and without Greg as a buffer!

How did this happen?

FOUR

'Poppy!'
Recognising Dom's unmistakeable voice, she promptly blinked back the tears that were threatening to spill over at any moment, took a deep breath, and smiled.

Dom was one of the few people she'd ever met who could put a person through so many emotions in such a short space of time. He was a perfect charmer, too. Not quite as tall as Greg – but certainly taller than Alfie – he had the enchanting boyish good looks that many men aspire to; blond hair with huge floppy curls and a wide, cheeky smile. At 45, he was the youngest of the founding members of Hawkins, Monroe and Sable, but this didn't detract whatsoever from his skill set. He may have liked to act as a bit of a 'jack-the-lad', but Poppy knew he was in fact a very astute and ruthless individual.

'Are you waiting for me, sweetheart?' he called out impishly as he approached her.

'Sorry to disappoint you, but I was just seeing Greg off.'

Dom frowned. 'Off? Surely you mean *in*?'

'I wish that was the case,' sighed Poppy. 'It seems that Marnie and the children have been involved in an accident and Greg's had to rush off. I... I don't know any more than that. He received a telephone call – the local police, I think – and then... Well, he's obviously gone straight to the hospital.'

Realising how upset Poppy was, Dom promptly set his case on the floor, putting his arms around her in a friendly, comforting manner. He knew that she'd become close friends with Marnie.

'Listen, I know you're worried, but let's wait to hear more from Greg,' he said eventually, his voice full of genuine concern.

Poppy's bottom lip trembled involuntarily as she failed to fully compose herself. 'He... er, Greg wanted me to tell you and Alfie, although he doesn't want a fuss made. You know, in case people think we're not in control.'

Despite everything, Dom laughed. 'Greg worries *far* too much about what other people think. Then again, I guess that's what makes him so successful, eh?' He grinned at Poppy, trying to lighten the mood. 'Come on, let's get you inside and we'll find Alfie. We can bring him up to speed on what's going on and then decide what we're going to tell our guests.'

He picked up his case, guiding her back to reception where he checked in, requesting that his luggage be taken directly to his room. Fortunately, he'd already dressed for the evening, so they were able to make their way quickly over to the guests.

Poppy soon spotted Alfie, who was listening intently to a group conversation. The concerned murmurs, she noted, must have been down to a discussion of the potential stock fraud relating to a well-known senior investor. The whole city appeared to have been talking about it lately but, as yet, factual details remained limited.

'Dom!' shouted Alfie, distracted by his partner's arrival. He greeted him warmly, with a hand shake and a pat on the back.

'Sorry, Alfie – I didn't mean to interrupt, but I just wanted a quick word before dinner, if that's okay?' Dom smiled at the others in the group, nodding at them in greeting.

'Of course.'

Alfie excused himself before following Dom into a more private alcove area, which was located at the back of the room. Poppy joined them.

A few minutes later, having put Alfie in the picture, they all concurred that he would be the most suitable person to take over Greg's place at dinner. This was mostly down to his connection with Oliver, but it was also due to the fact that he could reputably charm the likes of Greeta D'Angelo – a woman whose voice made Dom inwardly shake. Dom was to present Greg's speech in his absence – he'd written most of it anyway – and this left Ian Ellis, Dom's Head of Private Investors, to take over Alfie's role.

Poppy rushed off to make the last minute changes to the seating plan, then gave the banquet manager the nod to call the guests through.

Once everyone was seated, Alfie stood up, carefully but firmly tapping his glass to attract the guests' attention. 'Good evening, ladies and gentleman – can you hear me okay at the back?'

'We can hear you, but we can't *see* you too well!'

An eruption of laughter danced through the room at Harry Smithson's quip. He was, of course, referring to Alfie's small frame.

Alfie grinned playfully – taking the taunt in his stride as usual – before promptly delivering Greg's apologies at not being able to join them this evening. Poppy knew that it was imperative to move on before the guests had too much time to digest the information, and Alfie acted upon that same conviction.

'On behalf of the Hawkins, Monroe and Sable team,' he continued, 'we'd like to welcome you all to this evening's dinner, and to thank you for attending the day's seminars, which we trust have whetted your appetites. The aim of this evening is not only to celebrate our recent success, but also to introduce you to the investment services and analysis that we're now able to make available to our clients.' He glanced around the room, smiling. 'I'm pleased to say that this has already placed us far out in front of most of our top competitors. You'll learn more about this throughout the evening – and tomorrow – but for now, please enjoy the dinner and presentations. Dom and I very much look forward to having an opportunity to talk to each of you as the evening progresses.'

With that, he thanked everyone for listening, raising his glass and smiling widely.

Everyone gave him a round of applause, and then it was time for the first course to be served.

*

'I must have been a *very* good boy today.'

Poppy could feel the hairs on the back of her neck begin to rise. So far, she'd been busy making pleasantries with the other guests seated at their table, and successfully managing to avoid *Mr. Rude* save for a polite but impassive 'good evening, good to see you'. She desperately wanted to ignore him but she knew that she couldn't – it wouldn't exactly be very professional. More frustratingly, there was also a part of her that didn't wish to neglect him at all. And besides, she had to deliver Greg's message, didn't she?

Turning to face Oliver, she eyed him curiously. 'What do you mean?'

Oliver smiled. 'Well, I didn't expect to be sitting next to the most beautiful woman in the room, so I assumed that it must be because I've been such a good boy today.' He looked her straight in the eyes as he spoke, the small smile playing on his lips causing her to blush.

She dipped her head; she wasn't used to this (especially not in front of all the company's colleagues and clients) and she wasn't quite sure how to respond. Luckily, right then the first course was served, the interruption saving her from having to reply, but her relief soon vanished – how on earth was she going to eat this wonderful-looking food? Her throat felt so tight she was certain she wouldn't be able to swallow anything, and besides, her appetite had completely gone since Greg's phone call.

Clearly aware of her angst, Oliver seemed to realise that his teasing was a bit over the top. 'Hey.' He reached out his hand, placing it gently on her arm. 'Don't mind me, I'm only teasing – though what I said was true; you *are* beautiful.'

Yet again Poppy had no idea what to say, and yet again she was saved – Alfie's timing couldn't have been more perfect as just at that moment, he claimed Oliver's attention.

Relieved that there was no need for her to comment further, she began to relax, sitting back in her chair and trying to get comfortable. Even so, she was struggling to still those fluttering butterflies in her stomach.

What *was* it about him?

The rest of the dinner passed more or less smoothly. Oliver and Alfie's discussion continued, though Poppy noted how Oliver made a point of glancing sideways at her every now and then, as if to check she was still there. And she had to admit – she liked it.

Dom had delivered Greg's presentation perfectly, gaining the attention of every single person in the room. In fact, a number of them were now clambering to speak to him while several people were craving Alfie's attention. Some of the other delegates were breaking off into smaller groups, slowly sauntering through to the bar area, and finding herself now seated at an empty table, Poppy decided she may as well follow everyone else.

Within moments of reaching the bar, she heard a by now familiar voice.

'Here, let me get that.'

As he spoke, she could feel the warmth of Oliver's breath on her neck, like a fleeting caress, and trying to keep her composure, she turned to find him gazing at her. Briefly, she felt her knees go weak. Attempting to summon up the strength (which she knew full well she did not possess) to refuse him, she realised she still hadn't delivered Greg's message anyway.

Well, now seems as good a time as any.

'Thanks, I'll have a glass of red wine, please.' She smiled, though she hoped it came across as being a polite, professional smile and nothing else.

'Fancy sharing a bottle?'

Nodding her agreement, she watched as he gave their order to the waiter, taking the opportunity to examine him further. He really was very handsome, even if he was rude.

After ordering the wine, they wandered into the bar lounge, settling themselves onto one of the well-weathered leather sofas whilst they waited for their drinks – Poppy at one end, Oliver at the other. He seemed more relaxed now, and he happily placed himself at more of an angle so she would be in his field of vision at all times.

Feeling slightly awkward at the silence, Poppy decided that now would be a good time to deliver Greg's message. *Well, here goes.* 'I've been meaning to speak to you all evening, actually...'

'Oh?' he cut in. 'That sounds intriguing.' He rubbed his hands as if in excited anticipation, completely unaware of the inappropriateness of the action.

'Greg wanted me to pass on his apologies to you for having to leave without speaking to you himself,' she explained, feeling even more awkward now.

'Oh, that's okay.' He sank back into the sofa, slightly disappointed. 'I'm sure it must have been something unavoidable, knowing Greg. I'll call him in the morning – don't worry about it.'

Poppy bowed her head as she attempted to find the words to continue. 'It's just... he wanted me to tell you that an urgent family matter arose and that he'll call you as soon as he can.' She didn't know if the tears stinging her eyes were due to the relief of finally getting her words out, or because she'd been reminded of the accident and was yet to discover the aftermath of it.

Oliver surveyed her for a moment, bringing his hands together in a concentrated gesture. 'It's serious, isn't it?' he asked quietly, his earlier excitement having completely diminished.

She nodded. Just then the waiter delivered their wine, and Poppy waited as Oliver poured out two glasses. The action seemed to ease the tense atmosphere of a few moments ago, and when he handed her a glass, she smiled.

Picking up the other one himself, he held it out as he said, 'Let's make a toast!'

Confused as to where he was going with this, Poppy looked across at him quizzically.

'Let's drink to getting to know each other *better*.'

She raised an eyebrow in surprise, wondering how he had the audacity to be so artful. Even so, she allowed his glass to chink against hers and as their eyes met, he held her gaze, causing her heart to pound madly in her chest.

Suddenly, her mobile burst into life, ruining the moment as she made a quick grab to answer it, anxious to hear from Greg.

'Greg! What's happening? How are Marnie and the children?'

When he spoke, he sounded tired and stressed. 'They're okay; shaken up, of course, but apart from a bit of whiplash the kids are good, thank God.' He paused for a moment before adding, 'Marnie didn't get off quite so easily though.'

Poppy held her breath for a moment, anticipating the worst. She didn't dare speak.

'She's suffered quite a serious leg injury; the pain is excruciating. It's terrible to see her like this but at least they've started pain relief now. She's going into surgery shortly.' His voice was thick with concern. 'The surgeon says it looks as though they're going to have to pin it.'

'Oh, that's terrible, Greg – poor Marnie! Do you want me to come over? I can sit with the children whilst you stay with her.'

'Thanks Poppy, but there's nothing much that anyone can do at the moment. The kids are being kept in overnight, just as a precaution, so I'm going to stay with them and then I can be here for Marnie once she comes round from the operation. I'll call you in the morning once I know more.'

After Poppy said goodbye, Greg rang off. For a few seconds she just sat there, staring into the distance, and then she seemed to remember where she was. Tucking her phone away, she picked up her glass and took a large gulp of the warming beverage.

'Everything okay?'

She looked across at Oliver, for the first time appreciating the softness in his voice. 'It's Marnie, Greg's wife. There was an accident earlier... the children are a bit shaken up, but Marnie's got to have surgery.'

He sat up straight. 'How serious is it?'

Poppy shrugged. 'It's her leg, I'm not sure of the exact details. Greg says they might have to pin it...'

He reached his hand out, resting it on her arm for the second time that evening. 'I know you're worried, but I'm sure she'll be fine. She's in the best place.'

She looked back at him cautiously, unsure of what to say.

He smiled. 'Seriously, I know I've spent most of the day teasing you, but that's only because you intrigue me. And, of course, because I'm attracted to you.' His smile widened.

She was quite taken aback; no one had ever been this forthright with her before. Ever. *And anyway, what did he mean she intrigued him?*

Irked, she turned to look at him, her eyes flashing dark with anger. 'I'm not a plaything, you know.'

He burst out laughing at her unexpected response, which only infuriated her further. 'I'm sorry,' he said, once he'd got control of his laughter, 'I'm not trying to annoy you; I'm attempting to pay you a compliment. Perhaps I've been out of the circuit too long...'

'What? And you think I'm *on* the 'circuit', do you?' she retorted, still fuming.

Oliver shook his head, trying not to laugh again. 'I'm not doing very well here, am I? What I *mean* is that I don't usually spend time trying to chat up beautiful women – and *yes,* that's exactly what I'm trying to do now.'

His words took her by surprise again, making her realise with embarrassment that she'd got the wrong end of the stick.

Seeing her relax slightly, he attempted to placate her further. 'Why don't you tell me about yourself? Do you live in London?'

After thinking for a moment, Poppy responded tartly, 'Why don't you tell me about *yourself?*' She couldn't help it – she didn't mean to be rude; she just wasn't used to being hit on like this. She simply wasn't sure how to react.

He laughed again, clearly enjoying their exchange. How he liked a woman with spirit! 'Well...' he started, before pausing and grinning. It was then he decided to try and amuse her by responding in the style of someone appearing on one of those dating shows, like *Take Me Out*. 'My name's Oliver, I'm twenty-nine years old, and I'm from Surrey. I have a flat in Chelsea and I work for a stockbroker in the city. I love eating sushi, I enjoy red wine, and I love nothing more than curling up with a book in front of a roaring log fire, though I don't get to do that very often. I'm allergic to milk and I have a small birthmark on my back that resembles Africa.'

As he spoke, Poppy became more and more relaxed, and not just because of the wine making its way through her body. She had no idea if any of what he'd just said was actually true, but she found herself enjoying listening to him all the same.

He refilled their glasses. 'Come on, your turn,' he encouraged, smiling as he watched her cheeks start to colour up with yet another blush; he liked that all of this seemed new to her.

'*Well*,' she said, leaning forward, 'my name's Poppy and I'm twenty-five. I was born in a small village not far from the Cotswolds and I'm an only child. I share a flat in Wood Green with a lovely girl called Orla, who is incredibly messy and incredibly noisy but has a massively kind heart. My favourite food is pasta, mainly because it's quick to cook when I get home late. I love red wine and cats – though I don't believe I could eat a whole one.'

Oliver laughed out loud again, clearly pleased she was showing a more relaxed side to herself. And she was funny!

Appearing to have broken down the barriers that had been there before, they spent the next couple of hours chatting together like old friends, with Poppy completely overcoming her earlier shyness. It was a while before they realised that most of the other guests had retired to bed, but when they did, Poppy glanced at her watch.

Placing her empty glass down on the table, she stood up. 'Time for bed, I think.'

He jumped up too, a mischievous glint in his eye. 'I couldn't agree more. Shall we go to your room or mine?'

She couldn't help but laugh at his cheeky suggestion. 'You *wish*.'

Oliver smiled. 'Well, I suppose we really *should* wait until our second date, at least...'

She gasped. *Second date?* Her bristles were now well and truly up. 'What do you mean?'

He held up his hands in mock surrender. 'Okay, okay. Just kidding! But how about we go out on a first date then? Unless, of course, there's a *Mr.* Poppy somewhere?' He raised his eyebrows in an impish, questioning sort of way.

She eyed him suspiciously again. She did rather like him; she just wasn't certain how serious he was. Or what he really wanted from her.

As if reading her thoughts, he continued to plea his case. 'Seriously, I would really like to get to know you better, if that's what you'd like too. How about joining me for dinner one evening next week?'

Feeling satisfied that he did, in fact, appear to be genuine, Poppy accepted his invitation and they exchanged numbers, with him promising to call at the beginning of the following week. When he took a step or so forwards, she could feel the warmth exuding from him, the scent of his spicy-yet-musty cologne filling her nostrils and causing her to feel quite heady.

'I'll call you, then?' he murmured, before leaning forward even further.

Poppy froze for a moment, unsure of what he was about to do – though inwardly she was willing him to kiss her – and as she felt his lips brush against hers, a rush of emotion surged through her entire body.

He pulled away, and when she opened her eyes she found him smiling widely. 'Goodnight, Poppy. Until next time.'

In moments he was gone, having disappeared down the corridor, and Poppy finally came out of whatever spell he'd seemingly cast on her. Looking around, she saw she was the only one left in the lounge.

Back in her room, she found herself leaning against the door, her hand against her burning mouth where his lips had brushed against hers. She'd been kissed before – it's not like it was her first time or anything – but she hadn't experienced feelings quite like *this* before.

She hugged herself, grinning; a late night phone call to Sally was *definitely* in order.

FIVE

Greg returned to the office following Marnie's recent surgery, having been working from home in the meantime to help care for her and their children. What Marnie needed now was rest, as it would be several weeks before the plaster cast could come off and a few more still before she'd be fully mobile again. In the meantime they'd taken the decision to employ a temporary housekeeper and nanny, whom Marnie was quite enjoying having around. In fact, she thought she might well try to talk Greg into keeping her on longer.

Poppy was relieved everyone was alright and that Marnie was recovering well. She'd been keeping her friend amused during her convalescence with regular text messages, joke emails, and of course, plenty of phone calls, but for some reason she'd been somewhat reluctant to tell her about Oliver. Then again, what *was* there to tell, exactly? It wasn't like they'd slept together or anything.

Her heart weighed heavy as her thoughts drifted back to him, as they often had in the past few weeks. Despite all his attention and somewhat keen interest in her on the night of the Gala dinner, she'd neither seen nor heard from him since, and as far as she was aware, Greg hadn't either. She tried not to feel too disappointed, but it was hard.

She recalled her late night telephone conversation with Sally on the night of the Gala dinner, when she'd excitedly demanded to know each and every detail. They'd so giggled at the prospect of Poppy being wooed by such a handsome suitor, particularly as Sally had then delivered some rather unexpected news of her own by announcing she was getting married. Poppy couldn't have been more pleased for her.

The air had been electric with the emotion stirred up by the two friends, and Poppy had drifted off to sleep that night with a huge smile on her face and a heart full of hope. It all seemed rather silly now.

Oh well, it's obviously just not meant to be.

Greg's voice interrupted her thoughts. 'Aren't you leaving early? I thought you'd have shopped half of Oxford Street by now.'

Poppy laughed. Things weren't that bad really, were they? Earlier that day she'd received a glowing appraisal from Greg, who'd not only given her a salary increase but had also delivered the exciting news that she'd earned a generous bonus too. Her hard work at streamlining systems and re-organising the secretarial team, together with handling events after Greg's unexpected departure from the annual conference, had definitely paid off. She'd certainly not been expecting anything like that, but she was more than happy to accept.

'Just shutting everything down,' she replied, smiling merrily.

Leaving the office early for once, Poppy headed off towards home, having decided to grab something nice for dinner on the way. She intended to spend the rest of the day relaxing rather than shopping. Orla was away at a conference so she had the place to herself for a couple of days; a rarity not to be missed. She picked up a newspaper and a big bar of fruit & nut, chiding herself one minute for her frivolity but then reminding herself the next that she'd earned it.

Once home, she packed away her shopping before running herself a hot bath, even adding a few drops of lavender oil and lighting several tea lights, something she hardly ever did.

She sank into the bath and soaked herself for almost an hour, decadently topping up the hot water every now and then whilst immersing herself in the latest *Milly Johnson*. She could feel her body physically relaxing, joint by joint, limb by limb, and she realised with a sigh that it had been far too long since she'd treated herself like this.

Once dried, she slipped on a pair of loose-fitting tracksuit bottoms and an oversized t-shirt then collapsed onto the sofa, having already applied a cucumber face pack.

This is Heaven.

Relishing having the place to herself, she soaked up the silence, for the moment completely content. There was no radio or TV blaring like usual, no noise of any kind in fact – well, once you blocked out the noise from the traffic outside, that was. It was sheer bliss.

As she lay there, several thoughts filtered through her mind, reminding her of her new financial status. With one thought leading to another, it soon occurred to her that she could now afford to rent a place *on her own*. Maybe something even nearer to the office, she fancied. As much as she loved Orla, it would be great to have her own space, to be able to do this whenever she wanted.

She certainly wouldn't miss picking up after her flatmate – Poppy got increasingly frustrated by the wet towels Orla left around the place, not to mention that Orla never did her share of the shopping, cooking, or cleaning; she just didn't see any of these things as being a priority, whilst Poppy was the complete opposite. She was used to living in a clean and tidy home and that's just the way she liked it too, even if she was a bit OCD about it. Well, who wanted to live in a pigsty?

With renewed enthusiasm, she jumped up and raced into the bathroom to wash the face pack off, before stopping at the kitchen on the way back to pour herself a big glass of red. It was a bit early in the evening but after all, she told herself, she was celebrating, wasn't she? Settling on the floor in front of the gas fire with the local paper, she spent a few minutes searching through the sections on available properties to rent, before deciding to text Sally and Marnie to see what they thought of the idea.

Marnie texted back straight away.

'Gr8 idea! Come over this w/e we can look 2gether. Goin crazy here ;) xx'

She hugged the phone, delighted at the unexpected invitation. It'd been a while since she'd seen Marnie in the flesh and it would be good to have a face-to-face catch up. After all, it didn't look as if she was going to get any other offers that weekend, did it?

After sending a quick reply, Poppy leaned back against the edge of the sofa, a big smile on her face.

Her own place. She couldn't wait!

SIX

It was a beautiful, cold, crisp morning, the rays of the autumn sun streaming through the branches of the trees; long shards of bright light akin to fingers of a giant hand guiding Poppy as she steered onto the driveway of Greg and Marnie's Surrey home. Just seconds later, their children ran out to greet her, having all been eagerly awaiting her expected arrival. She embraced the three of them together in a big hug, laughing as she looked at them each in turn. Justin, the eldest, was the spitting image of his father, as was his younger brother Matt, and then there was Louisa, who was just *incredibly* cute.

'I've got a surprise for you, my lovelies,' Poppy said once they'd all stopped hugging her, 'let's go inside and see what's in my bag.'

The boys made a grab for her bags and she followed them into the house, carrying Louisa in her arms.

'Hello stranger,' Greg welcomed, his quip referring to the fact that they'd only seen each other the previous day. 'Come and see the invalid! She's desperately in need of some adult company; some *female* adult company, that is.' They laughed as she followed him through the house to find Marnie.

Upon entering the living room, Marnie shouted, 'Poppy!' and, having set eyes upon her friend, she frantically attempted to get up and greet her.

Greg rushed forward before she could get much further. 'Er... no you don't!' He settled her back down onto the sofa, placing a few more cushions behind her back for added support. 'You're not going anywhere, my sweet. You're to stay *exactly* where you are.'

She mock scowled at him, which made everyone laugh, and Poppy fondly greeted her friend, much to Louisa's disgust. She was now watching them with a scowl on *her* face, her arms tightly folded across her chest, annoyed at having been put aside in favour of her mum.

'It's so good to see you, Marnie,' Poppy exclaimed. 'How are you?'

'I'm okay, actually – *surprisingly*. I can't tell you how frustrating it is though having to lay here most of the time, but it gets a little easier each day, so I can't really complain.' She shrugged. 'Anyhow, it's nice to have everyone running around after me for a change.'

Poppy laughed, although she knew Marnie was only teasing; she loved being wife to Greg and mother to their three children, and an excellent wife and mother she was too. Poppy so envied her at times. She often fantasized about settling down and having children of her own one day. A nice home. A loving family. Of course, right now she was far too busy enjoying her career, and besides, didn't she need to find a partner first?

That was easier said than done.

*

The girls had been chatting away for ages when Greg re-joined them, having left the children busily occupied with the treats Poppy had bought for them. 'So, c'mon then,' he teased her gently. 'Tell us what you've spent all your money on! New clothes, I suppose?'

The girls giggled.

'Actually, Poppy's decided to get her own place,' Marnie announced proudly, glancing across at her friend.

Greg looked impressed. 'Oh, really? That's a very sensible idea, are you looking to buy then?'

'Oh no, I can't afford that just yet. I'd still be renting, but I'd prefer somewhere on my own, you know what I mean? Having my own space and not having to worry about anyone but *me*.'

'Yes, I *do* know what you mean,' Marnie sympathised. 'When you flat share, once the initial novelty wears off it can get quite irritating. Little annoying quirks can turn into huge, intolerable problems.' It sounded like she was talking from experience.

'Have you thought about investing?' asked Greg.

Poppy looked at her boss, biting her lip. 'Can't say I have, to be honest. I might work for a major Investment Stockbroker but I haven't a clue about that sort of thing. Anyway, don't you need hundreds of thousands for that?'

He chuckled. 'You can invest as little or as much as you want, there's no limit. If you were to invest half or two thirds of your bonus, for instance, you'd be surprised at the return you could make in a relatively short space of time. Think about it; you'd soon have the deposit for a property of your own, maybe more depending on how you invest it.'

She mulled over his words for a moment. 'I suppose when you put it like that it *does* sound quite attractive.' She looked at him and then at Marnie, who smiled and nodded at her encouragingly. 'Okay, well I'd certainly consider it, but I still wouldn't know where to start.'

Greg smiled. 'That's where I come in. Let's talk you through some options and you can go from there.'

Greg made lunch for everyone, and with the children having been despatched to play for an hour or so, the three of them sat down whilst he and Poppy discussed how to get the best out of her money. It all went a little over her head, but she listened attentively, grateful for Greg's expertise.

Once the business discussions were complete, he decided to leave them to more girlie time.

Which was exactly what she needed.

*

'Phew.' Greg returned sometime later, displaying mock exhaustion. 'That's Louisa bathed.'

'Thanks for taking care of the children, darling,' Marnie said, smiling at him gratefully.

Poppy watched them exchange looks, their eyes meeting as they smiled that deep, knowing smile that only two people who are truly and deeply in love can experience. She so wanted to share a look like that with the love of *her* life. Perhaps one day she would, though that day seemed pretty far away right now.

Everyone's attention was suddenly drawn towards the kitchen as small padded footsteps could be heard approaching. A moment later in came little Louisa, dressed ready for bed in her cute fairy pyjamas and her favourite rabbit slippers. She was sucking her thumb and twisting her hair round and around with her free hand. 'Please read me a story?' Having ripped her thumb out of her mouth for a moment to speak, she looked up hopefully at Poppy, who gazed down fondly into her big blue eyes; how could anyone say no to such a cutie?

'Of course, I'd love to.'

Louisa excitedly clapped her hands in response, causing everyone to laugh.

'She's got you sussed,' said Marine. 'Now, come and say goodnight to mummy please, Louisa.'

Louisa threw herself against her mother and planted a big, sloppy kiss on her lips. 'Love you mummy, night, night.' With that she popped her thumb back into her mouth and took hold of Poppy's hand, leading her upstairs to her room where she picked out one of her favourite *Kipper* books.

Poppy read through the story, using different voices for each character much to Louisa's delight, who chuckled away happily until eventually she relaxed and fell soundly asleep.

Poppy leaned over and stroked the hair from her forehead, smiling; she was such a beautiful child and she so hoped to have a daughter like her one day. After kissing her gently on the forehead, Poppy stepped quietly out of the room.

*

'Everything okay?' Greg asked, handing her a very welcome glass of wine.

'Oh yes, she fell asleep, bless her. Although I don't know if you want to check on her?'

Greg and Marnie smiled at her concern. 'I thought my wife was a worrier over Louisa, but you only left her a second ago.'

'I just wanted to make sure she's lying in the right position and everything,' Poppy explained rather uncertainly.

He laughed aloud. 'Huh! If she's anything like her mother – who can't keep still all night – it won't really matter.' Marnie playfully threw a cushion at him. 'If it makes you feel better though, I'll go and check.'

As he headed towards the stairs, Marnie chuckled. 'You know, he'd have done that anyway; to be honest, he's worse than me.'

Just then, the sudden interruption of the doorbell echoing throughout the downstairs caused them to exchange looks of curiosity.

'That's *never* the door, is it?' Marnie exclaimed. 'We're not expecting anyone else.'

Poppy nodded. 'I believe it is; should I answer it?'

'Please, although I can't imagine who it could be,' replied Marnie. Evidently they didn't get many callers appearing out of the blue.

Smiling, Poppy made her way to the front door, wine glass still in hand as she reached out for the handle.

It was hard to tell who was the most shocked, really. Poppy, because she'd been completely knocked off guard, or Oliver, because the very last person he expected to be answering Greg's door was his PA, particularly with a glass of wine in her hand.

Her mouth dropped open.

He opened his mouth and then closed it again, attempting to gather his scattered thoughts.

Poppy could feel her heart hammering in her chest, her stomach fluttering overtime. No one had spoken in what felt like forever, but she couldn't for the life of her think what to say.

'Oliver!' They were *both* startled then by the sound of Greg's voice booming out as he came down the stairs. 'I'd quite forgotten you were coming over, please do come in.'

Poppy stepped aside as Greg welcomed Oliver into his home. She didn't know where to look, what to do, how to act... her mind had just gone blank.

'Would you like a drink? Some wine?'

'A glass of wine would be great, thank you,' Oliver replied, smiling politely.

Greg took his coat whilst Poppy made her way back to Marnie, who was keen to know who their visitor was – she was mouthing the words *who is it?* at her.

Knowing that the two men were right behind her, Poppy put a finger to her lips as Greg brought Oliver through to greet them both.

'Darling, I'm so sorry,' he said, 'I'd quite forgotten that Oliver had called this morning to ask if he could drop by some papers. He's heading off to Europe for a while so this is the last chance he thought he'd get.'

Marnie gave Oliver a welcoming smile, offering her hand to him, which he readily accepted. 'That's no problem at all, darling. Hello

Oliver, lovely to meet you. I can't get up, though, I'm afraid.' She indicated her leg, which was covered from thigh to toe in plaster.

'Good to meet you too,' Oliver replied, smiling. 'Oh dear, that looks rather painful.' He nodded towards her injury as he shook her hand.

She nodded in return before gesturing at her friend. 'Do you know Poppy?' she asked, unable to miss the look the two of them exchanged. Something about it made her intensely curious, especially when she noticed her friend blush.

'Of course; I had the pleasure of meeting Poppy at the conference a few weeks ago, actually.' He turned towards her. 'It's very nice to see you again.' He smiled and took her hand, which made her blush even more, just as he knew it would.

She smiled politely but said nothing; she really did *not* trust herself to speak, especially not in front of Marnie and Greg. So instead she took a rather too large gulp of her wine, which went down the wrong way and caused her to start coughing and spluttering. Smooth.

Oliver smiled again, but to himself this time, enjoying the reaction his presence appeared to have evoked in Poppy. Greg – who appeared completely oblivious to it all – invited Oliver into his office so they could continue their discussions, but his wife was a lot harder to fool.

Marnie never missed anything, and as soon as the men had left the room, she patted her friend's back, eager to gather the details. 'Poppy Jackson, just what have you been up to?' She smiled curiously at her friend, her eyes twinkling mischievously.

Poppy gulped some more wine – this time very much relieved to find that it went down the right way – and wiped her eyes, which had smarted tears from all the coughing. Once she had composed herself, she hissed back at her friend, 'I don't know what you mean.'

'Oh please. I *saw* you.' Marnie was grinning; she was enjoying this.

Poppy knew full well that she wouldn't be able to talk her way out of this one, especially after the way she'd reacted, but she just wasn't sure what to say.

Marnie seated herself more upright as she asked, 'You two have something, don't you? The way you looked at each other... come on lady, spill!'

Poppy's blush intensified. 'It's nothing really,' she started, before finally giving in and rather matter-of-factly explaining all about their something-or-nothing liaison.

'No way! How exciting!' Marnie exclaimed. 'So, let me get this right. He makes a play for you, then you spend the whole evening getting to know each other, and he even *kisses* you, but there's been nothing since?'

Poppy shrugged. 'It was only a quick peck really, and yep, that's about the long and short of it. Story of my life.'

'Hmmmm.' Marnie looked across at her, deep in thought. 'I'm not so convinced; I think there's more to it than that. He seemed pleased to see you, and you can't easily fake looking at someone the way he looked at you, my darling. Trust me.'

Poppy liked the sound of what Marnie was saying – indeed, she wished her words were true – but Oliver's lack at making any attempt to contact her told a very different story.

'I have to say,' Marnie continued, 'I don't really know that much about him, although I believe his parents live a few miles or so from here. They own a rather garish Sixteenth Century Manor House they seem to be forever renovating; such is the talk in the village, anyhow. He doesn't actually live there himself though I don't think.

'He did mention he had a flat in Chelsea, actually.' A thought suddenly struck her, causing Poppy to wince. 'Perhaps he's married?'

The horror of such a predicament had not crossed Poppy's mind until then, although it would at least explain why she hadn't heard from him.

Marnie was quick to note the look of disappointment on Poppy's face and her heart went out to her; she was clearly far fonder of him than she was letting on. 'I don't know, to be honest with you, sweetie.'

Since Poppy had started working for Greg, they'd developed quite a friendship that went from strength to strength. Marnie thought back. When Greg had first come home after interviewing Poppy, he'd been so enthused about her – singing her praises and talking about her potential – that Marnie made a decision: if there were to be two women in her husband's life, it was best for everyone if they got on with each other. She just hadn't expected on meeting someone like Poppy; they'd clicked right from the off.

However, Marnie *was* astute enough to recognise that Poppy was quite naive in some respects, and when she discovered that it had been some time since she'd had a female influence in her life – since the death of her mother – she'd felt a strong urge to take her under her wing and to provide some much needed support in the areas of her life that weren't centred around the office. In fact, Marnie felt as though Poppy were the sister she'd never had. 'I know,' she said after a few moments of silence, 'let's invite him to join us for dinner. What do you think?' She winked mischievously at Poppy, an excited smile spread across her face.

'What? *No!* Are you crazy?'

Marnie giggled; this was just the kind of distraction she needed.

'Okay, well say we *do* invite him to join us… I mean, why? What good would it do? Didn't Greg say that he was going away for a while – who's to know that it isn't with his wife or girlfriend?' Her voice rose slightly in exasperation as she spoke.

Marnie was still smiling. 'Well, if we ask him to dinner then we can find out, can't we? Wouldn't you rather know now?'

Poppy rolled her eyes upwards, sighing; she knew there was no use arguing with Marnie when she got an idea into her head. So instead, she went off to set another place for dinner, her stomach fluttering excitedly the whole time.

SEVEN

Being the only child of Anthony and Martha Sullivan, Oliver had a lot to live up to. His father was both a highly successful and respected investment banker and a senior partner at the London-based firm, Fletcher Holmes Securities. In fact, he was so successful that Oliver had lost count of the number of times when, upon realising whom his paternal father was, people became far more interested in the possibility of him acquiring them an introduction, rather than actually working with Oliver himself.

It didn't help that he appeared to be a constant source of disappointment to Anthony, who consistently made comparisons expressing his frustration at how Oliver never seemed to achieve what he himself had at a similar age. But Oliver *did* have ambition; he was determined to build a successful career and was working hard to get there too. Anthony may have set the bar high, but by his own volition, Oliver was determined to raise it even further.

Having left the family home three years ago, Oliver had soon found himself an apartment just off the Kings Road, equidistant to both Chelsea and South Kensington, which suited him perfectly. It cost an arm and a leg, of course, and he worked damn hard to make sure he could afford it – which, at times, was incredibly tough. For instance, in his role as an Investment Stockbroker for Artimedius UK, he'd made some bad judgements of late, which he'd only managed to get through by the skin of his teeth whilst still managing to keep himself in the running for the Partner vacancy. He may yet earn his father's respect, he thought, and finally prove just how capable he really was.

His mother Martha was the third of five children born to Lord and Lady Haversham of Northumberland. Being a middle child, she was predisposed to 'middle child syndrome' and never once, in her opinion, felt loved and nurtured until she met Anthony – then she couldn't wait to become his wife. They were delighted when Oliver came along, and Martha embraced motherhood wholeheartedly. He became the very light of her life, much to her husband's disappointment and later, annoyance.

She loved and cherished her son as she herself had so longed to have been loved and cherished by her own parents, but did not anticipate nor recognise that far from creating the idealistic loving home life that she yearned for, her actions were in fact creating a harsh competitiveness between the two most important people in her life; whilst Anthony adored Martha, he began to grow tired of having to constantly vie for her affections. In fact, he soon began to fear that this was one battle he would never win.

Oliver had travelled to his parent's home on Friday afternoon, arriving just in time for Martha's birthday dinner. It turned out to be quite convenient, as he could kill two birds with one stone, so to speak. He'd been reviewing an investment opportunity presented to him by Greg Sable, and if he stayed an extra night, he could deliver the signed paperwork in person as his parents' house was just a couple of miles away from Greg's. Besides, he was keen to get the wheels in motion what with being seconded to Artimedius' French office for the next three months.

He drove over to Greg's the next evening – having spoken to him earlier that day – and as he pulled his car onto the driveway, he was oblivious to the shiny yellow one that was also parked there, somewhat askew; he was far too busy thinking through the investment opportunity he was hoping to take part in and trying to work out how quickly he'd be able to get a return on his money.

In fact, he was so focused on it that he was completely dumbstruck when he looked up to find Poppy answering Greg's door. And so, it seemed, was she. Thankfully, Greg appeared just in the nick of time, but her appearance had really thrown him. Just for a split second – for a nano-second, really – Oliver had been fearful there might be something going on between the two of them. Office affairs were rife in the city; well, everywhere really, or so it seemed.

He was relieved, however, to quickly discover that this wasn't the case at all, and he mentally kicked himself for not having been in touch with her yet. He just hoped he might get a chance to put things right this evening. He wanted to explain to her all about the nightmare he'd returned to at his office following the conference in Worcester; he'd walked into a complete disaster, which had to be resolved fast or he'd be at risk of some serious repercussions.

Having set up an investment portfolio for a large client, things hadn't gone quite as planned and he'd spent several fraught days trying to rescue it all. Then, by the time he'd pulled it off and had the client singing his praises again, he was immediately presented with two new clients and he'd barely had a moment to himself since. If he really *was* determined to go after the position of Partner, he had to remain focused, and this didn't leave much time for socialising outside of client entertaining, investment seminars, or the many lunches and dinners one had to get through in order to network and attempt to bring on more clientele (not to mention keeping the current clientele happy too).

Nevertheless, he had genuinely wanted to see Poppy again, and now she was here, at Greg's house, and so was he.

Even so, he really needed to focus on this deal…

EIGHT

'**G**reg, darling, could you help me change into some fresh clothes before dinner?' Marnie asked – as much as she hated to admit it, there were some things she just couldn't do for herself.

Greg scooped her up in his arms, helping her upstairs whilst muttering to her playfully, 'I'm sure this plaster cast weighs more than you do.'

Finding themselves unexpectedly alone, Poppy and Oliver looked at one other, their hearts thudding in their chests.

'Well... this isn't at *all* awkward,' Oliver said, breaking the silence and hoping his light-hearted approach would relax the situation.

Poppy, however, looked past him and headed for the kitchen to fetch more wine, hoping the gesture would help to disguise how suddenly nervous she'd become.

Without a second thought, he went after her. He wasn't about to give up quite so easily, and besides, he might not get another chance to catch her alone. But despite his bravado, he was quite uncertain how to approach the elephant in the room. Clearing his throat, he attempted to gain her attention. 'I've been meaning to call you, actually.'

She raised an eyebrow, glaring at him, her eyes flashing dark. 'Oh please, spare me!'

He just loved her fiery nature. Struggling to keep a straight face, he replied, 'No, seriously, I have – I'm not just saying it.'

'Don't feel you need to explain yourself on my account,' she responded tartly. For a brief second, though, her heart filled with hope. *Maybe he does have a genuine reason for not calling.* But then again, he was probably just trying to save face. Trying to avoid having to listen to his wishy-washy excuses, Poppy turned her focus to pouring the wine.

'It's not like that, believe me,' he said as he took the bottle out of her hand, placing it on the nearby counter. Then he lifted his other hand to her face, turning her to look at him and causing a rush of emotion to surge through her body. He suddenly became very serious. 'I *have* wanted to call you, honestly I have. I've just been so backed up with problems at work that I really haven't had a moment to think of anything else.'

His gaze fell to her dark hair, cascading gently around her face and shoulders. She was so beautiful; all he really wanted to do was to envelope her in his arms. 'Of course, it doesn't really help that I'm being seconded to France for three months tomorrow.'

Poppy gasped, touching Oliver by her reaction – maybe he was still in with a chance.

She had heard Greg mention that Oliver was off to Europe for a while, but for three months? It seemed that their relationship was doomed after all.

Oliver placed his hands on her shoulders, gaining her attention again. 'Surely, Poppy, you have an understanding of the difficulties that can arise in our line of business? The markets change all the time and I've certainly had some tough issues to deal with of late. I *do* want to get to know you better Poppy, truly. I swear.'

Pushing his hands off her shoulders, she started to walk away. 'Seriously?' she shot back, 'If that were true, Oliver, surely you could have found the time to ring me?'

Now very much exasperated, he took hold of her again, turning her around and taking her by surprise. Now *he* seemed fired up, a look of sheer determination crossing his face as he said, 'We've got something between us, you know we have. You felt it that night as much as I did. You can't give up on us so easily; let's at least discuss this properly before I leave for France. What do you say?'

Just then, Greg and Marnie's voices drifted over from the stairway, indicating their return.

Poppy felt rushed, but she didn't want their discussion to end. 'Okay, okay. Call me tomorrow. We'll talk then.' She turned away from him, trying to compose herself as Greg and Marnie re-joined them. 'I love your outfit, Marnie,' she blurted out, complimenting her friend a little too quickly, though she did look stunning having swapped her earlier outfit for a burnt orange-coloured kaftan.

'Thanks honey, it covers up this wretched plaster cast quite nicely, so I sort of feel normal again.'

Greg began preparing dinner whilst the others made small talk, and once Oliver began to relax, he soon regained his earlier charm, keeping them all amused with little anecdotes from his mother's birthday dinner. Despite this, he found himself inwardly wishing his conversation with Poppy had turned out better. If only they'd had more time alone!

Eventually they took their seats, settling down to an enjoyable and entertaining dinner as Greg joined Oliver in sharing some amusing stories of his own. Every now and then Oliver glanced across at Poppy, pleased to see that she too seemed more relaxed and had allowed the real Poppy to shine through. He noticed she was quite shy at times, and he loved the way her eyes widened when she became animated about something, or the way her voice softened whenever she became emotional.

Greg seemed oblivious to it all – as usual – but Marnie certainly wasn't; she was very much enjoying watching them interact. It was clear that Oliver was quite taken with Poppy, and she was intrigued that he'd appeared reluctant to take things further – it was just so perplexing, watching him now. *Maybe after tonight things will be different* she thought, mentally plotting a way to leave them alone again.

'Oops, sorry everyone!' Marnie's voice rang out, dramatically claiming everyone's attention. 'Greg, could you take me to the bathroom, darling? The wine's gone right through me and I'm not sure how much longer I can hang on.' Of course, this wasn't entirely true.

Once they were out of earshot, Oliver quickly turned to Poppy, taking his chance. 'It's been a lovely evening; I'm glad I stayed for dinner,' he said, fighting the urge to take her in his arms and kiss her. 'I'll call tomorrow, I promise – I don't intend to make the same mistake twice.' With that, he lifted her hand to his mouth and kissed it briefly, having heard their hosts returning.

After thanking Greg and Marnie for dinner, Oliver bid them all goodbye, giving Poppy one last look before he left. She then busied herself clearing the table whilst Greg saw him out.

'Well,' hissed Marnie, who'd hobbled with great difficulty into the kitchen and was now clutching the counter top for support, 'anything to report?'

Poppy smiled, enjoying the attention, especially now that she *actually* had something to tell. 'Don't think I didn't notice what you did, Marnie Sable. And don't think I'm not grateful either.' She winked at Marnie, who let out an excited squeal.

'Oh my God, tell me, *tell me!*' She pretended to jump up and down with excitement; just like little Louisa had done earlier.

'Ssshh, of course I will; I just don't want Greg to know about it until there *is* something to know, if you see what I mean.' With that, she eagerly relayed the evening's brief, but interesting, exchanges.

'Well Poppy,' said Marine with a smile, 'I have to tell you that judging by the way he kept glancing at you through dinner, well… it's just like Greg and I. He likes you, Poppy, I'm certain of it.'

With that, Greg entered the kitchen, and after settling Marnie back onto the sofa, he helped Poppy clear up whilst Marnie read aloud some details of potential flats they'd highlighted earlier that day.

As she listened, Poppy couldn't help but smile, thinking of the new place she might have – and the new man.

*

The following morning on the drive home, Poppy reflected on her conversations with Oliver. Her stomach kept fluttering as thoughts of him filled her head, and her cheeks flushed when she recalled how he'd taken her hand and pressed it to his lips. She'd spent a restless night tossing and turning, churning all kinds of thoughts and feelings through her mind, though she knew one thing for certain: she wanted to see him again, and if he really meant everything he'd said last night, she was now eager to get home and await his call.

NINE

Poppy stretched out luxuriously before snuggling further into the duvet. She felt like the luckiest girl on earth right now and she wanted to relish the feeling a while longer.

Two months had passed since she'd moved into her new home and she still absolutely loved it. Situated on one of the streets off Clapham Old Town, and within walking distance of the tube station, she'd managed to find a large ground floor Victorian conversion to rent with a small, private garden.

It was completely perfect. She'd viewed a number of properties, but upon walking into this one, it just felt right. The owners were a lovely middle-aged couple, the husband of which had been relocated abroad with his job, prompting them to decide on letting the property out rather than selling it. The neighbours seemed friendly too, with everyone greeting and waving at each other whenever their paths crossed. There was a gentleman who lived above her – in his 50's, she'd guess – who introduced himself as Professor John Smedley and told her he worked as a university lecturer. In the flat above Professor Smedley lived an adorable lady called Maisie, an eccentric cockney well into her 80's with eyes as bright as two shiny buttons. All in all, Poppy felt she'd done rather well for herself and was delighted to finally have her own space. In fact, most things had been going very well for her lately.

As promised, Oliver had telephoned the day after he'd joined them for dinner at Greg and Marnie's house. They'd shared quite a long conversation too, where she'd patiently listened as he explained the reasoning behind his lack of contact, which was purely due to his stressful work schedule and certainly not because he wasn't interested in getting to know her better.

If she were honest, she saw this sort of thing in her own workplace all the time, a fact which did indeed help fill her with confidence that his explanation was plausible. Since then, their relationship had seemed to go from strength to strength – despite Oliver being on secondment – and they both looked forward to their regular long distance telephone chats, which, in a serendipitous way, afforded them an opportunity to get to know each other in a far more enriched way than perhaps they might otherwise have been able to do. Not only that, but she'd been delighted when he'd even managed a couple of surprise trips back to London, where he'd taken her out to dinner and to the theatre. Now he was due back from his secondment and she could hardly wait, literally counting the hours until he returned.

Marnie and Sally had been such a great support, both of them always pleased to receive regular updates on her blossoming relationship with him, which now appeared to be going very much in the right direction. She'd been particularly delighted to catch up with Sally over Christmas, and was excited to hear all about her and Dave's wedding plans. Sally had selected a stunning bridesmaid dress for Poppy and she could hardly wait for the big day to arrive herself. She so hoped her relationship with Oliver would continue to flourish so that she could invite him to come along as her guest.

Only time would tell, she supposed.

*

Oliver relaxed as he settled into the taxi; it seemed like forever since he'd actually taken the time to sit still and unwind. He was so looking forward to seeing Poppy again; he'd really missed her.

He thought back to when they'd first met – or more accurately, when he'd basically hijacked the Hawkins, Monroe & Sable Annual Conference at the *Friars Retreat* in Worcester. He'd spotted her through the glass windows of the corridors as he was making his way to the meeting room, and was immediately enchanted. He smiled as he recalled her blushes at his teasing, surprising himself as to how taken he was with her.

Up until then, he hadn't had much time for relationships as such. Certainly he'd had plenty of one-night stands, some of whom had made many an attempt to date him further, especially when they'd discovered his family connections. But he wasn't really interested – he was far too focused on his career instead. Once he'd got to where he wanted to be, there would be plenty of time for romance, but until then, he was more than happy with the odd liaison here and there – well, he had been until he'd met Poppy.

He was acutely reminded that he'd nearly missed his chance with her too. He'd really had to pull out all the stops to rescue the Ellhart deal – which was not only a lucrative deal for him but for Artimedius UK too, and, more importantly, a deal that would go towards helping him gain both the promotion and security he'd been working hard to attain. Given the success of his recent secondment, it looked as though he wouldn't have to wait much longer, either.

He took a deep breath, relaxing further. He certainly saw Poppy as someone he wanted to spend more time relaxing with – he'd really enjoyed getting to know her better over the past few months, which surprised him. Not being one to usually have long telephone conversations with girlfriends, he was somewhat taken aback at his keenness to maintain contact, and was also pleasantly surprised at how much he looked forward to and enjoyed their conversations. Even from the beginning, they seemed to have a lot to talk about; him telling her all about where he was working and staying, and her telling him all about her hunt for a new home.

Gradually their telephone calls had become more frequent, with each of them revealing a few more personal details here and there, and of course, it helped that he'd made a couple of trips back to London, which had set some foundations from which their relationship could develop even further. He'd certainly grown quite fond of her and he hoped she felt the same way too.

Despite being from completely different backgrounds, they'd both strived hard to build successful careers and they both had a lot of ambition. He really liked that she wasn't looking for someone to be dependent on – that was certainly not something you could say about Poppy. He'd long since grown tired of all the usual girls he seemed to hang out with in the past, whose Daddy did this, and Mummy lunched with that, them both holidaying here and dining there. It had all become rather tedious and pretentious, and he was certainly not attracted to these types of women, no matter how much money their parents had.

Whilst he could be a ruthless businessman, he had a soft inner child that yearned to be loved and nurtured – a side of him even he was only just getting to know. One thing he *did* know was that Poppy seemed to bring out this undiscovered side of him more, and he was finding it far from unpleasant.

*

Poppy was trying to calm what felt like the thousand or so butterflies that were currently fluttering around frantically in her stomach. Having carefully planned the evening ahead, she'd booked a table at the local bistro, within walking distance of her place. She was certain Oliver had had quite enough travelling for a while, and there were a couple of bottles of *Veuve Clicquot* chilling nicely in the fridge, ready for their return. She couldn't wait for the evening to start.

Just then she was alerted by the familiar sound of a black taxi pulling up outside, and gulping, she started nervously chewing on the edge of her bottom lip. *Oh God, he's here – he's really here.*

She rushed to fling the door open, stretching a beaming smile across her face just as Oliver was approaching the doorway, appearing somewhat taller than she remembered but still oh so handsome. *He just has the most gorgeous blue eyes.*

She hesitated for a moment, unsure of what to do, though fortunately for her, Oliver knew *exactly* what to do – he stepped towards her, enfolding her in his arms. His mouth was gentle upon hers, yet he kissed her with an intensity she'd never before experienced. They parted, taking just a moment to look at each other and soak up each other's presence, and then Oliver cupped her face in his hands, totally surprising her by whispering, 'I could so easily fall in love with you, Poppy.' Then he kissed her again; a long, slow, but deliciously moreish kiss that she never wanted to end.

It wasn't long before they found themselves lying side by side, kissing and gently exploring each other, both of them knowing exactly how far they wanted to go but unsure of whether to make the next move or not.

Oh, the best laid plans!

Later, as they lay in each other's arms, he thought how for the first time in his life he'd actually experienced the joy of making love with someone he truly desired and cared for, rather than just having 'sex'. For some time now he'd realised he was entering a new phase of his life, which promised to be more grounding and fulfilling than he'd ever experienced before. It felt pretty good.

Realising Poppy had fallen asleep, he leaned over her – she looked so peaceful and happy it made his heart swell. 'I don't know about you, Poppy Jackson,' he whispered into the darkness, 'but I have a feeling this could be the start of a very promising and lasting relationship.'

TEN

It was almost the end of April, and with less than two months until Sally and Dave's wedding, Poppy was heading back to her hometown for a dress fitting. Thoughts of Oliver swirled ecstatically through her mind as she drove along.

Since his return from France they'd spent every weekend together, and she couldn't wait to tell Sally all about it, particularly the bit about inviting him to the wedding. She was practically bursting with excitement at the thought of introducing him to everyone.

Pulling onto the driveway of her birth home caused a pang of emotion to rise in her throat; she always felt emotional coming home, but she'd left it a bit longer than usual since her last visit and she suddenly found herself engulfed by an additional rush of guilt.

She glanced up as the front door opened, and as she watched her father, Percy, step out excitedly to greet her, she suddenly noticed just how tired he looked; indeed, he appeared somewhat older than his 65 years. She knew he still missed her mother dreadfully and she wished he'd socialise more, but no matter how much she tried to encourage him, it was a losing battle.

Stepping out of the car, she rushed over to hug him. 'Hey Dad, it's good to see you!'

'Hello lovely! Do you know, it seems ages since you were last here? How are you doing?'

'Yeah great,' Poppy replied enthusiastically. 'How are things with you?

'Oh, I'm good thanks, love, you know – *still here*,' he quipped, trying to sound light-hearted even though there was no mistaking the tinge of sadness in his voice. 'C'mon inside, then; here, let me get those bags.' He reached for her overnight bags, pausing to feel the weight of them in his hands. 'Staying for a month then, lovely?' he quipped again, but this time a smile lit up his face and he winked at her teasingly.

'You know me, Dad, I like to travel light.'

They both laughed as they went inside the house, Poppy heading straight to the kitchen to put the kettle on and feasting her eyes upon the lunch her dad had set out ready for them.

After taking her bags upstairs, he joined her in the kitchen. 'Tea?'

'Kettle's on,' she replied, smiling. Tea was a staple in the Jackson household – not much time ever passed without a cup of tea being made. 'Oh wait, I just need to get something, back in a mo.' She turned and quickly sprinted off upstairs, remembering the parcels she'd brought with her. She returned just as Percy was pouring their tea.

'Sit down, love, no need to tell you to make yourself at home; you don't need to be reminded of that.'

'Thanks, Dad. This all looks very tasty, is that pâté?' She loved pâté; it was one of her favourite treats, but it wasn't so easy to find in a little village like King's Oak. He must have gone to one of the larger supermarkets at Midford County – or perhaps even further afield than that – to buy it.

'It is; I know how much you like it, Poppy. Actually, you'll be surprised to hear that big department store in Swinford St. George has just started selling food, posh stuff like, not your every day bits and pieces they sell up the local shop here. I spotted that in the deli contestant section and remembered you telling me how much you liked it.'

She giggled at his mispronunciation of delicatessen. She so loved her father and his quirky ways; he was very old-fashioned and very traditional, for him to buy pâté was quite a big deal. 'I even brought some of that stuff too.' He pointed to a plate of the finest Prosciutto Italian dry-cured ham that she also adored.

'Now I *am* impressed.' They helped themselves to crusty bread, which she proceeded to smother with the delicious pâté, and as they ate, the two of them chatted about her job and what they'd both been up to since her last visit. It wasn't long before Percy steered the conversation around to Oliver, clearly eager to learn more about the young man his daughter appeared quite taken with.

'So, how's your young man, then? Pleased he's back now?'

She had, of course, already told him all about Oliver and their blossoming relationship – well, not *all* of it. The very mention of his name made her face flush and her stomach flutter, causing her to wish that she hadn't eaten with so much gusto. She took a few sips of her tea to settle her tummy back down again.

'Well,' her father added, 'I can see you're sweet on him by that reaction.'

She smiled at his teasing. 'Well, I like him a lot actually, Dad, but we're just taking it slowly – you know, getting to know each other.'

'Oh ah, what does that mean? Friends with benefits?'

She gagged at this, nearly choking on the slice of ham she'd just popped into her mouth. 'You've been watching too many American sitcoms, Dad. It's not like that, it's more like…' She trailed off. *Should she say boyfriend and girlfriend? Was he her 'partner'? No, that didn't seem to sound right either.*

Just then, Percy's voice cut into her thoughts. 'What *is* it like then, Poppy?'

'Well, relationships are different these days, Dad,' she tried to explain. 'We *are* dating, but we're just taking things one step at a time. It's difficult with Oliver's job and the fact that he sometimes has to go off at short notice, although I know he doesn't want me to feel as though he just 'picks me up and puts me down' whenever it suits him. He wants our relationship to be more than that. It's just, well, I guess he doesn't feel ready to commit to anymore than that right now.'

'How do you feel about that then?'

'I'm good with it.' She paused for a moment before continuing. 'Don't forget, it's been a while since I dated anyone myself, so the last thing I want to do is to rush into anything, but I'd be lying if I said I hadn't developed strong feelings for him.' She paused again, for the second time that day feeling quite emotional.

Percy Jackson surveyed his daughter, his only child. He was so proud of her that there were times when he had to stop himself from shouting out to the world how wonderful she was. She was headstrong, though, just like her mother. Oh how he missed his dear wife so!

'I'm very proud of you, Poppy, and I know you've got your head screwed on right – I just want you to be happy, that's all. I'm just looking out for you, love.' He reached across the table, picking up her hand and squeezing it reassuringly. 'Anyway, truth be told, I just want to meet this fella.' They smiled at each other. 'Will he be coming to the wedding then?'

His reference to Sally's forthcoming nuptials presented the ideal opportunity to discuss her concerns over whether to invite him or not, and she was glad she did as they both decided that, with Poppy being chief bridesmaid, it would do no harm to mention it and see how he reacts. Then she could take it from there.

With the problem solved, or as good as it would be for that day, she picked up the two packages she'd taken from her bag earlier and presented them to her dad.

'These are for you.' She pushed the packages across the table towards him, watching as he surveyed them with great interest.

'Oh, what we got here, then?'

She felt like an excited child at Christmas as she watched him open up the first package, smiling as he gasped in appreciation at the gift inside.

'Oh Poppy, you really shouldn't be spending your money on me, love.' However, by the look on his face and the way his eyes were already scanning the cover, she knew she'd been right to do so. Her father was a poetry buff and – after a long and hard search – she'd managed to obtain a first edition copy of Thomas Hardy's *Wessex Poems*.

'I'm speechless, Poppy, speechless!' he exclaimed as he carefully teased the book from the blue cloth-covered compartment that had been snugly protecting it. He proceeded to examine the book tenderly, completely lost for a moment, enthralled to be holding such a treasure in his hands. She watched him carefully reinsert the book back into its case and then tenderly place it back inside the protective wrapping.

'Thank you, Poppy – you know how much this means to me. I shall enjoy looking through this is more detail when I'm on my own.' He then moved his attention to the next package. 'I certainly hope you've not wasted more of your money on me, Poppy.'

His attempt at scolding her was soon short-lived, however, once he'd parted the wrapping on the second package. His voice immediately dried up, and as he put his hand to his mouth, she was touched to notice there were tears in his eyes. Indeed, tears had already sprung to her own.

In his hands was an antique silver frame containing the picture that had been taken when he and Grace, her mother, had first become engaged. He was standing proudly beside her, holding her hand and showing off the single set diamond ring he'd saved up for just over a year to buy, big smiles on both their faces.

The black and white photograph depicted a much younger Percy, of course, dressed in his smart grey suit, with a white shirt and dark-coloured tie. His light brown hair appeared blond and was slicked firmly back in place, off his forehead – such was the style of the day.

The picture had been taken at the end of Grace's parents' garden, in front of a gooseberry bush. Poppy recalled her mother telling her how she'd howled with embarrassment when the photograph had been developed, and everyone had teased Grace and Percy mercilessly about how many children they would find under the gooseberry bush.

As he looked at it with his teary eyes, the picture invoked such a strong surge of emotion in Percy that he almost broke down. He was so proud when Grace had agreed to be his wife; they had both been so happy.

He hadn't seen this photograph for years. In fact, he'd quite forgotten it even existed, and he was deeply touched at Poppy's thoughtfulness in having the picture reframed.

Getting up from the table, he came around the other side as Poppy stood up to meet him, and then they just hugged and held each other for a moment.

'Thank you.' His voice was thick with emotion. 'This means so much to me, my lovely, thank you.'

He left to go upstairs then, to have a moment on his own. Poppy knew he missed her mother deeply, as she herself did, but it was different for him and she always tried to remember that. She couldn't imagine being with someone for as long as her parents had been together, and then to lose one of them so suddenly, without even having the chance to say goodbye…

It didn't bear thinking about.

*

As she walked the short distance to Sally's house later that evening, a couple of bottles of red tucked into her bag, Poppy reflected on the day's events, and how blessed she felt that her relationship with her father now seemed stronger than it had ever been. Initially after her mother's passing, life with Percy had become unbearably strained; they struggled to interact with each other at times, having become suffocated by the melancholic atmosphere they'd built up.

Her father was a cautiously proud man who kept himself, and his feelings, to himself. Grace had been the centre of his universe, after all, and he felt completely lost without her. As hard as it was at the time, Poppy knew that leaving home had been the best decision for both their sakes; they'd both readjusted, and as a natural consequence, had rebuilt their relationship not just as father and daughter, but also as friends. It had taken time, but in the end, it had been worth it.

After lunch earlier, he'd surprised her by talking about a new housing development situated on the outskirts of Swinford St. George that he was considering moving to. He was lonely now, living in such a big house, and the many memories it held whilst happy, were also painful.

Initially Poppy expressed her concern that his reason to move was because he was struggling financially, much to his amusement – he quickly assured her this wasn't the case at all. He explained that it was a retirement development he was interested in, and by moving to somewhere like that he hoped to make new friends – both male as well as female – which was something she'd wanted him to do for a long time. Sure, she'd be sad to see the family home go, but she knew it was the right decision and she gave him her full support.

She noticed afterwards that their discussion really seemed to lift his spirits, with him revealing that it hadn't been an easy decision to make and that it was one he'd been wrestling with for some time – which probably explained why he was looking so tired.

I don't know why we Jacksons are such worriers.

'Poppy!' Sally wrenched open the front door, enthusiastically throwing her arms around her friend. 'It's *so* good to see you, come on in.'

Poppy followed, giggling at how excited Sally seemed to be. 'Woo, you're looking pretty chic,' Poppy complimented her, as she took in her new look. Sally was quite petite like her at only five feet tall, and now she'd had her dark hair cut into a short crop which really emphasised her elfin-like features.

'You don't look half bad yourself, missus.' She patted the space next to her on the sofa. 'C'mon, sit down and tell me all about your gorgeous man and what you guys have been up to.'

Sally's excitement was infectious, and the two friends spent the next few hours chatting, gossiping, eating pizza, and drinking red wine. They laughed, they cried, they laughed some more, but most important of all, they had the best catch up ever. It was perfect.

When it was getting late Poppy set off home, promising to catch up by telephone during the week. It was such a lovely clear night that instead of walking straight back to her dad's house, she felt inspired to take the longer route, which would take her all the way around the village. It'd been a long time since she'd walked the streets of King's Oak and she was curious to see how much things had changed.

As was usual for the time of night, the village was deserted. The odd yellow light could be seen here and there – bursting through the crooks and crevices, illuminating someone's front door or shining out of an upstairs window – but otherwise all was quiet. She heard an owl hoot every now and then as she walked along, and she was intrigued to notice someone else out and about late at night too – someone who was now heading towards her.

As the figure neared, she realised it was in fact a policeman; he was wearing a long dark coat over his uniform.

As they approached each other, he greeted her politely. 'Evening Miss, everything alright?'

She realised he must think it strange for her to be wandering around at this time of night – after all, it was well after midnight. 'Yes, fine thanks, just enjoying the night air.'

'No problem, I just wanted to make sure you got home safely – you don't seem to be local?'

She smiled at hearing this. Well, she supposed she wasn't local to King's Oak anymore, but of course she was staying at her father's so she still was in a way.

'I'm staying with my father, actually,' she explained, 'he lives on the King's Oak estate. I've just been visiting friends so I thought I'd take the long way home. It's been a while since I've walked around the village.' She smiled. 'My father's Percy Jackson, do you know him?'

At those words, the policeman took a closer look at the young woman in front of him. He had clearly seen from the way she was well groomed and smartly dressed that she wasn't local. He'd been concerned that she might be lost, in trouble, or worse; she could well have ended up in trouble if she continued to wander the streets of King's Oak at this time of night.

But he hadn't quite bargained for this.

'Poppy Jackson? Surely not!'

She gasped, completely surprised that he knew her name.

He laughed. 'You don't recognise me, do you? Well, I suppose it *has* been a few years.'

'Surely you're not PC Hudson?' Poppy asked, remembering a face from long ago.

'Please, call me Matt.' He touched the tip of his hat with his right hand.

'Ohhhhh,' she groaned, placing her face in her hands in complete embarrassment. The realisation of who he was evoked memories of her youth, and the mischief she and her friends had got up to.

'Well, unless you've been playing knock and run tonight or worse, you've got nothing to worry about,' he joked.

She couldn't help but laugh at that. 'My goodness, what must you have thought of us?' Even more memories flooded into her head then, making her cheeks flush. She was just glad it was dark so he couldn't see her red face.

'You certainly look as if you've come a long way since those days, Poppy, I'm pleased to say! And from what your father tells me, you're doing pretty well for yourself too; right proud of you he is.' As Matt took in the image of the young woman in front of him, he marvelled at how this once angry, mischievous, and belligerent teenage girl had significantly blossomed into a fine young woman – and quite a stunner too, he couldn't help but notice. He took a moment to pull himself together; he was on duty, after all.

'I can't believe you're still the village bobby for King's Oak,' Poppy marvelled.

'Oh, I don't just look after King's Oak; I'm the local PC for all the surrounding villages here now, including the Hamptons and Swinford

St. George. To be honest, I usually patrol this area in the station car but there's been a few reports in the past couple of weeks of kids hanging around late at night – drinking, using drugs, and being a general nuisance – so I thought I'd walk around the village. The sight of the car either makes them run or hide or both.' They laughed again. 'I'm hoping for a promotion later this year too. I've been a PC for long enough now,' he added.

'That sounds great, good for you. So, tell me, are you married? Do you have any children?' She thought he must be married by now, having guessed he was in his late thirties.

'No, not quite found the right one yet...' His voice trailed off, making her wish she hadn't asked.

After a bit of an awkward silence, Matt noticed that Poppy had started to shiver. 'Here,' he offered, shrugging off his long, black, and incredibly warm police issue overcoat. 'Put this around you and I'll walk you home.' She accepted the coat, grateful for its warmth against the cold night air. 'This time we'll take the short route back, shall we?'

When they reached her family home, she gave him his coat back, thanking him for the loan and for walking with her too. He was looking at her quite intently, as though he was trying to see right inside her. 'It's been really good bumping into you like this, Poppy. It'd be good to have a proper catch up sometime. Goodnight.'

She bid him good night and let herself back into the house, quickly becoming engulfed by the warmth from the central heating. She was careful not to make too much noise as she locked up, then she crept quietly upstairs, quickly undressing before snuggling down into the oh-so-familiar flannelette sheets and thick wool blankets that covered the bed, making her feel safe and secure.

Sleep came quickly, but not before she'd given out thoughts to Oliver – and not for the first time that day, either. She was really looking forward to getting back home to see him.

Home? Funny, she had once thought of here as home, but now her home was in London.

On that thought, she drifted off into a deep slumber.

*

Matt Hudson shrugged his thick warm overcoat back on and continued his checks around King's Oak village, using his torch to illuminate any suspicious shapes or dark areas.

His nose was suddenly filled with a pleasant aroma, which he soon realised was the same fragrance he'd smelled on Poppy earlier – it must have transferred off her when he'd placed his coat around her shoulders to keep her warm. He couldn't help but breathe in the pleasing floral aroma, feeling a slight fluttering in his stomach at the same time.

He'd certainly had a surprise at seeing her this evening; she was the last person he'd ever expect to find wandering around King's Oak in the early hours. He recalled back to when he'd first started out as a young PC, some 14 or so years ago.

Poppy was part of a group of children from King's Oak that he'd spent time mentoring when he'd first been posted to Midford County. He smiled, remembering how he used to spend every Thursday night at the local youth club in the village, working with the kids to help keep them on the straight and narrow. Truth be told, they were a good bunch of kids, with nothing more than just high spirits at times.

Things were far different these days, though, and Poppy was no longer a teenager. Indeed, she was a young woman and a beautiful one at that. She must be, what? 24 or 25 now, he guessed. Aged 34 himself, he felt it was about time he met someone and settled down. He'd love to start a family too. *If only I could find someone like Poppy, I'd have no problem.*

After re-joining his patrol car at the junction of King's Oak Road and Hampton Ash, Matt set off for his nightly patrol around the rest of his area.

He usually hated the night shift, but tonight he was exceptionally pleased to be on duty.

ELEVEN

Poppy felt incredibly nervous as she came down the stairs; she noticed that the inside of her palms had started to perspire, and her stomach fluttered nervously.

'Oh, I *do* like that, lovely.' She smiled as her father complimented her choice of blouse. 'That colour really suits you.'

He could sense she was nervous. Since late afternoon, he'd noticed that the closer the time crept towards Oliver's arrival, the jumpier she'd become. He went up and patted her shoulder reassuringly. 'I'm not going to eat him alive, I promise.'

Poppy, however, wasn't in the mood for such light-heartedness. *What if Percy didn't like him? What if Sally and the others thought he was too posh? What if this was all just one big mistake?* They often teased her about how she'd grown from being a country mouse into a girl about town, and she didn't want her family and friends to believe that she thought herself better than anyone else.

Please God, help and guide everyone to get on.

'Ready then?' She grabbed her bag and keys, and heading outside, they both got into her car, ready to set off for Swinford St. George station to collect the other, very important man in her life.

*

Percy chose to wait in the car at the station, as he wanted to give her a moment alone with Oliver – he still remembered what it was like to be young and in love, after all, and he was pretty sure that Poppy was in love with her young man. The question was, *is her young man in love with her?*

Well, thought Percy, that was what he hoped to find out over the next few days.

*

Poppy paced nervously up and down Platform 3 whilst waiting for Oliver's train to arrive, stopping every now and then to rock back and forth on her heels – she was trying to distract her stomach from fluttering nervously and her heart from pounding wildly, but she was facing a losing battle. She was glad that her father had chosen to wait in the car.

Suddenly the train sprang into view, and as it trundled into the station Poppy swallowed, noticing just how dry her mouth had become.

As soon as she saw him, her breath caught in her throat. Here, in these surroundings, he was even more handsome that she'd remembered. He was wearing denim jeans matched with a blue shirt, the first couple buttons of which were undone, and his hair was both neat and a bit scruffy at the same time, like he had 'bed head' that had probably taken him quite a while to achieve with gel.

As he stepped off the train, his suit bag in one hand, she watched as he turned back to retrieve his overnight bag. She felt completely weak at the knees for a moment and she didn't know whether to go running into his arms or to just walk steadily towards him.

She continued to watch him as he placed his bag on the ground so he could rearrange his suit bag, and then he looked directly at her, a big smile stretching across his face as he held out his arms towards her. She ran over to him and he caught her in a big hug, laughing and embracing before he gently released her, looking at her appreciatively.

'It's so good to see you, darling, you look stunning.'

She glowed from his compliments, glad that she'd chosen the jade-coloured blouse.

He pulled her towards him again and kissed her gently, yet with a desire they both recognised. 'I've missed you,' he whispered into her ear, before smiling and gazing lovingly into her eyes. 'I know it's only been a few days since we were together, but it feels *so* much longer.'

She mentally hugged herself; she loved the fact that he'd missed her, and especially the fact that he'd *told* her – it wasn't the kind of thing he usually said. 'I've missed you too, Oli; I've been completely antsy all day waiting for you to arrive. I can't tell you how good it is to have you here! Come on, come and meet my dad.' She bent down to pick up his overnight bag.

'Why don't you take this?' Oliver suggested, offering her the much lighter suit bag. 'And then,' he paused again, this time reaching for her hand, 'I can take *this*.'

She giggled, returning his smile.

They walked out of the station hand in hand, looking every bit the perfect couple, Poppy holding her head up high and strutting proudly beside her man.

Once they came into his view, Percy got out of the car in anticipation of greeting Oliver. The truth was, he was a bit nervous himself; he didn't want to let Poppy down and he hoped Oliver would think him a decent sort of fellow. As the two men caught sight of each other, they smiled, and Poppy quickly took care of the introductions.

Oliver returned Percy's welcome with a warmth sincerity. 'It's a pleasure to finally meet you, Mr. Jackson.'

'Oh, you must call me Percy, and it's good to meet you too. Goodness knows Poppy's gone on about you enough.'

Poppy wanted to cover her face with her hands, but she relaxed as Oliver laughingly replied, 'Well, if she's half as proud of me as she is of you, Percy, I'm a very happy man.'

Delighted, Percy looked over to his daughter, and as their eyes met, they smiled knowingly at one another.

He likes him.

'Come on, you two, let's get to the church,' she mock chided them as they settled into her car, heading towards Hampton Waters.

During the short journey, Percy was pleased to learn that Oliver wasn't familiar with this part of the Cotswolds, making a mental note to tell him all about the interesting and historic parts of the surrounding villages that he thought Oliver would like to see, having perceptively decided he was the sort of chap who would be interested to learn more about it.

Arriving at St. Michael's, they noted there were already quite a few cars parked outside. So, they pulled up alongside the others and went inside the church, where most of the bridal party were already in situ. All eyes were upon them as they approached the aisle.

'Poppy!' Sally came bounding towards them. 'Alright, Percy?' Sally greeted, kissing him enthusiastically on the cheek. 'And you must be

Oliver.'

Poppy chuckled as she watched Sally. She was beaming up at Oliver and kept looking him up and down, and up and down again –a as if she wanted to devour him but didn't know where to start first.

'Hello Sally, it's a pleasure to meet you. I've heard so much about you.' Oliver, ever the gentleman, shook her hand and smiled brightly at her, charm oozing out of every pore.

This caused Sally to blush and go all giggly before turning to shriek to the rest of the bridal party, 'Gawd, Poppy! I didn't realise he was such a *dish*, yum – meeee!' She then proceeded to shout down the aisle towards her husband-to-be, in her best thick West Country accent, 'Oi Davy Boy, you'd better watch it or I might just marry the wrong man tomorrow.' Then she promptly fell about laughing, *very* loudly.

Yes, I'm definitely going to crawl away and hide. Poppy immediately started searching for an escape route.

Oliver, on the other hand, was clearly loving the attention, and he laughed along with Percy, who knew Sally only too well – in fact, this was quite tame for her.

'Huh!' Dave retorted loudly. 'He'll soon give you back when he finds out you snore like a stuck pig.' This caused everyone else to fall about laughing, even Sally.

'What's he like, eh Poppy?' Sally nudged her friend, winking at her at the same time and making her shudder to think what she'd say next. 'Come on then, Oli, come and meet the rest of the gang.'

Poppy cringed as she watched her friend grab Oliver by the arm and drag him towards the waiting group at the front of the church. She followed them cautiously, hoping that an overly-excited Sally would not say nor do anything that might cause any offence – after all, they were in a church. She watched her gaily introducing him to everyone else, wincing each time she referred to Oliver as *'Poppy's bit of stuff'*, and occasionally adding, *'he's a bit of alright, 'aint he?'*

Oliver seemed completely unfazed by it all, though, and was clearly still enjoying the attention.

Needless to say, Poppy was quite thankful when Reverend Fisher arrived, feeling quite sure that his presence would bring some calm and order to the occasion. The Reverend approached the front of the church, gathering everyone together and gently guiding them to their places. He then clasped his hands together in a prayer motion and, as dramatic as ever, smiled and nodded towards the happy couple.

'How blessed it is to see so many of your family and friends here this evening,' he announced, 'welcome one and all. Now, everyone, I'm sure each of you – like me – would like tomorrow to be as perfect a day as possible for Sally and David.' Poppy watched Sally and Dave gaze into each other's eyes; it was good to see her friend so happy and about to marry the man she clearly loved. 'Tonight,' continued Reverend Fisher, peering seriously across the top of his spectacles and sweeping his gaze across the small gathering, 'we will be holding a *brief* rehearsal in preparation for tomorrow's festivities, after which we can all pop along to the Maide of Honour for a quick drinkie, if anyone's interested?'

His announcement was met with a cacophony of cheers and whoops of excitement – as he well knew it would be – and now he was grinning proudly, lapping up everyone's approval.

Poppy glanced over at Oliver, who seemed perfectly relaxed, having taken a seat on a nearby pew. He was busy watching the proceedings with Percy, the both of them laughing along at the excited banter flying back and forth across the church, clearly enjoying the whole situation. Poppy was glad.

An hour later, having been put through their paces by Reverend Fisher, everyone made their way to the Maide of Honour public house; the most popular pub in the village, which was owned and managed by the fabulous Marcus Brett and Piers Lynes. Oliver and Percy fetched the drinks – much to everyone's delight – whilst Poppy took the opportunity to chat to Sally's cousins Paige and Emmy, the other two bridesmaids.

A while later, Oliver placed a large glass of wine in front of her. 'Thought you might appreciate this.' He delivered her a knowing smile. *Oh, how he makes my stomach flutter so.*

'I can't,' she replied, disappointed. 'I'm driving.'

'Oh, don't worry about that, my darling – I'll drive us back. Your need is greater and all that.' He sat down next to her, placing his arm around her shoulders and planting a kiss on her lips. She smiled in response, feeling perfectly content.

The next hour or so passed far too quickly for Poppy's liking, with everyone in high spirits, excited at the impending nuptials. The evening was in danger of heading towards a lock-in, though, and as much as everyone would have liked that, it was decided they should try and keep as clear a head as possible for the following day.

Sally came over, giving Poppy a goodbye hug. 'You was alright with me earlier, wasn't you? Me teasing about Oli and everything?'

Poppy smiled, the wine having helped relax her, and she hugged Sally right back. 'Of course. You're okay, Sally – if he stills wants to be with me after this weekend then at least I'll know it's for real.'

'Well, if it's any help, I can tell by the way he looks at you he's keen, alright. I mean,' Sally paused, raising her hands up in the air for added effect, 'my Dave's never looked at me like that and we're getting married tomorrow.' The two friends laughed and hugged again. 'Seriously though, Poppy, I can't wait for tomorrow – I'm so glad you'll be there to share it with me.'

'I wouldn't want it any other way.'

'Well, just you remember me when it's your turn, eh?' Sally joked with an over-emphasised wink, nodding in Oliver's direction.

Poppy couldn't help but laugh.

*

On the drive back to King's Oak, the three of them laughed as they exchanged anecdotes from the rehearsal and subsequent impromptu gathering.

'Well, if tonight was anything to go by,' Percy chuckled, 'tomorrow should be a blast.'

'God help us!' Poppy averted her eyes, making Oliver laugh, and he reached across to hold her hand reassuringly.

'It's going to be great, I promise.'

Back at her dad's, she helped Oliver with his luggage whilst Percy poured them all a night cap.

'Here's to a fabulous weekend *and* to new friends.' He looked across at Oliver as he spoke and they raised their glasses together.

Oliver smiled. 'To new friends.'

TWELVE

The following morning Poppy made her way to Sally's house, having left Oliver and Percy looking through the book of poetry she'd presented him with a few weeks previously.

Percy was so proud to own a first edition and he couldn't help showing it off, but what she hadn't realised was that Oliver was also a poetry buff – he even went on to quote some works from his own collection which then evoked a deep discussion between the two men.

Deciding to leave them to it she kissed them goodbye, reminding them that a car would be arriving at 2.30 p.m. to take them to St. Michael's church as the wedding was due to start at 3 p.m.

As she walked along, she bounced on the balls of her feet with excitement, pleased that Oliver and Percy seemed to be getting on so well. She visualised walking up the aisle later that day in support of her friend, the vibrant purple colour of her bridesmaid dress emanating around her like the wings of an angel, drawing Oliver's focus to her and her alone. All of the emotions swirling around her body threatened to overwhelm her as she hugged herself in anticipation of the day ahead.

Chaos reigned as usual at *chez* Knight; Poppy let herself in to find everyone bustling about, trying to get ready for the wedding. Sally's dad, Arthur, was sitting at the dining table watching TV as he polished his shoes and Deborah, Sally's mum, was acting like a contestant on *MasterChef* with just a minute to spare as she frantically threw ham and cheese into finger rolls, wanting to ensure everyone had *a little something inside them* before the off. Deborah was well known for cooking up a range of delicious treats, but not normally in as rushed a manner as she was today.

Calm restored once again, the bridal party began to assemble, everyone having been primped and preened to within an inch of their life and all dressed in their finery. Deborah appeared first, looking very chic in a pale pink-coloured close-fitting dress, matched with a long jacket to which she had pinned a corsage of freesias of the most vibrant blues, purples, pinks, and oranges – their rich aroma clung to the air around her. Deborah was quite a slim woman and at 54, still good looking too.

Arthur stood proudly in his morning dress whilst Deborah adjusted his cravat, which was matched to the same rich purple as the bridesmaids' dresses.

Just then, the doorbell rang. 'The cars are here, the cars are here!' Deborah shouted excitedly up the stairs, a flurry of footsteps sounding above as the girls rushed to complete their looks before each tip-toeing carefully downstairs, clutching their gowns so as not to fall before lining up ready for inspection.

'Oh girls – you *do* look beautiful,' Deborah gushed as she handed them each a white rose bouquet to complete their look. 'You've really done yourselves proud.' The bridesmaids' dresses were strapless with an elegant pleated side wrap in a rich, deep purple-coloured satin. Each of them also had a delicate diamante brooch, which sat at waist height, adding a touch of sophistication.

'Now now, *no* upstaging the bride, if you please.' A moment later Sally swept into the room, to many excited gasps. The white and elegant gown she'd chosen consisted of lace placed over satin, with long sleeves, a deep V-shaped back, and a chapel train.

'You look wonderful, Sally!' praised Deborah, dabbing at her eyes. Arthur also had to swallow back the lump in his throat as he looked admiringly at his daughter. He and Deborah had done a pretty good job raising Sally, he thought. She was a good girl and a hard worker and they were very, very proud of her.

'I'm feeling a bit nervous now, actually,' Sally confided as Poppy hugged her friend – well, as best as you *could* hug someone who was dressed in as elegant a gown as they both were.

'You look lovely, Sally,' Poppy said, smiling at her friend. 'And so beautiful! Dave's a very lucky man.'

*

Reverend Fisher was waiting patiently outside St. Michael's church, the warm afternoon sunlight reflecting off his bright white protruding teeth. He smiled broadly as the wedding party arrived, greeting them one by one as they lined up outside the church ready to pose for the waiting photographer.

'Righty-ho, everyone!' Reverend Fisher announced, grasping everyone's attention. 'I shall now make my way into the church and start the organ playing.'

'At least he's not going to play *with* his organ,' Sally whispered to Poppy, who almost gagged trying not to laugh.

'When you hear the organ play, that'll be your cue to start your journey up the aisle,' he explained, and then off he went, his clothing flapping in the warm breeze as he walked towards the church.

Deborah followed closely behind, having wished everyone good luck, and then the sound of the wedding march rang out as Sally took her father's arm. Feeling more proud than he ever thought possible, he led her up the aisle towards her husband-to-be and the start of their new life together.

Poppy followed, with Emmy and Paige behind her, and as they stepped inside the church she was engulfed by another sudden rush of emotion, causing her to swallow hard and blink back tears. She held her head high and continued onwards, astonished at the sea of faces before her; the church appeared completely packed.

As they turned and headed up the central aisle, she looked around for Oliver, and as their eyes met, her heart pounded and her stomached fluttered madly. She smiled as he winked at her discreetly, and then she placed her attention back on Sally, who was now standing next to a very proud-looking Dave.

Next to Dave were his four brothers; having not been able to single out any one of them for best man, he'd decided to ask them all, but it was Dan – his eldest brother –who was holding the rings.

The wedding ceremony was conducted perfectly by Reverend Fisher, who threw in a couple of tasteful jokes every now and then for good measure. Being a small village, most of the congregation were regular churchgoers, and they sang out wholeheartedly to the hymns they'd chosen to accompany the service.

Dave looked quite handsome, Poppy noticed; he was clean-shaven for a change and his hair had been freshly cut too. If fact, he looked quite dashing in his morning suit and, as he and Sally posed for their wedding photographs afterwards, she thought that they really did make a handsome couple.

As the wedding party made their way from the church to the reception, the invited guests took great pleasure in bombarding them with confetti, and Poppy had more than her fair share not only thrown over her but also stuffed into her gown. It was all good, innocent fun, and laughter rang out amongst the crowd as everyone walked towards the Hamptons Village Hall, situated just a few feet from St. Michael's.

Poppy had by now met up again with Oliver and Percy who, to her surprise and pleasure, was walking alongside Rosie Hunt.

'Fancy Rosie being here,' Poppy whispered to Oliver. 'That's the lady who showed Dad and I around Hazel Wood on Thursday.'

Oliver knew all about Hazel Wood, as Percy had taken great pleasure in proudly showing off the brochures and telling him all about his proposed new home. They were pleased to note that it looked as though Percy was making new friends already.

As soon as they arrived at the hall, Poppy joined the rest of the wedding party in preparation to welcome the guests, quickly slotting in beside Dave's parents as people started making their way into the hall.

The large room had been set out beautifully. There was a top table for the wedding party at the front, with round tables having been sporadically placed around the rest of the room to seat the remaining guests. There did seem to be a *lot* of guests, though, causing Poppy to wonder if there would actually be enough room for everyone to be seated. She supposed Sally must have worked it all out.

The tables looked absolutely perfect for the occasion, each covered in crisp white linen and matched with crisp white linen napkins – all courtesy of the Swinford St. George golf club, of course. And, as Sally and Dave both worked in catering, their respective managers had been only too happy to lend a helping hand, along with several of their colleagues, who were all in the kitchens busily preparing their wedding feast.

There were purple and cream-coloured helium balloons dripping with matching purple and cream ribbons at the centre of each table, as well as being spread along the top table together with floral displays of pink, white, and violet-coloured flowers, all aimed at complementing the colour scheme that Sally and Dave had chosen. There was a stage at the far end of the room, the opposite end to the top table, where a disco had been set up in preparation of the evening's festivities. Basically, everything was ready for people to start having fun.

Oliver and Percy came into view then, subsequently following the line of the wedding party. Rosie followed closely behind and Poppy greeted her warmly. 'Hello Rosie, fancy seeing you here.'

'Well, I must tell you dear, I'd no idea you were going to be here either – what a small world!' she exclaimed. 'I'm related to Dave, you see, dear – his father's my cousin. Can you believe it?'

Poppy couldn't, and she said so while smiling happily.

Later on, Poppy noticed how much more relaxed the atmosphere in the room had become after everyone had eaten, no doubt helped along by the many glasses of fizz that had also been consumed.

Soon it was time for the speeches, and everyone fixed their attention on the top table as Arthur stood up and began the traditional father-of-the-bride speech. It was heart-warming listening to him speak, clearly proud of his only daughter and proud too of Dave now that they'd gained a son. Everyone cheered as he toasted the happy couple, and Poppy got quite teary again.

Next up was the best man's speech, but as there were four of them, it wasn't quite as traditional as Arthur's had been. Nevertheless, it was absolutely hilarious; the four brothers told their captivated audience the tale of how Dave had come to team up with Sally, who was yet to realise that she hadn't just gained a husband, but also four brothers, who were all partial to a bit of home cooking.

The foursome performed like it was open mic night at the *Comedy Club,* and soon had their audience in complete fits. The air was charged with excitability, happiness, and positivity, and there wasn't one person in the whole room unaffected by it.

Next up was Dave, commencing his speech with the usual '*my wife and I*' causing everyone to cheer, shout, and be generally raucous. He paid tribute to his brothers' best 'men' speech and went on to compliment his bride, expressing his deep joy that they were now man and wife, which had everyone 'oohing' and 'aahing'. After proposing a toast to his new wife, he completed his speech by colourfully complimenting the bridesmaids, causing each of them to glow with pride. Poppy blushed when her name was said, and Sally smiled at her from her position next to her new husband.

Then there was a bit of a break, the guests reassembling in the main hall in time for the evening's festivities. It was well known that many a wild night had been held at the village hall in the Hampton's, and Poppy guessed – by judging the events of the day so far – that anything could happen.

She re-joined Oliver and Percy, who were sitting at one of the round tables along with Sally's parents and Rosie Hunt. 'Hello stranger,' she whispered, leaning down over her man.

Oliver stood up to greet her. 'I've missed you, can I take it that you're all mine now you've finished with your bridesmaid duties?'

She laughed, hugging him back. 'Absolutely. I hope so, anyway, because I haven't seen much of you today.' She snuggled into him.

'Don't worry about that; we've got the rest of our lives together. It's good for you to have an opportunity to catch up with your friends, and they're a great crowd too – I must say, I haven't laughed so much in ages!'

Poppy, however, wasn't listening by that point. She was too busy re-running *we've got the rest of our lives together* through her head.

Had he really just said that?

For Poppy, that was when the wedding *really* started to get fun.

THIRTEEN

A hot and sunny Saturday afternoon towards the end of July found Poppy and Oliver on their way to his parents' house. Relieved that the antics of Sally and Dave's wedding hadn't scared him off completely, she'd been thrilled when he said he wanted her to meet his parents. In fact, he seemed to have been more attentive and caring towards her ever since that weekend. He told her it was the first time he'd felt really welcomed anywhere, and that he'd thoroughly enjoyed being around people who didn't suffer any airs and graces.

She thought back to the memories he'd shared of his own childhood, when he'd never really been allowed to play, shout, scream, or run about, as everything had to be so serious all the time. Of course, now she was anxious about meeting *his* parents and had asked him over and over again all about them, their house, and what to expect. She just wanted to be prepared.

Even though he'd told her to relax and be herself, she couldn't quite settle her jangling nerves. It didn't help, of course, that he'd told her his mother, Martha Sullivan, was the daughter of Lord and Lady Haversham of Northumberland – in Poppy's book, this was as close to the Queen as she was ever likely to get!

She'd dressed carefully for the occasion, but demurely, having chosen a pale lemon sundress and putting her hair in a chignon. She'd applied only a little subtle make-up and had finished the look with a pair of lemon pumps – no clonking high heels to fall off this time.

Oliver glanced at her as though reading her mind. 'Honestly darling, you look perfect.'

She smiled back. 'Well, you would say that, wouldn't you? I just want to make a good impression, that's all.'

'To be honest,' replied Oliver, with a cheeky smile on his face, 'I couldn't give a flying fuck whether my parents like you or not.'

She gasped at his retort as, like her, he rarely swore. She was surprised at his sudden outburst.

'What I mean is, whether they approve of you, like you or not, whatever. It doesn't matter to me. All that matters is how *we* feel about each other; that's what's important, my darling.' He raised her hand to his lips and gently kissed the back of it. 'I love you Poppy Jackson, and that's not something I say lightly.'

She hugged herself as her heart swelled with joy, thinking back to the first time he'd said those words to her, on the evening of Sally and Dave's wedding. Percy had decided to share a taxi home with Rosie Hunt so they'd been able to have some time alone together.

Oliver had taken her into his arms, looking earnestly at her. 'Being a part of this weekend with you, Poppy, has made me realise how much more I love you than I did even yesterday; if that's at all possible.' He kissed her then – slowly and gently – and she thought she would just about burst with happiness.

Bringing her thoughts back to the present, she looked across at him. 'I love you too.'

He smiled. 'Then, no matter what happens this weekend, remember that. Nothing is going to change it.' His eyes held hers for a moment longer, and although she did feel a little better, her apprehension and nervousness grew as they drove slowly towards Stone House.

As the car crunched its way along the gravel driveway, Poppy took in the surrounding scenery; it was breath-taking. With it being July, the shrubbery was bursting with bright flowers and lush green leaves, and she gazed in awe at the beautiful oak trees lining either side of the long driveway.

The house soon came into view, every bit as lovely as Oliver had described it – a pretty 16th Century Mansion. There were four bedrooms in the main house, he'd told her, with a further two in the renovated barn, all set in approximately seven acres of land.

Once he'd parked she exited the car, smoothing down her dress just as a large, black Labrador came bounding towards them, rushing first to Oliver and then to Poppy, wanting to greet her, its tail wagging madly.

'Hello Ben.' Oliver stooped down to stroke and pat the dog, who was clearly delighted to see him. 'Come and meet Poppy.' Ben wagged his way over towards her, appearing to completely understand everything Oliver said, which made her laugh. She petted him too, making a real fuss, glad of the unexpected distraction.

'Let's leave our bags here for now and go on inside,' Oliver said as he held out his hand, wanting to ensure that she felt fully supported. His mother could be rather difficult when it suited her, and he was certain that today would be no different – particularly given his conversation with her earlier in the week when he'd called to inform her he was bringing Poppy along at the weekend, amongst other things.

They headed over to the door, and Poppy was amazed at just how vast the inside of the house was; it really was quite spectacular. They soon heard footsteps approaching – a loud clip-clopping sound on the wooden floors – and then a woman, whom she guessed to be Oliver's mother, appeared.

'Oliver, *darling!*' Martha Sullivan gushed to her one and only son. She held out her arms to embrace him, and Poppy noticed him tense up immediately. It was something that did not escape Martha's notice either, given her subsequent glance at him through pursed lips.

'Hello Mother,' he responded, although not quite as enthusiastically as Poppy had expected. 'May I introduce Poppy?' He held out his arm to coax Poppy forward, who politely shook his mother's proffered hand.

'Nice to meet you, Poppy.'

'Lovely to meet you too,' Poppy replied. She was tempted to add that she'd heard so much about Martha from Oliver, but decided against it at the last second.

'Do come through to the drawing room,' Martha ordered as she turned to walk in the direction of said room. 'I thought you might be in need of a spot of afternoon tea.'

She led the way into the large room, which housed period furniture and featured some exquisite decor. Oliver, having retaken Poppy's hand, guided her to one of the sofas, which they sat upon together, while Martha chose to sit on a matching one opposite. On the coffee table placed between the two there was a pot of tea waiting, together with some daintily prepared sandwiches and tea cakes.

'Tea, Pippa?' Martha enquired.

'It's Poppy, Mother!' Oliver snapped, thinking to himself that it was a bit early for her to start acting up.

'Oh, I'm so dreadfully sorry,' she replied, although she didn't sound *that* sorry. 'My apologies... tea, Poppy?'

'Yes please.' *It's an easy mistake to make... Pippa / Poppy... sort of the same, I suppose.*

Poppy and Oliver watched Martha expertly pour tea and offer sandwiches and cakes, which they both declined; Poppy decided that if she attempted to eat anything, she may well choke, which wouldn't be a good look at all. It didn't help that the air of tension between Martha and Oliver was so thick she was beginning to wish she hadn't come at all – and they'd only been here a few minutes.

Oliver passed Poppy her tea and then reached for his own.

'So Oliver,' his mother said, turning his attention to him, 'tell me, how are you, darling? How is business?'

The two of them had a brief – and somewhat stilted – discussion about his work before Oliver asked, 'Where's my father?'

'Oh, he's not due back for an hour or two. He had a business engagement last night in London so he decided to stay at his club,' she explained. 'He'll be joining us for dinner this evening.' She turned her attention to Poppy. 'Well Poppy, tell me, do you work?'

Poppy tried not to show complete surprise at her question. 'Yes I do, I work in the city too, actually.'

'Oh? Are you an investment banker as well?'

Oliver blew air through his teeth in exasperation. 'Poppy works for Greg Sable, Mother. You know, *the* Greg Sable? As his assistant, amongst other things.'

Martha was well aware who Greg Sable was. Hawkins, Monroe and Sable were one of her husband's major competitors. 'Oh, you're his secretary?' she asked, raising a quizzical eyebrow.

'Well, there's rather more to it than that,' Poppy replied bluntly – she was beginning to feel a little riled now.

Martha raised an eyebrow again but chose not to comment further; instead, she took to questioning Poppy about her background as Oliver fumed inwardly. Having upset his mother earlier in the week, he was disappointed to find that she appeared to be venting her anger from their altercation towards Poppy, rather than at him.

'Poppy comes from a small village in the Cotswolds actually, Mother,' he interrupted, thinking that might be enough to shut her up.

'Oh, you're a village girl, are you?' She enjoyed taking the opportunity to sniff, disapprovingly.

'I think it might be an idea for us to go and freshen up after that drive, Poppy,' Oliver said, who couldn't even look at his mother anymore.

Relief flooded through her as Oliver stood up, and retrieving her cup and saucer, he placed them both onto the coffee table.

'What a good idea,' agreed his mother. 'I've had the green room made up for Pip... er... Poppy, and your old room's all ready for you, Oliver.'

He looked at her in complete exasperation. 'Are any rooms in the barn made up?'

'Yes, of course, the Braithewaites are coming to stay next week.'

'Then that's where we'll stay,' he insisted, and with that, he marched Poppy out of the room, leaving his mother aghast.

Once outside, neither of them exchanged a word. Poppy was so uncomfortable by this time that she just wanted to leave anyway, and Oliver didn't exactly know *what* to say after that little introduction.

They made their way to the barn, heading upstairs and along the landing area until they came to an oak door, which Oliver opened for her. Impressed, Poppy stepped inside and admired the surroundings. The room really was quite beautiful. The furnishings were very rich and the walls beautifully decorated in white wallpaper patterned with tiny pale lavender flowers. The main feature of the room was a rather grand four-poster bed, and there were huge lavender chintz curtains hanging at the windows. It all looked incredibly comfortable and relaxing – which was exactly what she needed after the run-in with Oliver's mother.

She sat down on a nearby chaise longue whilst Oliver placed their overnight bags on the plush, cream, freshly vacuumed carpet.

'So,' he said, allowing a gasp of air to escape between his teeth in exasperation. 'That went well.' Oliver paused, and Poppy smiled at him – she was sympathetic to his discomfort. 'As you've no doubt gathered, my mother doesn't like the thought of having to share me with anyone. In fact, she's so over-fucking-protective it makes me sick to my stomach.'

He sat down on the bed and pushed his fingers through his hair in frustration. Poppy was concerned that the stress of the situation would cause him to develop a full-blown migraine; something he'd told her he'd suffered with since his early teens. 'I'm almost thirty-fucking-years-old for Christ's sake.' He looked up at her then, taking a deep breath and reaching out, bringing her closer to him. 'I'm sorry, darling. I hope her behaviour hasn't upset you.'

'If I'm honest, Oli, I *do* feel a bit uncomfortable, but I got the impression she'd already made up her mind about me.' Poppy shrugged.

'Oh, but you must know it's not you, my darling.' He stroked some stray curls away from her face. 'Believe me, it honestly wouldn't matter *who* I brought home. No one would ever be good enough for me in the eyes of my mother.'

She nodded. She *did* understand that. Martha's behaviour had been worse than a scorned child, only Poppy was not privy to what had triggered such childishness.

'However,' Oliver continued, 'I do unfortunately still need to address a matter with her that cannot wait, and I think this is best tackled by me alone. Will you be okay here for a few minutes? It shouldn't take long.' He paused, thought for a brief moment, and then said with half a smile, 'We could always take Marnie and Greg up on their offer?'

This thought brought a welcome relief. When Poppy had told Marnie she was going to *meet the parents*, they'd joked that she and Oliver could always go and stay with them if things became unpleasant, given that they lived nearby.

Poppy smiled at him. 'I realise that I don't know your mother that well, but my guess is she'd actually love us to do just that; indeed, she'd think herself the stronger person if we did. Why don't we just stick it out and head off early in the morning? We could have breakfast at Marnie and Greg's instead.'

'Do you know,' he pulled her gently towards him as he spoke, 'that's one of the many reasons why I love you, Poppy Jackson. You always try to make the best out of a bad situation.'

Their embrace was so sweet and longing, she didn't want it to end.

Eventually – and rather reluctantly – they pulled apart, and he kissed the top of her head, slightly distracted. 'Now, let me get this business out of the way. Are you okay to unpack and make yourself comfortable whilst I go and do another round with Mater?'

She laughed. 'Of course, I'll be fine.'

'Okay, it shouldn't take long, back soon.' He kissed her quickly on the lips and went off.

The room seemed so quiet when he'd gone, and Poppy sat pensively on the edge of the bed. She hadn't met his father yet, and she wasn't really looking forward to it much; out of the two of them, she'd imagined Martha would've been the easiest to get on with, given the apparent tension between Oliver and Anthony. *Oh Lord, I guess I'm to expect fireworks at dinner then.* She rolled her eyes upwards before becoming distracted by a bleeping sound in her pocket, indicating an incoming text message. Retrieving her phone, she was delighted to find a message from Marnie.

'How's it going? Handbags at dawn? M x'

She texted back. 'Not brill, just had round one. You up for early breakfast? xxx'

Marnie was quick to reply. 'Absolutely, want all the gory details. Enjoy x.'

Poppy smiled wryly, wondering just how 'gory' things were going to get.

Her attention was suddenly drawn to some commotion, which appeared to be coming from the floor below. Not wishing to pry – but being concerned for Oliver – she tiptoed towards the door of their suite, listening carefully and realising it was actually someone screeching, and pretty hysterically too by the sounds of it.

She opened the door slightly, enabling her to catch the raised voices that she quickly realised belonged to Oliver and Martha, and not wishing to hear anything bad about herself, she gently closed the door and returned her concentration to unpacking – more to occupy her mind if anything, as she wasn't entirely certain they'd be staying much longer now.

She couldn't hear what was being said – just that voices were raised – and after a few moments of indecision, she decided to go into the en-suite to freshen up, relieved to discover that once inside, she couldn't hear them anymore. A short while later she caught the sound of the bedroom door being opened, signalling Oliver's return, and as she peered out of the doorway to greet him, she saw him place something into his overnight bag. For some reason, it seemed like something she shouldn't have seen, so quickly but silently she retraced her steps, deciding to wait for him to seek her out.

'Hey gorgeous,' he called out, and despite the light-hearted approach, she couldn't help but note he seemed flustered.

'Everything okay?' she asked, coming out of the bathroom. She didn't want to mention she'd overheard him arguing with Martha; she didn't want to pry.

'Yes fine, Mother says dinner will be at 7 for 7.30 p.m. Fancy a walk in the meantime?'

Poppy readily agreed; it would be good to get out and walk off their frustrations, so grabbing a cardigan, she followed him outside, taking his proffered hand. 'Come on Ben!' he called out to the black Labrador that had greeted them earlier, 'You can come too.' Ben bounded a quick greeting towards them before running on slightly ahead, sniffing along the side of the verges as he went.

They walked slowly along, hand in hand, chatting easily and relishing their beautiful surroundings with Oliver calling out to Ben every now and then, ensuring he didn't disappear too far out of view. Neither of them referred to either his mother or father – instead, Poppy took the opportunity to update him with the latest gossip and news about Sally, who appeared to be deliriously happy with Dave. She also mentioned that Percy was moving into his new home the week after next, having found a buyer for their old family home.

'I'm so pleased,' said Oliver, 'but not at all surprised the house sold so quickly. It's a good-sized family home, and King's Oak is a nice village too, although I do prefer Hampton Waters.'

She had to agree with him; Hampton Waters was such a quaint, picturesque part of the Cotswolds, and steeped in history. There were only 190 residents in the village, which is why it had been merged with Hampton Ash – which boasted 357 residents – about two years ago.

'Does your dad need a hand moving?' he asked innocently.

'He's booked a removal company... but many hands make light work and all that; what do you think?' Poppy was excited at the prospect of an impromptu visit.

'Give him a call and arrange it. We could stay at the Maide of Honour so your father doesn't have to worry about putting us up.'

Delighted by his unexpected suggestion, Poppy chatted eagerly with him about their plans as they continued on their walk. Ben soon picked up on their excited chatter and came bounding back towards them, wagging his already over-wagged tail even more enthusiastically, if that were at all possible.

By the time they got back to Stone House, it was after six, and feeling refreshed after their walk, they showered and put on fresh clothes, both now feeling much better.

'You look gorgeous, darling,' Oliver complimented her as she came out of the bathroom, having dressed in a navy blue chiffon cocktail dress. Nothing too formal, but dressy enough for dinner.

Spraying herself liberally with *Chanel's Crystal*, Oliver watched her for a moment before taking her head gently in his hands and kissing her tenderly on the lips. 'I love you, Poppy, don't ever forget that.'

As they made their way downstairs for dinner, Poppy steeled herself for round two – she felt as though they were walking towards a lion's den. It was still a warm evening and the French doors in the drawing room had been opened to invite in the last of the evening's sunlight.

'Ah. Here they are,' Martha greeted them with somewhat more warmth than she had earlier that afternoon, offering them both a glass of champagne. 'My, don't you look lovely, dear.'

Poppy accepted her compliment warily just as someone entered through the opened French doors, taking her by surprise. It was obvious he was Oliver's father; the likeness between the two of them was uncanny and he was almost just as handsome, it had to be said.

'Evening Father.' She watched Oliver greet him with sincere warmth, which seemed pleasantly reciprocated; they shook hands and patted each other on the back.

'Oliver!' Anthony exclaimed, his voice slightly deeper than his son's. 'It's good to see you.'

Oliver beamed, turning to introduce Poppy, but Anthony was one step ahead of him – he stepped forwards and took her hand. 'You must be Poppy.' Anthony took her hand and placed it to his lips, kissing the back of it. *Like father like son.* 'It's lovely to meet you,

Poppy. Oliver's told me nothing about you at all so I look forward to hearing all about you from *you*.'

Oliver smiled to himself. He knew what an old charmer his father was and he found her blushing reaction quite endearing.

'Right!' Martha cut in, trying to garner everyone's attention. 'We really ought to think about going through for dinner.'

'There's plenty of time yet, Martha,' Anthony gently hushed his wife. 'Let's all go outside and enjoy our drinks on the veranda, shall we?'

They stepped out into the warm night to discover Ben bounding towards them.

'Not now, Ben!' shrieked Martha, in the hope of calming him down, but he was just too excited. They didn't get many visitors to Stone House and Ben wanted to make as much of the extra attention as possible. Anthony called Ben to heel next to the chair he'd since occupied, and the dog quickly plonked himself down, his long pink tongue flopping out of his mouth as he panted and panted, still wagging his tail as Poppy was amused to notice.

'I hear you've made Partner at Artimedius, Oliver?'

'That's right.' Oliver was delighted Anthony had picked up on his promotion before he'd had a chance to tell him. 'I only found out myself earlier this week. It seems my hard work has finally been rewarded.'

'Yes, quite. Congratulations son, I'm very proud of you.'

A look of pure joy crossed Oliver's face. Anthony had finally uttered the very words he'd so longed to hear. It had been a long time coming.

Martha clapped her hands a tad too dramatically and stood up to hug her son. 'What fantastic news, darling; simply superb.' She kissed him on both cheeks. 'This calls for more champagne!' she added, before disappearing to fetch another bottle.

Poppy, of course, already knew of Oliver's much longed-for promotion and was completely thrilled for him. In fact, they'd planned a romantic meal out the following week to celebrate as he'd been too busy with other work commitments since – or so she thought, anyhow.

Martha soon returned with a fresh bottle of chilled champagne, which Anthony expertly opened before proceeding to top up everyone's glasses.

'So Poppy,' Anthony addressed her, glancing over the top of his refreshed glass. 'May I ask where you originate from?'

'Oh, Poppy's a village girl,' butted in Martha, but no one paid her any attention.

'You're a country girl, are you? Which part?' his father asked her.

'A small village in the Cotswolds, actually, which you've probably never heard of. It's called King's Oak?'

Anthony thought for moment as he took another sip of his drink, and then his eyes lit up with recognition.

'Ah. Yes. King's Oak! Isn't that near Hampton Waters?'

Oliver and Poppy exchanged looks, both pleasantly surprised.

'Yes, that's right,' they choroused together.

'We attended a wedding there in June, actually,' Oliver continued. 'Poppy's best friend recently married at St. Michael's Church.'

'Oh well, I guess you know the Reverend Peter Fisher then?'

The three of them chuckled knowingly.

'Yes, he's quite a character – we had great fun with him,' Poppy said before catching a quick glance of Martha's thunderous face. With that she quietened down, fearful of some kind of repercussion.

'He certainly is.' Anthony seemed oblivious to Martha's displeasure. 'Did you meet his wife, Cathy? Lovely woman but a raving alcoholic, you know? Keeps draining all the stock for Holy Communion, which drives Peter completely bonkers.' They all laughed. 'Actually, do you know the Hambly-Jones'?'

Poppy thought for a moment. 'No, I don't think I do. The name does sound familiar, but I can't place it, I'm afraid.'

'Never mind, we shall have to go there one weekend and I'll introduce you.'

Oliver looked elated at the prospect of such an invitation from his father, and Poppy had to smile too – she was happy he was happy.

With such a positive start, the rest of the evening passed pleasantly enough, despite one or two cutting remarks from Martha, which appeared to fall on deaf ears much to her disdain. This caused Poppy to wonder if the real reason Oliver and his father hadn't got on over the years was because Martha appeared to continually play one of them off against the other. However, this was one battle Poppy did *not* wish to get involved in, so she just kept those thoughts to herself.

She was genuinely quite sad when the evening came to an end, as Anthony Sullivan's presence had made a significant difference to their visit. It was a surprise, but a nice one.

'What are your plans for tomorrow?' Anthony enquired as they headed off towards bed.

Poppy wished she hadn't been so hasty to arrange an early breakfast with Greg and Marnie, but then neither of them had anticipated the evening going quite as well as it had. 'We were planning on leaving early actually as we've made arrangements to meet up with some friends,' she explained apologetically.

'Well, that is a shame. Never mind, I do hope we'll see you both again soon, though. Give me a shout next time you're at the Hamptons and we can meet up. You've got my office details, haven't you?' Oliver nodded in confirmation. 'Great, I'll look forward to it. Sleep well, both of you.'

They went back to the barn, Poppy feeling relieved that they were returning to their room on a much higher note than they had earlier in the afternoon. Oliver looked relieved too, not to mention incredibly pleased.

The following morning, Poppy was surprised to learn that Anthony had already left for London, and she couldn't help wondering that if they'd planned to stay longer, whether he might have stayed longer too. Was all not well in the Sullivan's marriage?

After bidding a quick and stilted goodbye to Martha – and making a big goodbye fuss of Ben – she was grateful to be leaving Stone House behind as they drove out along the tree-lined driveway and towards the main road. There was definitely tension in the air again this morning and she was glad to be out of it.

They made the short journey to Greg and Marnie's home, spending a fun-filled morning with them and the children, playing games in the garden before filling up on the delicious brunch Marnie had organised for them all.

As they drove back to London, Poppy found it difficult to keep her eyes open, and soon she fell asleep whilst Oliver watched over her, guiding them both safely back home again.

FOURTEEN

It was a chaotic week as, being the end of July, most people were going off on their summer holidays and there seemed to be endless last minute jobs everyone wanted finishing off.

Poppy and Oliver were taking a few weeks off themselves, although they'd yet to book anywhere, having been given the holiday bug by Greg and Marnie who were off to Canada for three weeks to visit Greg's family.

Having talked through all eventual possibilities that may occur during their absence, Poppy sat down with a final cup of coffee of the day with Amanda, Dom's PA, pleased that it was both home time and Friday night.

'So, have you got any plans for your holidays then?' Amanda asked.

Poppy jiggled excitedly in her seat. 'Oliver's taking me out tonight for a special dinner, actually – you know, to celebrate his promotion. Then next week we're going to stay in the Hamptons for a long weekend, helping my father with his house move.'

'That all sounds lovely.' Amanda gazed into the distance, thinking about her own weekend; she'd just met a new man who was taking her out for dinner that evening too. She was excited, but a little nervous.

The two girls hugged as they said their goodbyes for the next few weeks and then Poppy set off for the tube station, excited at the prospect of the evening ahead. They were dining at a newly opened restaurant in Kensington that evening before spending the weekend at Oliver's apartment, where they were going to plan the rest of their holiday. *Until then, I shall relax.*

She climbed into an already over-packed tube train headed for the Chelsea Embankment, and as the station neared, she readied the key Oliver had given her to his apartment – not that she really needed it.

Whenever she arrived at Priory Court, either Huw or Frederick – whichever of the two porters were on duty – always escorted her to the apartment, opening the main door for her. It always seemed very opulent to her.

'Good evening, Miss,' Huw greeted her warmly as she stepped through the automatic glass doors into the lobby area. 'Good week, I trust?'

Poppy always appreciated his polite chatter; now she'd taken to staying at Oliver's most weekends, the porters always greeted her as though she were a missed family member.

'Yes thanks, Huw, although a bit hectic this week with everyone going off on their summer holidays.'

Having already called the lift, he took hold of her overnight bag and case, and when the lift reached the second floor, Huw stepped aside to allow her out first before opening the apartment door. The porters held keys for every apartment in the block, not just to let the cleaners in twice a week but also to facilitate any work or repairs that may need to be undertaken – or indeed any deliveries, as it seemed was the case today, much to her delight.

'There's been a delivery for you, Miss,' he explained, smiling.

She entered the lounge where a huge, stunning floral display welcomed her.

'Oh my word, these are amazing!' She bent to breathe in the perfume from the mixture of floral delights.

'I'll leave you to it,' Huw added politely. 'Have a pleasant evening and do call if you need anything.'

After saying goodbye, Poppy reached for the card as he let himself out: *My darling Poppy. A small thank you for your unending support and patience during my bid for promotion. Deepest love always, Oli xx'*

She was thrilled by his spontaneity. In fact, she'd noticed a change in him again recently and she wondered if he was finally beginning to relax now that he'd achieved the promotion he'd long desired, and indeed deserved. Either way, the flowers were beautiful.

She headed for the bathroom to get ready for the evening ahead, and after choosing a black cocktail dress she fashioned her hair up, adding a diamante hair slide just in time for Oliver's arrival.

'Wow-wee!' he whistled appreciatively, taking in her completed look.

She went over to him then, and placing her hands on his chest, looked lovingly into his eyes. 'The flowers are beautiful, Oliver. You really didn't need to do that.'

'I didn't need to but I *wanted* to, Poppy. I want you to know how much I appreciate having you in my life.' He walked over and sat down on the bed as he began removing his shoes, then he stopped briefly, looking back over at her. 'You've put up with a lot since we've met, and you've not complained once. What with all the last minute cancelled and rearranged dates, or not seeing each other at all, or only snatching a brief lunch or quick drink together here and there.' He stood up, walking towards her. 'You've been amazing – no nagging, no moaning… I never thought I'd find a girl like you, and I want you to know just how much I appreciate you not adding any additional pressure to our relationship.' He winked, taking her in his arms and twirling her around. 'And now all my hard work has paid off! I've got a promotion, a huge pay rise, a bonus, and I've got the best girl in the whole world to go with it.' He bent down, covering her face and neck with kisses.

She pulled away, laughing. 'I've had the odd drama too, but what's important is that we work at it together.'

Oliver smiled. 'My point exactly – we make a great team.' He went off to shower then, humming to himself happily whilst Poppy fetched a pre-dinner glass of wine.

By the time she'd returned he was selecting his outfit for the evening. 'Lovely, thank you,' he said, accepting the proffered drink gratefully. 'Let's drink to us.'

Poppy raised her glass, taking a sip. It tasted delicious.

'Ready?' Oliver began tapping his pockets, returning briefly to the dressing room before they made their way to the lobby. He then escorted her outside to a waiting car, ready to take them to the restaurant.

He's really pulled out all the stops this evening.

She revelled in the luxurious leather seating of the Bentley he'd hired for the night as he told her that he'd booked them a table at *l'ange*, a newly opened French restaurant situated along Kensington High Street. When they got there, however, she wondered if he knew it more intimately than he was letting on, given the greeting he received from the Maître d' on their arrival.

'Monsieur Oliver, welcome.' The Maître d' fussed around them, taking their coats. 'Your table is all ready for you. Please, come this way.'

Once seated, Oliver chose the wine whilst they both perused the menu. Poppy was concerned to notice that he appeared a bit distracted.

'Is everything okay, Oli?'

'What? Oh yes, darling, fine thanks – I'm just trying to decipher this menu.' He made a point of bringing the menu closer to him as if to convince her, but she definitely wasn't convinced. 'Thought I might start with the *Coquilles St. Jacques*,' he added, his French accent perfect.

'Ooh yes, I was thinking that too,' agreed Poppy. 'I can't decide between the *Filet de Dorade* or the *Magret a l'orange* for the main, though?' Her accent wasn't as good as his but he smiled and appreciated the attempt all the same.

'Well, *mon chéri*, perhaps we shall have one of each and then we can share, how does that sound?'

'*Parfait!*' she replied, causing them both to laugh.

Food ordered, they sipped their wine slowly, and whilst he began to look more relaxed than earlier, there still appeared to be something on his mind. It occurred to Poppy that he might be about to announce that he was going to have to cut their holiday time short and was, in fact, wrestling with how best to broach the subject with her. She contemplated this for a few moments more and decided to do her utmost not to look too disappointed when he did.

She was reminded of their earlier conversation in the dressing room, when he'd heavily complimented and praised her for being so patient when their plans had to change at the last minute, and she wondered now if perhaps he'd been preparing her for some more bad news. At that realisation, her heart sank a little.

'I don't know about you, but it felt so good leaving the office today for three weeks' holiday.'

Here we go. She braced herself.

'I know we said we'd go through our plans on Sunday, but have you had any thoughts at all?' He looked across the table, smiling into her eyes, but she wasn't sure what to say – she didn't want to set herself up for disappointment.

'Er... not really. I guess I thought we could maybe go on a few day trips and then, after next weekend at the Hamptons, perhaps we could go away somewhere for a few days, what do you think?' Although she'd asked, she wasn't sure she really wanted to hear his reply.

'Well, to be honest, it all depends,' he replied, somewhat pensively. He looked down at his hands before bringing his gaze up to meet her own, an extremely serious look on his face.

She swallowed. *Oh my goodness, here we go; he's definitely got bad news.*

'Depends on what, Oli?' she probed, attempting to keep her voice low so as not to make a scene – and also not wanting to hear his reply. The evening had been going so well; she'd felt like a princess so far with the way he'd treated her... the flowers, the private car, the glorious French restaurant... No, she didn't want to hear his answer; she didn't want their evening to be spoilt.

'It depends,' he began hesitantly, and she noticed him swallow and look around nervously. He cleared his throat again, and then, rather dramatically announced, 'It all depends, Poppy Jackson, on whether or not you would do me the complete honour of agreeing to be my wife!'

As he spoke he placed his hand into his inside jacket pocket, producing a tiny green-coloured leather box. It had a cute little button clasp that he flipped open to reveal the most amazing, beautiful-looking antique diamond and sapphire ring she'd ever seen.

She was completely lost for words, her hands flying to her mouth, which was open in shock and amazement.

Oliver looked back at her expectantly, a smile playing on his lips, unsure whether to break into one of his fully-fledged grins or not.

'Oh, Oliver, I'd be honoured to be your wife!' she exclaimed. Tears of joy fell down her face as he stood up and came around the table to take her in his arms, much to the delight of the other diners whom, having realised what was taking place, had been holding their breath in anticipation of her answer. They were now all standing and clapping, offering their congratulations.

'Champagne all round!' Oliver requested to the Maître d', bringing even more delight to the diners of the – thankfully – small restaurant. Luc (the Maître d' of *l'ange*), having already been given the heads up from Oliver a few days ago, appeared at their table in no time at all with a chilled bottle of champagne and fresh glasses, whilst his waiting staff served a glass each to the other diners.

'A toast to Oliver and Poppy!' Luc said, as everyone raised their glasses and joined in.

Poppy couldn't believe what was happening – she even had to pinch herself to check it was definitely real. She was engaged! Actually engaged!

Having offered his own congratulations, Luc went off to fetch their first course whilst Poppy and Oliver held hands, grinning across the table at each other. She felt a little more composed now and Oliver just couldn't stop smiling.

'You had me going there for a moment; I thought you were about to tell me you were going to have to cut our holiday short or something and return to work.' She laughed, and he did too.

Still smiling, Oliver took the engagement ring out of its silk nest and, taking her hand, slipped the ring onto her finger. 'How does it feel?'

She held her hand up, shaking it lightly and then gently turning it this way and that, admiring the beauty of the set gems. 'It feels rather good – a perfect fit, I think, and so beautiful!'

'I thought you'd like it. The ring belonged to my grandmother – my mother's mother – and when she died it was passed on to me. My grandmother was a very similar build to you, especially the slim hands.' He lifted her hand to his mouth, kissing it gently, then he took an envelope out of the inside of his jacket and handed it to her to open.

Inside, she was staggered to discover tickets and an itinerary for a 10-day trip to the Maldives. 'Wow!' she gasped in delight. 'Really? This is so amazing!' With excitement oozing out of her, she jumped up and hugged him.

'You deserve it – we *both* deserve it. We're due to fly out next Tuesday so we can still enjoy a long weekend in the Hamptons beforehand.'

'I can't wait to call my father,' Poppy said, the thought just occurring to her. She knew how delighted Percy would be at hearing the news. And then, of course, there was Sally, and Marnie. *They aren't going to believe this.*

'I think your father might not sound as surprised as you might think.' He winked knowingly. 'After all, I took the traditional route and asked for your hand in marriage before I proposed.'

Poppy sat back in her chair, astonished at what she was hearing. *What an amazing guy. So kind, so thoughtful, so caring...* She loved him deeply; not many people got to see this side of him and she was touched that he'd gone to so much effort on her behalf.

'I'd like to make a toast to you, Oliver, for being one of the most thoughtful and caring people I have ever met.' She raised her glass. 'Here's to a long and happy future together.'

'There's one more thing,' Oliver added quickly, placing his own glass down and reaching across the table to take her hands in his. 'Now that we're engaged to be married, will you move in with me? Say... tomorrow?'

She fell about laughing; they were practically living together anyhow. 'Are you serious?'

'As serious as I am about wanting you to be my wife.'

'In that case, it's another yes.'

With that, the two of them locked gazes, basking in the love emanating from one another.

FIFTEEN

Poppy pulled up the collar of her coat against the chilly November air as she waited for a tube to the Chelsea Embankment. She longed to be at home in their warm apartment, sitting in front of a cosy fire and sipping a glass of something red, but she still had shopping to do.

I can't really complain given we've got a long weekend ahead of us.

She mentally hugged herself; she was so looking forward to completing the final plans for their forthcoming wedding in the spring. Percy had already met with Reverend Fisher, who was only too delighted for them to marry at St. Michael's, having met them both now on several occasions, the most recent of course being the weekend they'd visited the Hamptons following Percy's house move.

Reverend Fisher had quite taken to Oliver and Poppy and was particularly pleased when on the Friday evening of their stay, Poppy's family and friends hosted an impromptu engagement party at the Maide of Honour. Of course, Reverend Fisher had been most delighted to attend, especially as it was the usual night of fun and debauchery one had come to expect of a get together in the Hamptons. Poppy smiled as she recalled the events of that weekend and the holiday that followed; it really had cemented her relationship with Oliver and now she couldn't *wait* to become his wife.

She was genuinely grateful that Huw was on hand to help her into the apartment when she arrived home – she'd been quite unsure how she'd managed to even carry so much that far in the first place. He took her bags through to the kitchen before making his way back to his desk in the lobby.

Slipping off her shoes, Poppy rubbed her arms, sensing a chill in the air as she made her way to their bedroom to get changed into a cosy tracksuit. They hadn't planned on going out and the evening was just perfect for snuggling up to Oliver in front of a roaring fire.

She'd no doubt Oliver would appreciate it too, given the hectic few months he'd had. Now he was a partner his responsibilities had practically doubled, and he spent at least three nights out of every seven away, building up a new side to the business and attracting new clientele. Of course, she knew it wasn't going to be like this forever, and certainly he'd be taking plenty of time off for their wedding and honeymoon.

There was also Christmas to look forward to before then and she was particularly excited about it given that Anthony and Martha were due to meet Percy for the first time. She just hoped the meeting went well.

Right. Wedding planning first.

Poppy went through to the living area to light a fire in anticipation of Oliver's arrival – he'd been away since Tuesday and she'd missed him dreadfully – and she'd just started unpacking the shopping when she heard the front door go.

Realising he was home, she dropped everything and rushed off to greet him. 'Hello, my darling!' she enthused as she ran to the hallway, but a second later, she was stopped abruptly in her tracks.

He looked awful. His skin looked extremely pale, and she could clearly see how exhausted he was, but he still did his best to smile and greet her lovingly – he allowed his bags to drop to the floor as she gathered him in her arms.

'Oli?' Poppy's voice was thick with concern as she put her hand gently to his head. 'What's wrong? You look terrible.'

'I've an awful headache, Poppy,' he replied, his voice hoarse. 'I feel dreadful; I really need to just go and lie down.'

'Of course, let me make you more comfortable.' She guided him through to their bedroom. 'Leave those bags; I'll sort them in a minute. Have you taken anything?'

'Actually, I think it's a migraine. It came on yesterday and I thought I could work through it, but it got much worse just before lunch.' He placed his head in his hands, groaning as he sat down on the edge of the bed. 'It's really painful now and I feel quite sick. I don't know how on earth I got through the flight...' His voice trailed off as she slipped off his shoes and helped him out of his coat.

'Maybe I should call the doctor?' She asked, wondering if he'd picked up a virus or something.

'No, no need for that, it's just a migraine – I used to get them all the time. I just need to take some tablets and sleep it off.'

Poppy coaxed him out of the rest of his clothing, doing her utmost not to jar him too much and make his headache worse. After settling him into bed, she went to fetch his migraine medication from the bathroom, as instructed, and then helped him to sit up so he could take the tablets.

'I'm so sorry, Poppy.' As he spoke, she could tell that he was trying to meet her gaze but the light from the bedside lamp appeared to be hurting his eyes.

'Sssshh, it's okay. We've got all weekend together, remember? Monday too.'

'I know, but we were going to call your dad tonight and everything...' His voice trailed off again and he laid back down whilst she placed the glass of water on the bedside table.

'I know you were looking forward to it, Poppy, we're planning the wedding...'

'Don't worry about that now, we can start all that tomorrow. How about I get my laptop and join you? Then I can keep you company whilst I look up wedding bits and pieces on the internet?'

'Make the calls, Poppy. I'll be okay, it's best I just sleep it off anyway, darling.' He turned his head, looking up at her. 'I love you so much, Poppy,' he added as he lifted up his hand to stroke the side of her face.

'I love you too.' She kissed the inside of his palm before placing another one gently on his forehead. 'Get some sleep, my darling. I'll leave you to rest and join you later. Just call out if you need anything.' She tucked him up, switched off the bedside lamp, and then crept quietly out of the room, leaving the door slightly ajar so she could keep an ear out for him.

When she got back to the kitchen, she pondered for a moment as to what to do. She'd never known him to be ill and he certainly wasn't one to moan and groan about aches and pains or things like that, but then, she hadn't really known him that long, had she? And he *did* seem pretty certain it was a migraine. Sally suffered with migraines from time to time too and the only thing she could do if and when an attack came on was to go home, take some medication, and go to bed to sleep it off.

Having thought this through several times, Poppy accepted that for the time being this was the only thing that Oliver could do too. How awful it must have been for him, though, flying home with such a terrible headache!

Having decided she was making too much of it, she focused her attention back on putting the shopping away, though once she'd finished she felt a bit lost – she'd planned such a fun-filled evening for them, it didn't feel right to continue with Oliver in the bedroom and her out here. Unless he was away on business, or she at a conference, every minute they were together was spent *together*, which she loved.

She thought about going and joining him in bed after all but then considered that her tap-tapping away on a laptop whilst he was trying to rest really wasn't very considerate, and anyway, she *did* need to make those phone calls. If she got those out of the way, she decided, tomorrow they could concentrate on the other decisions that needed to be made.

Just then her stomach rumbled, reminding her that she'd not eaten a bite since lunch and it was now getting on for eight o'clock. She made herself a quick chicken wrap and poured herself a large glass of Merlot before going off to enjoy them in front of the now roaring fire that she'd lit earlier in the evening.

As she ate, she flicked through some magazines she'd brought earlier, then realising the time, she started making her calls. She spoke to Reverend Fisher first, who was enthralled to hear her voice, he told her, having been expecting her call as Percy had spoken to him beforehand. He'd already picked out three available dates and times for her impending nuptials.

'I shall keep all three for you, my dear, until I hear from you otherwise, how does that sound?' He was, of course, as charming as always.

'Thank you so much, Reverend Fisher – that sounds perfect,' Poppy replied happily. 'We're hoping to make a decision in the next day or two, so I shall call you back certainly by Monday, if that's okay?'

'You really must call me Peter, my dear,' he replied, although somehow, calling a man of the cloth by his Christian name didn't seem quite right to Poppy, even though she appreciated the gesture.

They said their goodbyes – with Reverend Fisher asking that his good wishes be passed on to Oliver – and next she called Percy, going through the possible dates with him.

'Well lovely, it's not as if I've got anything else going on, is it? I shall just be delighted to see you get wed.'

Hearing the emotion rise in his voice took Poppy back to when she'd telephoned him on the night Oliver had proposed. They'd both cried into the phone, delighted with the news, both wishing there was someone else to share it with too.

'Thanks Dad, in that case I think I'll get Oliver to choose when he's feeling better, and then that's the one we'll go for.'

'Is Oliver not well?' Percy asked, his voice filled with concern.

'He seems to be suffering with one of his migraines, so I've given him some tablets and packed him off to bed. Hopefully he'll feel much better in the morning.'

'Ah well, best thing for those migraines is rest, lovely.' Hearing this made her feel slightly better, she had to admit. 'Well, give him my best, and give me a call when you've settled on a date.'

They said their goodbyes, and she picked up the phone again, this time ready to call Sally. However, noticing that it was half past nine already, she decided to go and check on Oliver instead, and when she tip-toed to the bedroom door, she could just about see him sleeping, the light from the living area illuminating the bedroom.

Satisfied that he was okay, she pulled the door ajar again to shut out the light and then settled back down to call Sally, having refreshed her wine glass along the way. Disappointed there was no reply, she telephoned Marnie instead, who was thrilled to hear from her.

They went through the suggested dates and Marnie laughed as Poppy relayed her earlier call to Reverend Fisher. 'I am *so* looking forward to meeting him,' Marnie exclaimed. 'He sounds like a real character.'

'Oh he is, you're just going to love him. Now, there's something else I've been meaning to ask you, actually.'

'Ooh, I think I might know what it is!' Marnie squealed excitedly. 'You do?'

'I think you might be asking little Louisa to be a bridesmaid?'

Poppy smiled into the receiver. 'Well, yes and no.'

'Oh?'

'I – or rather, *we* – were hoping that you'd be a bridesmaid too, along with Sally, and then little Louisa would be a flower girl.' Even before she'd finished speaking, she heard Marnie gasp.

'Me?' She was clearly taken aback, and emotion crept into her voice as she asked, 'Surely I'm too old for all that?'

'Certainly not! And anyway, age doesn't matter. So what do you think?' She guessed from the sobbing that Marnie was delighted. *What is it about me making everyone so emotional tonight?*

She listened as Marnie told her how she'd longed to have been a bridesmaid but had never before been asked, and this gave Poppy another idea – she asked if Marnie would like to help choose the colour and style of the dresses, which equally made her squeal with delight. Needless to say, she liked that idea a lot.

They chatted excitedly for a good hour or so before saying their goodbyes, with Poppy promising to call and confirm the wedding date as soon as Oliver had been able to check them out.

Once she'd hung up, she pondered for a few moments over their conversation. She loved Marnie very much – and Greg and their children, for that matter – and they'd become really good friends over the years. She was delighted how Marnie had responded to being asked to be part of the wedding, and now she was looking forward to the day even more, if that was at all possible.

Although it was quite late by then, she decided to try Sally again as she didn't want her to be left out of the planning, and this time Sally answered, having just got back from a late shift. She was just as thrilled as Marnie at being asked to be a bridesmaid, and they also had a good, long chat until Poppy noticed it was after twelve and decided to draw their call to a close.

'Give Oli my best,' said Sally, 'although I'm not surprised he's got a headache what with all the shagging you do.'

Poppy let out a shocked laugh. 'You're a fine one to talk. What about you and Dave? I'm surprised you haven't cooked up a little something of your own yet!'

'You're joking, ain't you?' asked Sally, laughing. 'We've only been married six months and I practically have to beg for it as it is – it'll be a long time before we start a family!'

They both roared with laughter. Poppy so enjoyed her telephone calls with Sally, and she came off the phone in high spirits, eager to share the news from all her calls that evening with Oliver – though she'd wait until the morning to do it.

She felt chilly again now that the fire had died out, and by now she was quite tired too. So, she collected up her plate and glass and went through to the kitchen, where she fetched a glass of water before carrying it through to the bedroom, trying to stay as quiet as possible as she slipped into bed next to Oliver.

She desperately wanted to snuggle up close, but she didn't want to disturb him. *Best to let him sleep.* So instead she rolled over onto her side and gently drifted off, all sorts of wedding plans, conversations, and ideas busily whirring through her mind.

The nightmare woke her quite suddenly.

She'd been dreaming of their wedding day, with her arriving at the church dressed in a huge, white flowing gown and a long, elegant train that was billowing in the breeze and kept tugging her backwards.

As she walked up the aisle, proudly taking her father's arm, she noticed all sorts of people in the congregation whom she didn't altogether recognise, along with old school friends and previous work colleagues. When she got to where Oliver was supposed to be waiting, he wasn't there, and no matter where she looked, she couldn't find him. She began searching frantically, running around and calling out his name, but he was nowhere to be found. She began to sob.

The people in the congregation surged forwards, circling her and laughing, and then three black bats appeared from nowhere, flying at her and clipping her hair with their wings. She was so terrified she began screaming and crying hysterically... and then she woke up.

A glance at the clock revealed it was 3.33 a .m. She was bathed in a film of sweat and a sob rose in her throat, such was the intensity of the experience. She took a few sips of water and laid back down, her heart pounding madly, before glancing over at Oliver, thankful that she didn't appear to have disturbed him. For several moments she replayed the nightmare over and over in her mind, before finally deciding to put it down to the stress of organising the wedding. Pushing her arm under the duvet, she searched for Oliver's hand in order to gain some comfort.

As quickly as she'd reached out, she withdrew again, sensing that all was not well. Her heart pounding crazily in her chest, she jumped up and switched the light on, immediately knowing that something was dreadfully wrong. She tentatively moved around to the other side of the bed, her eyes focusing on Oliver's face, thinking that if he suddenly woke, she wouldn't want to startle him.

He appeared, however, to be staring at her, only his eyes were still; he wasn't there.

A cry of hysteria rose quickly in her throat, her hand trembling as she placed it to her mouth to stifle her cries. She sank to her knees beside him, attempting to rouse him with her other hand. It wasn't working.

She began to shake uncontrollably, realising she could barely breathe she whispered, 'Oli!' She practically choked out his name. 'Oli, can you hear me? Please speak to me!'

By now tears were cascading down her face as the reality of the situation began to take hold. He was cold; he wasn't breathing. He wasn't responding. Realising she needed to get help urgently, she reached for the phone, but she was shaking too much and the glass she'd placed on the bedside table earlier fell to the floor unnoticed, spilling the contents onto the carpet.

Whilst just managing to press 999 on the telephone keypad, Poppy struggled to control the receiver – it quivered in her hand as shock surged through her. The emergency operator, being expertly trained in such moments of distress, was soon able to ascertain the situation and had quickly dispatched the necessary services.

After hanging up, Poppy called down to the Porter. They would need to unlock the main doors.

'Hello, Miss?' Huw became immediately concerned, having noted how upset she sounded. Poppy sobbed into the receiver, quite unable to control her distress. 'I need help. It's Mr. Sullivan...'

Huw grabbed the spare key before calling the lift, and Poppy came to meet him as he entered the apartment. She was very distressed, tears pouring down her already tear-stained face as she babbled, 'He's dead, I think he's dead!' She was sobbing, wiping fresh tears away with the back of her hand.

Huw guided her to the sofa before going into the master bedroom, returning a short while later. Being ex-military he was trained to handle all sorts of situations and he immediately took control. Having collected a blanket from the end of the bed, he went through to the lounge and placed it around her shoulders, which was just as well; she'd started trembling again.

'Have you called for an ambulance?' he asked, trying to make his words as clear as possible.

She nodded her head in confirmation and started to sob again.

He yearned to put his arms around her to comfort her, but instead he rubbed her shoulders, trying to offer some form of comfort to her that way. Despite his experience, he was still shocked himself; goodness knows what *she* was going through.

It looked to him as if Oliver had died in his sleep, but he was no doctor. There certainly did not, however, appear to be any foul play at hand. 'I need to go downstairs so I can open the doors for the ambulance,' he explained, kneeling in front of her. 'Will you be okay for a few minutes?'

She nodded and he reluctantly left, reaching the lobby just in time for the arrival of the on-call doctor. He briefly explained his understanding of what had happened whilst guiding the doctor back to the apartment, and when they got inside they found Poppy rocking gently back and forth, sobbing her heart out.

Huw directed him straight to the bedroom before going to make a cup of hot, sweet tea, hoping that the beverage would help calm her.

The doctor soon returned, and going over to Poppy, he crouched down on his heels, placing his bag down on the floor. As he took in her tear-stained face and obvious distress, his heart went out to her; she must have been completely devastated at having found her beloved partner in such a horrendous way.

'Hi Poppy,' he said softly and slowly, 'I'm Colin, the duty doctor on call.' He paused, giving her a moment to take in his words. 'I'm sorry to confirm that Oliver appears to have passed away in his sleep.'

This, understandably, brought forth a fresh outburst of emotion. It was never the easiest part of his job, of course, but it was always far worse when it involved a life taken well before its time.

He swallowed, waiting patiently and empathetically for her to calm before continuing, 'We'll have to wait for a post-mortem, but from what you've told us, it appears there is a possibility that Oliver suffered some sort of aneurysm.' The doctor went on to explain further. 'Poppy, experience tells me that even if you had got him to a doctor or sought medical advice earlier, the damage had already been done, and I doubt that anything would have prevented its outcome.' He paused again, wondering if any of this was sinking in for her. 'Now, you can't stay here tonight. Who can I call to take care of you?'

She peered up at the doctor, her face now blank of any emotion.

'Hello?' Greg reached out groggily, grabbing the shrieking phone before it woke the whole house up.

'Hello, is that Mr. Sable?'

Greg sat up, suddenly alert – he didn't recognise the voice on the line. Glancing at the clock, he saw it was four forty-five in the morning. His stomach immediately started churning. 'Yes, this is Greg Sable.' Marnie had woken up by now and was also beginning to sit up, wondering what on earth was going on.

'I'm sorry to call you so early in the morning, Mr. Sable – it's not good news, I'm afraid.' Greg's mind went into overdrive, concerned that something had happened to his parents. 'My name's Colin. I've been given your number by Poppy Jackson,' the doctor explained, making Greg's mouth go dry. Slowly, he climbed out of bed.

Oh my God, what the hell's happened to Poppy? By now his heart was thundering in his chest.

'Go on,' Greg encouraged.

'I'm afraid, Mr. Sable, that Poppy's had quite a devastating shock; I'm sorry to tell you that her fiancé, Oliver Sullivan, has passed away.'

Greg sat down on Marnie's dressing table chair, unable to believe what he was hearing.

'Would you be able to come and collect her?' asked the voice on the end of the line – Greg couldn't remember his name. His name was unimportant right now. 'It's not really possible for Poppy to stay here for the next day or so and she really needs some support right now.'

'Of course.' Greg gulped, not really taking it all in, but doing his best to, for Poppy's sake. 'We'll be there as soon as possible. How's she doing?' As soon as he'd asked the question he felt immediately stupid. He imagined she'd be hysterical – utterly devastated and hysterical.

He ended the call and turned to look at Marnie, who was sitting bolt upright with her hands over her mouth, looking at him expectantly.

'It's O-Oliver,' Greg stammered, making her eyes widen in horror. 'He's dead.'

SIXTEEN

Poppy slumped against the side of the bath; she would be glad when today was over. All this upset. All this stress. Everything. It was almost two weeks since her beloved Oli had passed and she was still having bouts of sickness and frequent episodes of crying; she realised it was going to take some time to come to terms with her grief.

She'd taken the tablets the doctor had prescribed for a few days, which helped, but then she realised she could all too quickly come to rely on them too much, so she hadn't asked for any more. She didn't want to go down that road, no matter how depressed she was feeling right now.

She recalled how devastated she'd been when her mother had passed away; distressed that she hadn't been there with her, and thinking that maybe if she had been, she might have somehow been able to help her – to save her, even.

Then, there she was, in the same house as her darling Oliver, drinking wine and gossiping on the phone whilst he'd been lying in their bed *dying*. What if he'd tried to call out for her? What if he'd tried to get her to help him? What if..? Question upon question raced through her mind during every moment of every day, continually torturing her.

One minute she was angry at herself for not calling the doctor earlier that evening, then she thought that she should've insisted on staying with him in the bedroom whilst he slept, and the next minute she was just angry that he'd been taken away from her. First her mother, now Oli! Tears trickled down her face; she really couldn't bear to be without him. Just what the hell was she going to do with her life now?

Just then she heard a gentle tapping on the door, followed by Marnie's voice asking if everything was okay. Poppy just sat there for a moment, completely unable to speak.

Concerned, Marnie let herself in. 'Oh sweetheart,' she cried, rushing to her friend and taking her in her arms. Today, she knew, was going to be hard on all of them, but more so for Poppy.

It was bad enough that she'd lost her fiancé, but Martha – Oliver's mother –wouldn't allow Poppy anywhere near the funeral arrangements. Poppy had asked if Oliver could be buried at St. Michael's Church in Hampton Waters, but his mother had gone apoplectic at the very thought of it.

Marnie had tried everything she could think of to get Poppy involved, even asking Martha if she could select a hymn for the service, but her requests were met with severe iciness to the extent that she realised it was better to just give up and go with it. On the one hand, she perfectly understood where Martha was coming from – after all, Oliver was her and Anthony's only son – but on the other hand, Oliver had also made Poppy his bride-to-be and had clearly loved her. She really should have been allowed to be involved in the arrangements of her beloved's last journey, at least in some small way.

'Come on, sweetheart,' Marnie said gently, 'Sally, Dave, and your dad have arrived – it's time to go. Come on, let's get you cleaned up.'

She took Poppy's hand and guided her to the washbasin, where she rinsed out a fresh cloth before wiping the tears from her face. Then, when Poppy was ready (or as ready as she could be), the two of them walked hand in hand downstairs to greet the sombre party.

Percy had already been to visit her the day after Oliver had died, of course, and the two of them now hugged, followed by Sally and Dave. The service was being held in the village church near to Oliver's family home, so they made their way there and waited outside St. Peter and St. Paul's as the funeral cortège approached.

Percy held his daughter's hand, squeezing it gently.

Poppy didn't really remember much of the service – she found it so distressing knowing that Oliver was lying only just a few feet away, yet she couldn't touch him or be with him. It just didn't seem fair. She tried to compose herself, but many of the words in the prayers, hymns, and eulogies were so touching she found it incredibly hard not to cry – though not as hard as she found it when she watched his coffin being lowered into the ground.

She was glad to have the support of Marnie and Sally; she felt quite sure that she would've collapsed had her dear friends not been there to support her, both physically and emotionally. Whilst the other guests made their way back to Oliver's family home, they took their time heading back to their own cars before Marnie spotted Martha walking towards them. She so hoped Martha was coming to invite them back to the house as well.

'Poppy,' Marnie whispered, 'prepare yourself – Martha's heading towards us.'

Poppy looked up and straightened, curious as to what Martha wanted. Sally stood up straight too; she hadn't yet met Martha and she certainly didn't like the look of the woman approaching them. She just had such a stern, cold face.

'Poppy,' greeted Martha coldly, stopping the trio in their tracks. Poppy said nothing; she just stared blankly through her. 'I think there's something you have that no longer belongs to you?' she continued, clearly impatient.

Poppy glanced at Marnie, somewhat confused as to what Martha was going on about. Marnie shrugged her shoulders – she had no idea either.

'My mother's ring,' Martha explained, holding out her gloved hand expectantly.

Poppy looked first at her hand and then back at Martha's face in complete amazement, her mouth dropping open.

'Martha, please,' urged Marnie, thinking her behaviour most inappropriate, but Martha held up her other gloved hand to silence her.

'This is none of your business,' she spat. 'Ring, Poppy, *now.*'

Poppy glared icily at Martha as she pulled her engagement ring from her finger, the engagement ring Oliver had been so excited to give to her; the engagement ring Poppy knew Martha hadn't never wanted her to have in the first place, hence the row with her son the weekend he'd taken her to meet his parents. Slowly, she placed the ring into Martha's outstretched hand.

'And the box?' she asked.

This was too much. 'That's enough!' Marnie snapped. 'You disgusting old witch, your behaviour is shocking!' With that she took hold of Poppy's arm, pushing past her while Sally guided her from the other side. Poppy was now in bits; if it wasn't for the fact they were on hallowed ground, Sally would've let Martha have a piece of her mind too. In fact, she was quite desperate to tell her exactly what she thought.

'As long as I get it by the end of next week,' she called after them, a cruel smile playing on her lips.

All with looks of disgust on their faces, the trio of friends reached the cars where the men were waiting.

'What the hell was all that about?' asked Greg, perplexed.

'I think,' replied Marnie, taking a deep breath, 'we had all better get back to ours before I explain that one; we're all going to need a very large drink.'

SEVENTEEN

It was the middle of December, a week before Christmas and three days since Poppy had returned to work. Almost a month had passed since Oliver's death and she was taking each day one moment at a time. She hadn't felt able to return to Priory Court just yet but she knew it wasn't fair to continue relying on Greg and Marnie's support for much longer. She'd decided to spend Christmas and New Year with Percy to give them some family time – especially as Marnie's parents were visiting from Scotland – and she intended to use the holidays to decide whether or not she should move back to the apartment.

Just then, her thoughts were interrupted by the shrill ringing of her desk phone, and having noted Oliver's private line flash upon the screen, she hesitated before gingerly lifting the receiver. 'H... hello?'

'Hi, Poppy?' said a cheery voice. 'It's Carrie, Carrie Bryant?'

Carrie was – or had been – Oliver's PA.

'Hi Carrie, how are you?' Poppy responded cautiously. She'd only been back at work three days – why would Carrie be calling?

'Yeah, I'm good thanks. Listen, I know things are difficult right now but I wondered what you wanted me to do with Oliver's post? I hate to ask in such sensitive circumstances, but there's quite a pile building up over here and some of it looks important.'

For a moment, Poppy was confused – why on earth was Carrie asking *her*? 'Surely there's someone else that can take over Oliver's responsibilities?' Poppy retorted tartly. 'Can't they deal with it?'

'I'm so sorry, Poppy,' continued Carrie, choosing her words carefully. She felt awful calling but she really couldn't put if off any longer. 'I should have explained, this is Oliver's private mail. You know, he had it on redirect to the office? Because he was away so much...' she trailed off, not knowing what else to say.

'Oh.' Poppy was taken aback; this was news to her. 'I didn't understand you for a moment; I should be the one apologising. Yes, of course I'll take it.' She paused to swallow, feeling nauseous again.

'Tell you what,' interjected Carrie. 'I'm off to lunch shortly. I'll gather it up and leave it in an envelope at your reception, shall I?'

'That'd be great Carrie, thanks,' Poppy replied, struggling with the emotions the phone call had brought up.

Thankfully the rest of the day passed quickly and Poppy was relieved when Greg popped his head around the door to collect her. As they departed through reception, the security guard handed her a very large and heavy brown envelope marked confidential. Greg raised an inquisitive eyebrow.

'It's just Oliver's post,' she reassured him, but hearing this made him raise his eyebrow even further, so on the way to the station she explained about her earlier conversation with Carrie.

Greg remained cautious. 'All the same, I think it's best we approach this together,' he suggested gently – he was damned if he was going to let anything upset her again.

They travelled in silence; her wondering what was in the envelope that could be so heavy, and him fearing there could be some unpleasant or spiteful communication from Martha, and if so, what it might look like so he could fish it out before Poppy saw it.

They were both glad of Greg's car once they reached the station at the other end, and he quickly drove the short distance back to the house, both of them still pondering their own thoughts. Poppy had felt sick again on the train and had realised it was probably because she was so hungry – she really needed to put more effort into getting her diet back on track, but she just seemed to have no appetite at all. Half the time she couldn't be bothered to eat, and the other half she simply forgot.

The house was all lit up as they approached, with Poppy noticing that the Christmas tree had been put up too. 'Oh, how lovely,' she exclaimed excitedly, causing Greg to smile; he always got excited at seeing the Christmas tree too, it being his favourite part of the festivities. Once inside, the children were bounding around the place excitedly, each wanting to explain what part they'd undertaken in the traditional decoration of the tree.

'Come on you three,' interrupted Marnie, 'there's pizza on the table, and garlic bread too.' They all laughed as three hungry children rushed off to claim their reward for a long afternoon spent putting up the decorations.

'The house looks great, Marnie.' Greg placed his arms around his wife's waist, greeting her with a kiss.

'It looks beautiful,' agreed Poppy, 'very Christmassy.'

Marnie smiled as she hugged her. 'Thanks guys, I thought it would be a bit of a cheerful distraction.'

'We could certainly do with one of those,' said Greg in reference to the large envelope Poppy was holding, before bringing Marnie up to speed with the latest events. 'Let's have dinner and get the children to bed before we tackle anything, what do you think?'

They all agreed, Poppy going off to get changed whilst Marnie followed Greg through to the kitchen.

'Is this a good idea?' she whispered as she watched him bite into a piece of garlic bread, unable to stave off his hunger even a moment longer.

Greg frowned. 'It's going to be a difficult one, admittedly, but at least we can go through it together. In a strange way, she may even find it quite cathartic – y'know, it might even bring her some closure.'

A couple of hours later, they retired to tackle the task in hand. Marnie poured them each a glass of wine, whilst Poppy opened up the large and bulky envelope, spilling the contents out onto the coffee table. There was certainly a lot of mail for such a short period of time, which in itself was rather intriguing.

'Okay, let's just open them all up and sort through them,' suggested Greg.

Poppy and Marnie nodded in agreement, and after getting to work, it wasn't long before a theme began to appear: bill upon bill upon bill. All demands for payment of one thing or another and many a lot older than just the few weeks since Oliver's death. An eerie silence developed between them, no one wanting to state the obvious.

Poppy gasped then, looking up from another letter she'd just opened. 'I think you'd better read this,' she said, handing the document to Greg.

He read through it, the women waiting for him to respond, and after a few minutes, he let out a low whistle from between his clenched teeth. 'Sheeeshh, this is a surprise.'

He looked from Marnie to Poppy and back to Marnie again, his face etched with concern as he finally asked Poppy, 'Did you know about the apartment?'

She shook her head. 'I just assumed, really...'

Marnie looked at Greg curiously. 'What is it?'

Greg took a deep breath. 'Well, it appears that the apartment wasn't owned by Oliver but rented – fully furnished – and it also appears that the rent and utilities haven't been paid for several months.' He flicked through the pages, scanning the details. 'It seems they've been writing to Oliver for some time, but as they had no response,' he continued, looking up again, 'they've started eviction proceedings; the apartment has to be vacated by the 19th of December.'

'But that's this Friday!' exclaimed Marnie.

Poppy placed her head in her hands. She honestly didn't know what to think.

'It's okay, it's okay,' Greg soothed, putting out a hand for support, 'I think it's better that you and Marnie go off to the snug and let me tackle the rest of this.' He gestured at the unopened post with his free hand. 'Leave me to properly assess what we're dealing with here. There certainly appears to be a side to Oliver that's new to all of us; let's just get the full picture and then we'll know what we're dealing with, okay?'

Poppy nodded – she was too stunned to argue otherwise – before following Marnie through to the snug, where they huddled next to each other on the comfy, overused, but much loved sofa.

Seriously concerned with how Poppy would cope with all of this, Marnie was desperate to reassure her dear friend. 'We'll help you sort this out, Poppy; you won't have to face this on your own, I promise you.'

Poppy smiled gratefully. She didn't know how she'd have managed these past few weeks if it hadn't been for Marnie and Greg, and she hoped she wasn't testing their support now.

It was a good hour later when Greg finally joined them, holding a notepad he'd written various figures and notes on. 'Okay,' he began, 'well, there's no easy way to say this, and remember – I'm not here to judge, I'm just presenting the facts.'

Poppy nodded in understanding, though she couldn't help but feel a little nervous.

'From what I've pieced together, Oliver was in a lot of debt.' He paused, looking through his notes before carrying on, 'There's stuff like utility bills, rent, phone bills and the like, that seemed to have been left unpaid for several months. Then there's a number of credit cards – all maxed out – some of which have been owed since last December, or even before that.' He paused, sighing. 'What I couldn't understand to begin with was why. It's quite clear from some of his bank statements that he was earning a decent salary, and certainly following his promotion he received a generous bonus and a salary increase.'

Marnie and Poppy had their eyes fixed firmly on Greg, trying to take everything in. Marnie nodded at him to go on.

'Then I found these.' He pulled forward some documents that he'd tucked at the back of his notepad. 'These are details of a number of investments he made, which sadly didn't go in his favour. I can clearly see he's made both good choices and bad, but hey, that's life. It's just that the bad choices were *really* bad, and he seems to have got himself into a situation he couldn't get out of – that's what's been draining his money, which is why all the rest of his finances started to get out of hand.' He paused to take a drink from his glass, then set it down on the table again.

'It's not all bad, though,' he continued positively, 'he still has several good investments, which I've roughly estimated will clear off some of the debt outstanding, but there's still a considerable sum left.' He paused again, looking straight at Poppy. 'The thing is, you're not responsible for Oliver's debt. I don't want to upset you, honey, but you're not his next of kin – God knows his dear mother has certainly made that clear enough.'

Marnie nodded in agreement as she reached across to pat Poppy's hand comfortingly. 'It's really not your problem,' she added.

Poppy cleared her throat, hugging her knees against her. 'I can't quite take it all in, to be honest. I mean, I didn't ever see or notice any of this, and certainly Oli never mentioned it; we never even discussed money.' She paused, thinking for a moment. 'Of course, when I moved into the apartment I offered to contribute towards the mortgage – well, rent as I now know,' she explained, 'and of course the bills, but he wouldn't hear of it. Instead he just suggested we save my money for our wedding, which was what I did. I had, of course, been buying some of our food, and...'

Greg gently interrupted her, 'You don't have to explain anything, honey; we're certainly not judging you.'

'Absolutely,' agreed Marnie, who was now holding her hand. 'That's neither here nor there.'

Poppy sighed. 'It's just that, well... I honestly didn't have a clue. Other than what I've just told you, we didn't discuss money at all, and I never really gave it any more thought either. God, what does that say about me?' She brought her hand up to her throat, as though trying to suppress the sudden and overwhelming feelings of guilt and sadness that were rising within her. 'The thing is,' she began, 'the *important* thing is, I don't want people to know this side of Oliver. I want people to remember him for who he was. He'd struggled with his relationship with his father for most of his life, and had only just felt as though he finally respected – and accepted – him...' Her voice trailed off, tears stinging at her eyes, but she wasn't going to let them take over. No, she'd already cried enough tears to last her a lifetime. 'I'll pay it,' she announced, making Marnie gasp.

'No, you can't do that!' she argued. 'Why should you?'

'Marnie's right, Poppy,' said Greg gently, 'this isn't your mess to clear up.'

'It is,' she shot back. 'I lived in that apartment too – it's only right I should clear the rent and utility bills, and I certainly benefitted from his credit cards and other monies. I mean, he frequently took me away, we ate out regularly, and I never paid for a thing. He bought me flowers, chocolates... all sorts. No, it's only right I clear it all and protect him. I want to protect him and his reputation,' she stated firmly.

'It's a lot of money, Poppy,' Greg gently informed her.

Fortunately, she'd always been good with her money and for years had been a keen saver. She'd bought a few shares, hadn't she? And she'd already had some savings when she moved in with him. Plus, there was the returned deposit on her flat in Clapham she'd given up, not to mention her having saved practically all of her salary since she'd moved in with him. That all came to a pretty decent sum.

Just then, another thought sprang to her mind. 'What about the money you invested for me?'

Greg mused over this for a brief moment. 'Yes, you could certainly use that. I mean, you won't get back as much as if you'd kept it there longer as we'd discussed, but it would certainly make a dent in all of this.'

'Then that's what I shall do,' Poppy replied, knowing in her heart she was making the right decision.

EIGHTEEN

It was a few days before Christmas Eve and Greg, Marnie, and the children waved Poppy goodbye as she set off to spend the festive period with Percy in Swinford St. George. It was an emotional parting but nevertheless a happy one, especially as the children were bursting with excitement at the prospect of a visit from Santa Claus. They'd all really bonded in the past few weeks and she hoped the presents she'd left for each of them under the tree would reflect how much they all meant to her.

As she drove, her thoughts wandered to the events of the past week, and at how much lighter she felt at having finally brought some closure to her life. Of course, she still had a long way to go; losing the love of your life was bad enough, but to lose them in such devastating circumstances was something she didn't think she would ever get over. However, she now felt she had at least reached a point where she could begin to move forward. All of Oliver's belongings had been returned to his family home, save for the shirt he'd been wearing when he'd come home on that Friday night, which Poppy had retrieved from the laundry and which still contained the smells she associated with him. She didn't feel right to have kept anything else, and anyway, she felt certain Martha was sure to possess a detailed itinerary of everything he owned – she could just imagine her ticking off each item as she unpacked it all.

I suppose I shouldn't be too hard on her, really – he was her only child, after all, and she must be just as devastated at his loss as I am.

After clearing out their apartment she'd arranged for most of her belongings to be put into storage, alongside the furniture she'd previously stored from the flat she'd given up when she'd moved into Priory Court; a good decision, as it happened, given that having now cleared all of Oliver's debt, her remaining funds were small. In fact, there was just enough left for a deposit and first month's rent for a new flat, together with some living expenses until next payday.

However, whilst she might not have much financially, she knew she had a lot more than that spiritually; she had total peace of mind that Oliver could now rest safely – in peace himself – and that was something that money could never buy. You just couldn't put a price on it.

As she pulled off the motorway and onto the country roads that would eventually lead to Percy's house, she slowed down – she was feeling quite dizzy, and had in fact been experiencing dizzy spells several times recently. Yet again she reminded herself that she still wasn't eating properly; she'd only had a banana at breakfast that morning as she'd been rushing around, trying to ensure she'd packed everything in an attempt to leave as early as possible.

She glanced at her watch, and when she realised that she still had at least half an hour to go of her journey, she switched on the cool air for a while.

*

'I see you're not staying long, then?' Percy teased as he helped Poppy with her luggage.

'I'm homeless, remember?' she joked back, before following him through to the house. It had seemed odd driving here, rather than to their old family home in King's Oak, but she liked the house; it smelled new and fresh.

'Good job there are two bedrooms,' he called out, 'although I'm not sure there's enough room for you and all this.' He gestured towards the many bags and cases that now covered the floor of the spare room.

Poppy laughed. 'Don't worry, Dad, I'll cope. Anyway, I hope by the time I go back to London, you'll have helped me find a new home of my own.' She rustled through a couple of bags until she came across some newspapers. 'I picked these up this morning,' she added, waving them at him, 'we can look through them together if you like and see what's about.'

Percy smiled at his daughter. 'Sounds like a plan,' he said before going off to the kitchen to make lunch.

Poppy followed after him, but she suddenly had to steady herself for a moment as the room started to spin, causing her to feel incredibly sick. She tried to swallow it back down but it was no good; rushing to the bathroom, she wretched over the toilet.

Percy quickly followed her, wiping his hands on a tea towel, concern etched all over his face. 'Are you alright, lovely?' Of course, he could see that she wasn't, and he leaned over to pull her hair out of the way.

She wretched several more times but nothing much came out, which wasn't surprising seeing as how all she'd eaten that day so far was a small banana, and that had been several hours ago. Leaning back onto her heels, she wiped her mouth with a piece of tissue paper, taking a couple of deep breaths.

'Sorry about that,' she managed. 'I haven't been eating properly and I think the long journey on such an empty stomach didn't help.'

Percy frowned. 'Wash your face and come into the kitchen, then – we'll get something inside you, alright lovely?' He helped her to her feet, and she nodded before rinsing out her mouth and dampening a wash cloth to run over her face, her reflection in the mirror displaying just how gaunt she looked. There were dark smudges underneath her eyes, and her cheeks had become quite drawn. She had lost a little weight recently, she supposed – which she'd put down to not eating properly – and with being sick on top of everything else, she wasn't entirely surprised to see herself looking so washed out.

I need to get a grip; Oliver wouldn't want me going on like this.

With that she mentally resolved to get her diet back under proper control; she was sick of being sick anyway. And besides, her dad was a great cook. They both had a yearning for stodgy puddings so she was sure she'd be sorted in no time.

After a couple of seconds she went to join him at the kitchen table, where they shared a plate of chicken sandwiches washed down with hot, sweet tea, and had fruit cake for afters.

It tasted like home.

The next few days just flew past, and on the Friday they attended midnight mass at St. Michael's Church, where Reverend Fisher had literally welcomed them both with open arms. He went on to invite them both over to the vicarage for tea on Boxing Day, which they readily accepted, and Poppy could slowly but surely feel herself healing.

On Christmas Day, after exchanging presents with each other, they set off to enjoy Christmas lunch with Poppy's Uncle Nicholas (her mother's brother) and his wife Annie. Her cousin Martin joined them too, proudly introducing his new fiancée, Kim.

Poppy felt more than a few pangs of nostalgia watching the two of them together, completely loved up, and quite rightly showing off the stunning engagement ring Martin had presented her with that very morning.

Poppy had been close to Martin when they were growing up; at 31, and just one and a half years older than her, she'd thought of him more like a brother during their childhood years. Even though their relationship had dwindled since she'd moved away to work in London, she still enjoyed his company and they had a good laugh reminiscing over their childhood, much to the delight of Kim, who was enjoying seeing a whole different side to her usually serious husband-to-be.

Martin had been relentlessly teased as a child for his shocking auburn hair, and as he'd got older, he'd sprouted even more hair on his arms, chest, legs – you name it, it seemed to get hair on it. What he didn't seem to appreciate, though, was the fact that his colouring just further enhanced his handsomeness; he generally suffered from a lack of confidence when it came to his looks.

He worked as an accountant for his father's company, Matthew and Cleary – which his father ran with his partner, John Cleary – and Martin very much hoped to become a partner with the firm one day too. Percy had worked with them for several years before deciding to take his chances working freelance, and had never looked back. He was pretty much retired these days, though, save for the odd helping hand he was only too happy to offer old friends.

*

Boxing Day tea at the vicarage was a complete hoot, and was just the tonic they needed. Poppy was delighted to finally meet Cathy, Reverend Fisher's wife, and their three sons, Michael, John, and

Gabriel – the latter being, at 13 (in Poppy's eyes, at least) a complete angel.

Poppy helped Cathy organise the tea, given that she appeared rather worse for wear when they arrived; her nose was glowing almost as much as her cheeks. She was a jolly woman, really gentle and softly spoken but with a sharp wit, delivering apt punch lines when you least expected it, which had everyone roaring – no wonder the Reverend was always so jolly.

The vicarage was in complete chaos, of course – with Cathy also being quite active in the community, Poppy thought it little wonder there wasn't much time to keep the house in order. Of the several rooms on the ground floor, Poppy could easily identify which was the kitchen and which room Reverend Fisher used as his office, but as to the others, she really wasn't sure. There was an eclectic collection of furniture and possessions spread all over the place, with a sea of black sacks everywhere containing books, shoes, clothing, or a mixture of them all. In fact, there was all manner of paperwork scattered here, there, and everywhere, though it didn't come across as disgusting or annoying – it just seemed endearing.

The Fishers had such a vibrant, positive energy, and by the time she and Percy got ready to leave, she found they had soaked it up too. Indeed, she felt quite light-headed as they went on their way, having been invited to return again soon.

The next day – having retrieved the newspapers she'd brought from London – Percy and Poppy began seeking out potential flats for her to rent. That was, until she shot off to the bathroom, completely unloading her breakfast in the process.

Percy stood in the doorway, watching her wretch and wretch, and decided it was time to take action; he called Dr. Anderson, the village doctor, and the person who'd delivered Poppy into the world.

'Aright Steph? It's Percy Jackson,' he greeted the surgery receptionist when she answered. 'Is Dr. Anderson free today?'

'I can get you in at three, Percy, if that's any good?' came the reply.

'Yes, that'll be fine, though it's not for me – it's our Poppy. I think he should take a look at her.' His voice was thick with concern.

'I'm sorry to hear that, Percy,' Steph replied politely.

He heard her tapping the keys of a computer keyboard as she typed in Poppy's details. 'All right, that's all booked – 3 p.m. today with Dr. Anderson for Poppy. See you then.'

By now Poppy had re-joined him. 'Dad? What are you doing?' she blurted out angrily. 'I don't need a doctor.' She started pacing up and down the floor, waving her hands about in an agitated manner. 'Oh my God, Dad! You're going to make me look really stupid – there's nothing even wrong with me.' She glared at him, a look of exasperation on her face. She'd come here to relax for Christmas, not get hauled over to the local doctor.

Percy walked over, calmly placing his hands on her arms to still her from pacing. 'Then Dr. Anderson won't mind checking, will he?' he told her firmly. 'You're seeing a doctor and that's the end of it.'

She stomped off to the bedroom to sulk, a few minutes later realising she was acting like a complete child. *I'm twenty-six, for God's sake! I shouldn't be acting like this.* She thumped the bed as she flopped down onto the covers, then had to steady herself as she became quite dizzy again.

Once stabilised, she got up and went back into the kitchen. Percy was back at the table, marking up adverts in the paper.

'I'm sorry, Dad.'

Percy looked up, carefully taking in her appearance. *God, she looks awful.* She'd clearly lost weight and her face in particular looked so drawn; he was really quite worried now. It wasn't that he thought it was anything sinister; he just thought that perhaps she wasn't coping with Oliver's death as well as she thought she was. He remembered back to when his dear Grace had died, the sheer immensity of it all. *You cannot judge until you've walked in someone else's shoes.* As he felt he had, he knew she needed some help, and after all, Dr. Anderson had helped him. 'That's all right, lovely,' he soothed, before trying to distract her. 'Come and look at the ads I've highlighted – if they're any good we could go and take a look at some next week.'

Dr. Jon Anderson had been the village GP for the past 27 years. He'd seen a lot of people come and go during that time, and had witnessed – and later become part of – many changes within the practice too. He was now Senior Partner at The Hamptons Medical Practice, based in their newly purpose-built surgery on the edge of King's Oak, and together with a team of partner doctors, nurses, and other staff, the practice serviced all the surrounding villages, amounting to some fifteen hundred patients, most of whom Dr. Anderson knew very well. He'd delivered many of their children and had nursed a number of patients through mild to severe illnesses – and sadly, had comforted the many left behind when their loved ones had passed on.

He was a popular character and well respected in the community at large, even though he had quite the reputation as being a bit of a lothario; although not in inappropriate circumstances. He might have been on his sixth marriage, but he still maintained an excellent relationship with his five previous ex-wives. He was such a charming, positive, and loving family man that it was impossible not to like and admire him.

Success hadn't been handed to him on a plate, however; he'd worked hard to achieve a place at Oxford in order to study medicine, and not having his parents' support to draw upon, he'd taken several part-time jobs to get himself through university and then medical school. Now he was a renowned GP who was respected for his knowledge in paediatric care, asthma, and cardiology, and he sat on many panels and committees as well as his being involved in clinical trials. His current wife, Lizzie, at the age of 32 was 28 years younger than he, which was what many of the locals believed kept him so young. They had two children, Millie and Sophia, 2 years and 6 months old respectively, and he had a further four children from his previous marriages as well. He fully supported them all, with most of them spending every other weekend at the family home situated in Hampton Waters, which thankfully was large enough to accommodate them all, albeit a bit of a squeeze at times.

That afternoon, Dr. Anderson was most intrigued to learn that his next patient was Poppy Jackson. It'd been some time since he'd last seen her – almost eight years he noted as he read through her records, when he'd treated her for a chest infection not long after her mother had passed away.

He'd heard she was now working for a firm of investment stockbrokers based in the city, whom he knew very well through his ever-growing network of friends, colleagues, and contacts. She was a stubborn young lady, he recalled, with quite a determined spirit, and he wondered what she was coming to consult him about.

He pressed the intercom to call her through, shortly after which there was a gentle tap on the door. In she stepped, closely followed – much to his surprise – by her father, Percy. He was momentarily taken aback as he took in her appearance; although she'd certainly grown, he could see she was looking tired and drawn.

'Hello Poppy.' He got up and greeted her warmly, shaking her hand. 'It's good to see you; come on in and sit down.' He guided father and daughter to the two chairs in front of him.

'Dr. Anderson,' Poppy politely acknowledged as she sat down.

'What brings you here to see me?' he asked, once they were all settled.

She started to blush. 'Well, I'm afraid I'm wasting your time really...'

Percy interrupted 'No, you're not.'

She blushed again, and a small smile played on Dr. Anderson's lips; he liked the way she spoke, so eloquent. She seemed to have shaken off her West Country accent completely, and it suited her.

'It's my father...' she began again.

'No it's not,' Percy interrupted again. 'It's not me, it's you, Poppy.'

Dr. Anderson caught her scowling at him and was glad to see that she hadn't appeared to have changed in every way.

'Take your time, Poppy, it's okay,' he said after a moment. 'I was sorry to learn about your fiancé; I offer my sincere condolences to you.' He hoped that by acknowledging Oliver's death it might help her to find the right words.

'That's not why I'm here,' she snapped.

Dr. Anderson stifled a grin. 'My apologies. Please continue.'

By now Percy was starting to get agitated, and he began tapping his knees with his hands.

'Well actually, now you mention it, maybe it has, I'm not sure...' Poppy hesitated, looking up at Dr. Anderson. He'd always scared her as a child and she didn't want to appear foolish in front of him. 'I can't eat,' she blurted out, 'and when I eat, I'm sick... that's it, really. I just keep being sick and feeling dizzy.'

'Dizzy?' Now Percy was even more concerned; he hadn't known that.

'Yes, Dad – *dizzy*.'

'You never told me about that.'

Amused, Dr. Anderson watched the two of them, thinking how much they reminded him of Percy and Grace many years ago. Of course, he didn't dare say that out loud. 'Okay, Poppy, let's get some more details. Can you tell me when your last period was?'

'What?' *Kill me now!* She wanted the ground to open in front of her and swallow her up. *How could he ask this in front of my dad!*

'Your period, love, he wants to know when you had your last period,' Percy prompted, as though this was a perfectly normal conversation to be a part of.

'Oh, for God's sake, Dad! Stop saying that.' She was turning a nice shade of red now and she had no way of stopping it.

'How about if you stepped outside for just a few minutes, Percy?' Dr Anderson tactfully suggested. 'It'll give me an opportunity to examine Poppy, and then I'll call you back in.'

Poppy breathed a huge sigh of relief at his suggestion.

'Besides, I'm sure Steph's got a fresh pot of coffee on,' the doctor added, smiling.

Realising he wasn't wanted, Percy got up, patted Poppy on the shoulder a couple of times, and then padded out of the room.

Once the door had closed, Dr. Anderson continued. 'No need to feel uncomfortable now, Poppy, it's just a few questions. Can you tell me when your last period was?'

'I, er... I don't know.' She bit her lip – as if that would help jog her memory –hating herself for having to answer such embarrassing questions from such a handsome but scary doctor.

'A month ago? Two?' the doctor asked.

'Oh, before that,' she answered automatically. Now she came to think about it, wasn't that a little strange?

'Okay, and when did Oliver pass away?'

'November 17th,' she answered straight away. That date would forever be burned into her memory.

'And you recall having no period since then?'

'No, none actually.'

The doctor nodded. 'What about before then, Poppy? I know it's hard with everything you've gone through during the past few months, but try and remember.'

She thought for a moment. 'Umm, September maybe?'

'Okay, well done. And what about the sickness? When did that start?'

'Just after Oliver passed away really.' She swallowed, her bottom lip starting to tremble. Dr. Anderson wasn't surprised to see her react like this; she'd been through more in her twenty-six years of life so far than many people ever experienced in eighty.

He handed her a tissue. 'It's okay. Take your time, there's no rush. Now, whenever you're ready, just talk me through what's been happening to you recently – physically, mentally, and emotionally.'

She let a few tears fall down her face and then slowly started to explain the events of the past few months. The sleeplessness, the nightmares, not being able to eat and then eating and being sick, everything. By the time she'd finished, she felt much calmer – getting everything off her chest was pretty cathartic.

'Any stomach pains or breast tenderness?'

She flushed red again, though she was glad her dad was no longer in the room. 'My chest has been a bit sore, I suppose.'

She watched as he typed a few things into the computer before turning back to look at her, smiling. 'Okay, I think that's everything for now. Are you able to provide me with a urine sample?' She nodded and he passed her a sample bottle. 'Please use the toilet located just out this door and to the left, then come straight back in here.'

She stood up and went outside. Thankfully, her father was deep in conversation with the receptionist, so hadn't noticed her coming out. She quickly made for the bathroom, grateful that she'd had a couple of glasses of water after being sick this morning. A few minutes later she returned back to Dr. Anderson's room and handed him the bottle.

'That's great, thanks. If you could please take a seat, I won't be a moment.'

He got up and went across the other side of the room to a washbasin that was surrounded with various trolleys containing all sorts of bottles and other medical supplies. He had his back to her so she couldn't quite see what he was doing, but she guessed he was testing the sample – she'd seen him unscrew the lid off the bottle she'd given him.

As the minutes passed she started to feel extremely nervous – she could feel her heart pounding quickly in her chest as she waited. Just then the doctor turned back to face her, and she could see by his expression that he was about to tell her something significant.

He's probably going to tell me I'm dying, knowing my luck.

She twisted her fingers nervously in her lap as Dr. Anderson washed his hands and sat back down at his desk, before turning in his chair to face her. 'Okay, the good news is I don't think there's anything ominous going on here – or anything that's of deep concern.'

She let out a breath, starting to relax a bit. *So far, so good.*

'From what you've told me, together with the tests I've performed...' He trailed off, pausing.

Yes, yes, spit it out.

'It appears,' he continued, 'that you are pregnant.'

Silence.

He watched her mouth open, and then close, and then open slightly again. She was staring straight ahead of her, clearly shocked at the news he'd just delivered. Of course, he'd known she would be, but in his experience the majority of patients who found themselves in such circumstances were usually thrilled that a part of the person they had so deeply loved was going to live on – indeed, this is usually what kept them going, helping them through their grief. He was certain that Poppy would take this attitude also, though he let the news sink in for a few more moments before speaking.

'What are your thoughts?' He leant his elbow on his desk, resting his head on his hand as he watched her reaction.

'Well... I, er... I don't know what to say. The word 'shocked' springs to mind!'

He gave her a few more moments before gently probing further. 'Good shocked?'

'Oh yes, yes, definitely yes.' Her anxiety-ridden face began to fade into an inquisitive smile as she started to process the clearly unexpected situation that had just been presented to her.

'My guess is – judging from what you've told me – that you were maybe five or six weeks pregnant when Oliver passed.' He paused for a moment. 'So this would mean you are roughly twelve or maybe thirteen weeks pregnant now. About three months.'

She gasped. 'Three months? Seriously?'

The doctor nodded. 'Let's organise an ultrasound scan as soon as possible to give a firmer idea of dates.'

She was gobsmacked… just completely flabbergasted. She hadn't really thought about children – except for knowing that she definitely wanted a family some day – but with Oliver gone... Her thoughts trailed off as a sudden realisation hit her.

'It's Oliver's,' she whispered. 'It's Oliver's baby, and that means a part of him will live on through me – that's incredible.' A tear trickled down her cheek then and Dr. Anderson learnt across, patting her hand in a fatherly gesture.

'That's right, and that's why we've got to make sure you're fully fit and well.' He returned to his computer, his fingers flying expertly across the keyboard. 'We'll need to run some blood tests right away; when are you due back in London?'

Oh my God, I'm pregnant and I've got nowhere to live. Her thoughts started to wander all over the place.

'Well, I'm due back at work on the 7th January.'

'That's good, I can arrange an appointment for your first scan before then; at this stage you're entering the second trimester, so the morning sickness should ease off a bit now – actually, from what you said earlier about not being quite so sick the past couple of weeks, it sounds like it already has.'

Poppy nodded, that shocked smile still on her lips. He was pleased to see she had a bit more colour in her face now, and he called Percy in to join them so they could tell him the good news.

'What's the verdict?' he asked as he sat back down next to his daughter.

'Well,' said the doctor, 'I've had a long chat with Poppy and I've run some tests… really, there's no other way to say this. You're going to be a granddad, Percy. My congratulations to you both.'

Percy's eyes filled with tears; clearly delighted, he struggled to speak for a moment. 'Oh Poppy, I'm so pleased for you, my lovely, so pleased! This is the best news ever, it really is.' Father and daughter hugged then, both of them wiping away tears of joy.

Dr. Anderson smiled fondly at them. They both deserved some good news after everything they'd been through, and he was delighted to be a part of it. 'Steph will call you later today or tomorrow morning with your scan appointment, okay? In the meantime, just try and get some rest.'

Poppy stood up with far more enthusiasm than when she'd arrived, grinning widely. 'Thank you, Dr. Anderson.' She smiled up at his six foot seven inch frame, and then turned to link arms with her father.

And with that off they went, a slight skip in their step, ready to plan the arrival of a new and very exciting chapter that would have a significant effect on both their lives.

For the first time in a very long time, Poppy felt excited about life again.

NINETEEN

Another month passed before Poppy noticed that her stomach had a definite 'baby bump', evoking great excitement as she twisted this way and that in front of the mirror, taking in the reflection of her growing and changing shape. It was a few more weeks still, however, before she noticed that her clothes were really beginning to feel a lot tighter. She felt more settled now that she'd moved back to London, and was thrilled to have found another flat just a couple of streets away from the old one she'd previously rented in Clapham.

It was so good to be back in familiar surroundings. It was a ground floor property with two good-sized bedrooms, and although she knew it wouldn't suit her forever, it was a perfectly decent first home for her and her baby.

She was pleased too that she could still catch up with her old friend Maisie, who was delighted to have her visiting again. Percy had, of course, pleaded with her to give up work and go to live with him so he could help and support her, but she wouldn't hear of it; she considered it unfair to burden him with both herself and a new baby, especially as he'd have to move out of his new home, it being a retirement property and all. Besides, she hadn't told him anything about paying off Oliver's debt or that her finances were currently critical; she had to at least try and make a living for herself and crawl back some funds in time for the new arrival.

Thankfully, as she'd placed all her furniture into storage when she'd moved into Priory Court, she'd managed to furnish her flat really nicely. All that was required now was to furnish the other bedroom and get the many bits and pieces needed for looking after and bringing up a baby. On that front she hadn't a clue where to start and was therefore delighted when Marnie offered to go shopping with her.

As she got ready for their outing, she placed her hands on her tummy and felt a slight fluttering; she wondered if it could be the baby moving but she wasn't entirely sure. She wondered then – and not for the first time, either – whether it would be a boy or a girl, but she knew it didn't matter either way; she just felt blessed to be carrying Oliver's child.

The sound of the doorbell jolted her back to the present and she rushed to open the door, greeting her friend.

'My goodness, look at you!' Marnie pulled her into a massive bear hug, admiring her growing shape.

'Marnie, it's so good to see you,' Poppy replied, smiling.

'It's looking great in here,' Marnie complimented as she had a quick look around the place, wandering in and out of the rooms. 'Ah, this is baby's room, I take it.'

The room had an old wooden chest of draws inside that Poppy had picked up from a second-hand shop just off of the King's Road. She'd since sanded it down and painted it white, matching it with a white wicker rocking chair she'd also picked up at a second-hand shop. The cot and Moses basket Marnie had lent her were still waiting to be set up, but she had washed and pressed all the tiny clothes she'd given her, which were now all neatly folded in one of the huge wooden drawers of the dresser. The walls of the bedroom had already been painted white and she'd put up a cute border – which ran around the middle of the walls – featuring Jemima Puddle-Duck, one of her favourite Beatrix Potter characters. Slowly but surely, the room was beginning to come together.

'I got you a couple more things, actually.' Marnie retrieved the carrier bags she'd brought in and handed them over.

'Oh, you shouldn't have, Marnie, thank you so much!' exclaimed Poppy as she pulled out packets of baby grows and vests together with cute little booties and bibs, all carefully colour selected to easily suit either gender.

Marnie smiled. She loved being able to help out and she knew that Poppy was sincerely grateful too. She loved children and a new baby was just what everyone needed right now; she was even tempted to suggest to Greg that they should consider trying for another addition themselves, but she'd decided to concentrate on Poppy's pregnancy first.

'It's only a few bits and pieces, and anyway, it's not my fault – you should blame the planners for placing a Mothercare next to Marks & Spencer's on that new business park they've just finished near us; I couldn't resist popping in there to have a look.'

They were soon on the tube, travelling to the west end where there was a really good undercover shopping centre. Marnie was certain they'd get most things they wanted there, and during the journey they discussed the best places to go, each making a mental list.

'Changing the subject,' Marnie began hesitantly, 'I don't want to upset you, sweetheart, but have you any thoughts as to whether you're going to tell Martha and Anthony about the baby?'

She'd been nervous about raising this issue, but nevertheless, it was something Poppy needed to think about and get out of the way before the baby was born. With the daunting task of being a new mother – and in Poppy's case, a working one at that – as well as dealing with all of those hormonal changes, Marnie didn't want Poppy having to wrestle with such a touchy subject once the baby came. Babies brought out all manner of emotions, and she knew Poppy well enough to realise she was just the sort of person to drive over to the Sullivan's house, baby in tow, and announce the arrival of their new grandchild like a slap in the face. She'd rather the matter was dealt with beforehand, before everything got completely crazy.

Poppy mulled over Marnie's question, which hadn't fazed her at all. She'd already been thinking about it anyway – of course she had. She certainly wanted Oliver's family to be part of their child's life, just as Percy was going to be, she just wasn't sure how to handle it. She explained as much to Marnie.

'Well, I agree it's not going to be easy; what about writing them a letter?'

They both agreed this would probably be the best approach, so Poppy said she'd put something together in the next day or so and they returned their thoughts to the job in hand – shopping.

*

It was almost two weeks later when she received a reply. She arrived home from work completely wet through, and letting herself into the flat, she shrugged off her coat and shoes, making straight for the bathroom where she undressed and stepped into a much-needed hot shower. Warmed and refreshed, she returned to the hallway and was just hanging up her coat when she noticed the mail on the mat by the front door.

Picking up the letters, she went into the kitchen to heat up a bowl of soup, placing everything on a tray before padding off into the lounge. She sat at the dining table to look through her mail while her soup cooled, and that was when she saw it. It was a handwritten letter – very nice writing too, although she couldn't tell who it was just from the envelope – but once opened, the Sullivan family crest leapt off the page in front of her. Her mouth went dry and she swallowed as she began to read the handwritten letter inside.

Dear Ms. Jackson,

We were somewhat taken aback at the arrival of your letter, particularly since you have not seen fit to contact us following the death of our beloved son and only child, Oliver. This lack of contact has been most disappointing considering that you had been engaged to be married to our son, and had professed to have been 'deeply in love with him'.

You can imagine, therefore, that this lack of contact – combined with the contents of your letter – has caused us immense concern. Do you honestly expect us to believe that after all these months you are carrying our son's child? And that you only consider it necessary to tell us the news now? We find this quite astonishing. If you are as far gone in your pregnancy as you claim to be, then Oliver would have been well aware of this and as such, would not have hesitated in sharing such delightful news with his devoted parents. It appears what is more likely here is that you have got yourself into a difficult situation and, clearly being an intelligent woman – and of course one who is well aware that Oliver was our only son and heir – now see fit to try and make a claim to what would have been his inheritance.

It is somewhat understandable that you have to try and make an attempt at obtaining a decent income now, especially as Oliver is no longer here to continue to support you, but I'm afraid that is not our problem. If you have now got yourself into some trouble then you'll have to find someone else to help you get out of it. We would be most grateful if you did not attempt to make contact with us again.

Yours,
Martha Sullivan.

She placed the letter down on the table, feeling as though she'd been slapped across the face, hard. Her cheeks flushed. Her hands shook. She gazed in disbelief at the words staring back at her from the luxurious headed notepaper, shaking her head slightly from side to side.

How could anyone be so vile? How could Martha be so cruel? She has the front to imply I'm some sort of evil gold digger when she has no idea of the lengths I've gone to in order to protect Oliver's reputation and memory – her precious son's reputation no less!

Poppy stopped herself then. Oh no, she didn't want to have thoughts like that about Oliver, and she certainly wasn't going to start now. She loved him, she always *would* love him, and she wasn't going to allow Martha to drag her down to her level. Still, she had to note her surprise that Anthony would take this stance, and she wondered if, in fact, he'd even known she'd written to them in the first place, given that he hardly seemed to stay at the family home. He probably had no idea about any of this.

She took a deep breath. She was upset, but she wasn't going to cry; she wasn't going to get distressed and upset her baby – *their* baby, her and Oliver's baby. Martha could think what she liked. She would be the one to miss out, not Poppy.

She folded up the letter and slipped it back into its envelope – intending to keep it as a reminder to herself that she'd tried to tell Martha and Anthony about their grandchild – before returning to her soup.

For a few moments she felt very lonely and very afraid, Martha's written words continuing to resound in her head, 'especially as Oliver is no longer here to continue to support you.' *The very cheek of it!* It was certainly true, of course, that she was worried about how she was going to manage financially, but she hadn't thought about that when she'd written the letter to them; she hadn't reached out to them because she'd expected some sort of financial support in return! She'd actually reasoned that Martha and Anthony would be delighted at the news, delighted that a part of the son they loved so dearly was going to live on.

She certainly hadn't bargained for being vilified in the process. Not at all.

Sighing, she tried to put the letter out of her mind.

FIVE YEARS LATER

TWENTY

'Lily! Lily Jackson! Where are you?' Poppy marched from room to room, trying to locate her daughter. She knew exactly where she was, of course, but this was a game Lily loved to play and Poppy was happy to humour her. As she could hear Lily trying to stifle her giggles from behind the bedroom door, Poppy began her 'mock concern' routine, which she knew would unearth her little bundle of mischief in no time.

'Oh, where on earth can Lily be? I've all these lovely cakes to decorate for Aunty Marnie too...' She paused, waiting for the pitter-patter of her daughter's feet as she ran out towards the kitchen, knowing she would not want to pass up such an opportunity. She was right on cue, too.

'Mummy, Mummy!' Lily came rushing into the kitchen. 'I'm here, Mummy – I was just playing.' She smiled up at Poppy, her face the very picture of innocence.

Laughing, Poppy picked up her cheeky monkey of a cutie daughter, swinging her round and round and making Lily squeal with delight.

'No, Mummy, stop it! It makes my tummy feel funny,' she squealed and giggled.

'Would you like to help me ice the cakes?'

'Yes please,' replied Lily, clapping her small hands excitedly.

Poppy demonstrated how to swirl the icing onto the fairy cakes she'd made earlier that morning, then watched Lily attempt to ice a cake of her own; she was kneeling on a chair so she could reach the table more easily, and with a look of pure concentration on her face she swirled icing onto the cakes, stopping every now and then to smear the mixture with her fingers when it didn't quite go the way she wanted it to.

Poppy smiled. Oh, how she loved Lily! As they often did, her

130

thoughts drifted back over the past five years, astonished at how quickly the time had flown. Lily would be five in July and due to start school before then, at Easter time; she was more than ready for the additional stimulation too. When she was born, Lily was so tiny that Poppy worried how she would ever be able to change and dress her without hurting her, but it was never a problem. Lily was such a happy child, always smiling, and if she was ever quiet, there was no doubt that she was up to mischief – meaning it was time to seek her out. It had become a bit of a routine with them.

Of course, Percy completely adored his granddaughter, and had been delighted when Poppy had chosen to name her 'Lily Grace' – Grace, of course, after her late mother.

Once a month, Percy travelled up to London for the weekend to see them, and on alternative weekends, Poppy drove Lily down to Swinford St. George to visit him. It worked really well, especially as Lily seemed to love going out and about, meeting new people and visiting different places.

Today was particularly exciting as it was New Year's Eve and they were travelling to Surrey to visit Marnie, Greg, and their children – Justin now 16, Matt 14, Louisa 8, and little Lottie 3. Poppy and Lily hadn't seen Marnie and the children since the end of November – as Greg had taken the family away to Canada for Christmas – so she was eagerly looking forward to a leisurely catch up.

Louisa always loved it when they came to stay too, because it meant that the girls could play schools and she could play teacher to Lily and Lottie, something that kept all of them entertained for hours.

Lily woke up just as they pulled onto the driveway of Greg and Marnie's home. She was a bit disorientated at first, but as realisation set in, she was soon wriggling about in her seat, desperate to get out of the car. Louisa – having kept watch for ages and ages, well, since breakfast anyhow – was now tapping ferociously on the car window and waving at Lily, who was giggling excitedly. Poppy released Lily from the car seat and watched, smiling, as the two friends ran off in search of Lottie.

'Poppy!' Marnie greeted her friend warmly, 'It's so good so see you; we've missed you.'

The two friends hugged and kissed before heading indoors,

carrying the various bags and boxes that Poppy had brought along.

'How was the journey?' Marnie asked, once they were sitting in the kitchen. They were hugging hot cups of coffee, the sound of the girls squealing with laughter in the playroom making them smile every now and then.

'Yeah, it was good, thanks. Lily slept most of the way so she's managed to regain all her energy.'

Marnie laughed. 'Tell me about it; Louisa's been awake since about six this morning but Lottie slept until eight – I don't know how she manages it with the amount of noise her sister seems to make.'

An hour or so later Greg came in, freshly showered. 'Hey stranger,' he greeted Poppy before going over to kiss and hug his wife. 'Isn't Lily adorable? I just overhead her telling Louisa and Lottie that she's starting school soon to be a doctor.'

Poppy smiled. 'I don't know where she's got that idea from, but I like it.'

The three of them laughed, then Poppy caught Greg and Marnie exchanging a knowing look. Curious, she wondered if Marnie was expecting again; something she herself would love but knew wasn't possible now Oliver was no longer here.

Greg cleared his throat, and looking from one to the other, Poppy became certain that something was up – only now she was getting a feeling in the pit of her stomach that she only ever seemed to get when something was *wrong*.

'You're freaking me out, guys,' she said after a pretty awkward silence, 'what's going on?'

Greg smiled nervously. 'We've got some news, Poppy. It's big news.' He shrugged. 'Good and not so good, but certainly not bad.'

She was on full alert now, wondering – with absolute horror – if one of them was ill. But he'd said 'not bad'. Honestly, she had no idea what to expect.

Greg drew a deep breath, smiling at his wife before explaining, 'As you know, I'm originally Canadian born and bred, and my parents, brothers, and sisters are all in Canada too...'

She nodded, uncertain at this point as to where the conversation was going.

'For the past couple of years I've not really felt fulfilled at work – I've pretty much achieved everything I can with the company. Sure,

Dom, Alfie and I have grown the company successfully over the past few years, but I don't think there's much left for me to do there anymore. I really need a new challenge, badly. I need to regain the thrill of building a business from scratch, and I don't feel I can achieve that being… here.' He paused for a moment, as though trying to find the right words. 'It's no secret that I've made a shed full of money, and to be honest, if I never work another day in my life we could all live quite comfortably off the profits and investments I've made, but there's no way I want to spend the rest of my life sitting around and resting on my laurels. So, it's been a tough call, but basically we've decided to emigrate to Canada, back to my hometown of Calgary.'

Poppy was stunned, staring blankly ahead as she tried to process what he'd just told her. He was right; it wasn't bad news, but it certainly wasn't good news either – at least not for her. How was this going to impact her and Lily? She knew that Greg was proud of his Canadian heritage, and he often talked about his family there and what life was like, but she never imagined he'd want to go back and actually *live* there. Marnie, either.

'Well, this is a surprise,' she managed to say after what felt like a long silence. 'I guess it will be great for the children to get to know their Canadian relatives.' She smiled brightly, trying to keep the disappointment out of her voice.

'Exactly. It will be a positive change for us all,' Marnie said, her words meant for Poppy too.

'There's more,' Greg continued, staring intently at Poppy. 'I've offered Dom and Alfie the opportunity to buy out my share of the company and they jumped at the chance.'

Okay, *now* she was concerned. She hadn't yet got around to thinking how this might affect her job. She gestured at Greg to go on.

'I know right at this moment you're probably thinking *'what about me?'* and you'd be right to do so. However, you've nothing to worry about, believe me. Dom, Alfie, and I discussed this, although there wasn't much to discuss really,' he joked. 'Apparently Amanda is leaving at the beginning of March – she's getting married and moving to the Lake District – so Dom immediately called dibs on you replacing her. However,' he laughed again, 'apparently there has been

– how shall we say – a somewhat embarrassing altercation between Alfie and Serafina, who has seemingly taken quite a shine to him, so he's keen to move her on. He also wants you to work with him.'

Poppy smiled wryly; Serafina was barking up the wrong tree there.

'I don't yet know how they intend to carve up all the roles and responsibilities, but either opportunity will be good for you, Poppy, they've both assured me.'

Just then she was feeling quite numb, and more than a bit lost, like she was being abandoned. She remembered feeling like this before, years ago, when she'd received that letter from Oliver's mother, Martha, although she wasn't about to allow her thoughts to take her back there. Not right now.

'Of course,' Greg continued, 'there is another option...'

He looked across at Marnie again, who smiled encouragingly at him, knowing how hard he was finding this.

'If working for Dom or Alfie doesn't appeal to you, then – much to our reluctance – we could offer you redundancy.'

She stared at him, horrified; surely he wasn't going to fire her? This conversation was just getting worse and worse.

'Now,' he added quickly, 'before you freak, it's not as bad as it sounds, believe me; we've put together a very attractive package, which is more than we'd do for most people. Besides, you've been with the company for some years now so I think it's certainly an option that's worth some serious consideration. Again, Dom and Alfie have asked me to try and dissuade you from taking it, but I know you better than they do and I think differently.'

Poppy really didn't know what to say. She was stunned. Amazed. Shocked. *Gutted.*

'You don't have to decide today.'

'When are you thinking of leaving?' Poppy asked, scared to hear the answer.

'We'll be moved by Easter...'

She raised her eyebrows. 'That fast?'

'The sale of my share of the business completes next week, but I'll continue to be around for a bit longer to help Dom and Alfie restructure slightly,' Greg explained.

'Well,' Poppy said, sliding forward off her chair and standing up, 'you've certainly given me a lot to think about.' She smiled, heading around to their side of the counter to give them both a big hug. 'I think congratulations are in order.'

She first hugged Greg and then Marnie, who kissed her on the cheek.

'I have to say, I perfectly understand your decision in some respects, more so now that I have a child of my own. I certainly appreciate that there are better or more opportunities in Canada perhaps than here; I honestly wish you all the best of luck.'

Marnie and Greg smiled; they knew each word was spoken with deep sincerity.

'However,' Poppy added, 'I'm not sure how Lily's going to take it.'

They laughed, welcoming the lighter atmosphere.

'Well, the girls will be able to Skype each other, which will be fun,' enthused Marnie, 'and of course they can email and stuff too; it's not like we'll never see each other again, is it Greg?' She looked to her husband for confirmation.

'Certainly not. I still intend to come to London from time to time...'

'...and we'll want to visit my family in Scotland too,' added Marnie.

'Yes, it'll be so good for the children,' Poppy agreed. 'How have they reacted?'

Marnie frowned slightly. 'Well, Lottie doesn't really understand, and Louisa's worried about missing her school friends, of course.'

'The boys are very keen though,' said Greg, 'but then I have promised them all sorts of exciting adventures when we get there, so that might've had something to do with it.' He winked, and despite everything, Poppy couldn't help but laugh.

Relieved to have finally been unburdened with what had not been an easy decision to make, Marnie and Greg felt as if a great weight had been lifted and that they could now really embrace the rest of the weekend. Poppy pushed her thoughts on the news aside for now, and instead just joined in the fun, determined to take her mind off things.

When they welcomed in the New Year, Poppy joined in wholeheartedly, wondering what the next 12 months would bring. One thing was for certain – it was going to be a year of great change for them all.

The following day she contemplated driving down to Swinford St. George. She hadn't had the best night's sleep – she'd tossed and turned until the early hours, trying to weigh up the various options in her mind, and had come to the conclusion that she really wanted a chance to talk things through with Percy before making any firm decisions.

She surprised herself too upon realising that she wasn't even actually sure she wanted to continue working at Hawkins, Munroe and Sable, or whatever the business was to be called, anymore. However, even with taking the generous redundancy package Greg had talked about into consideration, she knew her finances wouldn't last that long; she'd still need to work. Of course, she didn't have a problem with that. She loved her job, but maybe this was a sign – maybe now it was time for a change, time for her to find a new opportunity altogether.

This thought, however, just drew further concerns. What if her new employers weren't as understanding about Lily as Greg had been? What if she had to attend a lot of overnight conferences? If so, could she financially deal with that? After all, it would mean extra childcare for Lily. Moreover, did she really want to do that? It could mean spending less and less time with Lily and she was already trying to be both mother and father to her as it was.

After thinking for a while longer, Poppy picked up the phone and called Percy, telling him to expect them later that afternoon. She then set about packing a few things for their overnight trip, glad she'd made the decision to go.

Later that evening, once Poppy had settled Lily into bed at Percy's house, she joined her dad in the lounge and shared her news over a bottle of wine.

As she explained her predicament, he watched her carefully. He'd nothing but admiration for his only daughter, and he knew Grace would have been so proud of her too. She'd really picked herself up after Oliver's death, embracing motherhood wholeheartedly; this in addition to how she juggled a full-time career often amazed him.

He listened as she weighed up the pros and cons of continuing to work for either Dom or Alfie, clearly being able to tell by her expression and body language that this was not something she really wanted to do.

When she'd finished, she looked over at him expectantly, waiting for him to express his own thoughts. He certainly had some, of course, it was just that he didn't think she'd want to hear them; she could be a stubborn little so and so at times, just like her mother.

'You okay, Dad?'

'Well, I was just thinking... I'm not totally surprised to hear this. Greg's got an excellent mind for business and if things have gone a bit stale, there's no real incentive for him to carry on, is there? That's sort of why I left working with Uncle Nicholas – the challenge had gone and there was no thrill anymore, just the same old same old...'

As Poppy listened, she realised that she'd never heard him talk like this before, with him revealing a part of himself she'd not seen.

'...that's why I chose to go freelance,' he continued, 'which was hard enough, especially back then. I had to work bloody hard to drum up my own business; you can't afford to just sit back and wait for things to come to you, make no mistake about that. Admittedly, over the years, once I'd made a name for myself and my reputation grew, it *did* get easier, but still, I could never afford to take anything for granted.' He paused for a moment to gather his thoughts. 'The thing is, Poppy,' he added, 'I'm more than comfortable financially.'

She raised her eyebrows, curious as to where the conversation was going.

'We weren't too badly off when you mother died; we'd managed to put a fair bit by ourselves and I'd already built up a number of shares and investments. Then, of course, when your mother passed there was her life insurance.' He paused for a brief moment, lost in the past. 'Actually, I invested some of that money too – in fact, I used it to buy this house.' He gestured around the room with his hands. 'Then there's the house in King's Oak – which I got a good price for – and I've got a decent private pension too.'

He sat upright then, placing his wine glass down on the coffee table. 'I'm not getting any younger, Poppy.'

She looked at him, startled.

'It's okay,' he said quickly, smiling, 'I'm not ill or anything.'

Poppy breathed a sigh of relief.

'What I'm saying is, I would love to spend more time with you and Lily. She's going to be starting school this year and I feel as if

I've missed out so much on her development already.' He stopped to collect his thoughts again; he wanted to ensure she took him seriously. 'When I'm gone, Poppy, all this will be yours.' He chuckled slightly as he gestured with his hands again, following his corny remark.

'What do you mean, Dad?' she asked, still confused. 'What are you trying to say?'

'What I'm saying is that everything I have, will go to you. But instead of waiting for me to 'pop me clogs', why don't you let me share some of that with you now? That way, I get to help you and still be here to enjoy it too.'

'Are you trying to give me money, Dad?' She was cross now, and had sat bolt upright herself.

'If you mean buying a house for you and Lily to live in is giving you money, then yes, I suppose I am,' he responded, defiantly.

'No.'

'Why?'

'It's not right.'

'What do you mean, it's not right?'

'It's your money; you can't just go around buying people houses willy nilly!'

'I'm not giving it out willy nilly,' he retorted. 'I want to buy a home for my daughter and my granddaughter with money I can easily afford; I want to benefit from having you here whilst I'm still alive to enjoy it!' He was getting cross now too.

They glared at each other, neither speaking a word.

A few minutes of silence followed.

Eventually, Percy gave in, being the first to speak. 'You know you don't want to stay on without Greg. It's time for a change; you *deserve* a change, and you've worked long and hard all these years, so let me help you. If you let me buy you and Lily a home – and if you take the redundancy from Greg – it will easily keep you going for a year or so until you find something else you actually *want* to do.' He shrugged. 'You could even re-train if you wanted to.'

He looked at her with eyes full of hope whilst she sank back into her seat, then standing up, she went to fetch another bottle.

As she topped up their glasses Poppy said, 'I need to think about this.'

This made Percy relax a little – at least she was considering it. 'So think about it,' he said cheerfully.

'But what if you change your mind and want the house back?'

'I won't. I'll sign it over to you from the point of purchase.'

'What if your investments fail and you end up penniless?'

'Then I'll come and live with you, I hope.'

She smiled at him. 'Of course, I didn't mean that... but what if you get ill and need twenty-four hour care or a nursing home?' It was something she didn't like thinking about, but it was a possibility, wasn't it?

'I have insurances for that, lovely.'

Poppy frowned as she took another sip of wine. 'It still doesn't feel right, Dad. Taking money from you like this... it feels wrong.'

'Oh, for goodness' sake, Poppy, really!' he exclaimed. 'Would you enjoy it more if I was dead and you'd inherited it that way?'

She promptly burst into tears then; the idea of actually losing her father was something she definitely did *not* want to think about.

Percy went over, placing his arms around her. 'I'm sorry, lovely,' he said, giving her a hug whilst she sobbed into his shoulder. After a moment or so he stroked her hair – it had been a long time since he'd done that – trying to comfort her. 'I didn't mean for it to come out like that, it's just...' He paused, sitting down next to her. 'The older I get, Poppy, the lonelier I seem to get. I can't help thinking about getting old, and I would love nothing more than to be able to share what I have with you and Lily. It's only money, Poppy, and it doesn't always buy happiness... but it can be bloody helpful at times,' he quipped, making her laugh as fresh tears sprang forth from her eyes.

Poppy thought for a moment. 'I really don't want to go back there without Greg, Dad, you're right. I feel as though I've been fire-fighting with my life these past five years, and I'm just so *tired* of it!' She paused to wipe the tears from her face. 'Believe it or not, I don't get to spend that much time with Lily either, and I miss her too – although of course I do see more of her than you, I appreciate that.' She took a deep breath, trying to calm herself down. 'It's just that I'm frightened; I've been feeling a bit panicky about it all, in fact. You see, I have no back-up system, Dad – I have to support Lily and I'm frightened that I won't be able to get another job, especially not one with as understanding a boss as Greg has been anyway.'

'Well, that won't happen,' he instantly reassured her. 'At the very least your Uncle Nicholas would always give you work – you know that – but I have to say, you're far too good for him anyway.' He chuckled, and she managed a little smile. 'Seriously, I've no doubt whatsoever that with the excellent references from Greg, together with your skills and experience, you'd be able to find work anywhere.'

Poppy's smile grew larger. 'What if we were to move back around here?'

'Well, I was kind of hoping you would.'

He looked at her, waiting for his words to sink in, and then the two of them smiled at each other.

'Have you just tricked me, Dad?' she asked, her eyebrows raised.

'Yes, lovely.' He passed Poppy her wine glass and picked up his own. 'To new beginnings.'

'To new beginnings!' they chorused together, and Poppy felt her stomach flutter a little.

Now that was a feeling she *did* like.

*

'Sally!' she squealed excitedly into the phone an hour or so later. 'Have I got the *best* news for you!' After finally accepting her father's offer (much to his delight), Poppy was desperate to tell her childhood friend all about her impending move.

'Not before I tell you mine,' Sally cut in determinedly. 'Wait until you hear this: Dave and I are getting a divorce!'

TWENTY-ONE

Poppy took three long, deep breaths. In... and out... In... and out... In... and out. She felt *so* good. It was a beautiful sunny day and she was making her way to the Rectory, having already dropped Lily off at school.

She was meeting with Reverend Fisher and the church committee today to discuss the upcoming village fete, which she'd offered to help organise; although they'd only been living in the Hamptons for a few weeks now, she really wanted to get involved in the local community as much as possible.

She was feeling particularly light-hearted that morning too, as she'd planned a small celebration for Sally at the Maide of Honour for the following night. She was truly pleased that Sally had managed to move on following the trials and tribulations of her marriage breakdown, and she'd just signed the lease for a shop situated on Hampton Ash Road, which she intended to turn into a delicatessen and tea shop – something the local area had been crying out for.

There wasn't even one in the more upmarket Swinford St. George, which Poppy was surprised about given that it was the home of *Hambly-Jones*, the highly popular department store which housed all manner of luxury goods and designer clothing.

As she walked, she mentally planned to pop into the pub after her meeting that morning, just to check that Piers and Marcus had all the arrangements in hand.

'Poppy!' Reverend Fisher greeted her warmly, adding, 'A pleasure as always!' as he kissed her on each cheek.

'Good morning, Reverend Fisher,' she returned cheerily – she still hadn't got used to calling him by his Christian name, 'what a beautiful day it is!'

'Indeed it is, Poppy; the good Lord is rewarding us for all of our efforts here today,' he replied, making them both chuckle.

He led the way into one of the many chaotic rooms in the vast Victorian property, where several other ladies from the village had already congregated.

Poppy immediately recognised Rosie, of course, whom she'd struck up quite a friendship with since moving to Hampton Ash and who coincidently lived just across the road from her and Lily at Oakdene, with her big beautiful ginger cat, Mr. Boo. Lily *loved* Mr. Boo.

'Ah, Poppy,' Rosie welcomed her enthusiastically. 'I was just telling the ladies all about you, dear – come and sit down next to me and I'll introduce you to everyone.'

Reverend Fisher felt a tinge of disappointment at that – he'd hoped to have Poppy sitting next to *him* – and sulkily returned to where he'd been seated earlier, collecting a cup of coffee and a plate of biscuits on the way.

Introductions complete, they commenced their discussion on the forthcoming church fete, and in no time at all Poppy began to feel like a real part of the group.

'We like this committee to be known as COG, Poppy – the Church Organisation Group,' Beryl Madison announced proudly. Poppy had met Beryl before as her husband Ian ran the local butcher's shop. 'We like to think of ourselves as the cog that keeps the church going, so to speak.'

A few sniggers rippled around the room, and Poppy smiled politely in response.

'It took some convincing to get them to change the word Committee to Group, mind you,' interjected Charlotte Palmer-Reid dryly. 'And drop the C in favour of a G – for obvious reasons.' She raised her eyebrows, her eyes flashing brightly.

Poppy had to bite her lip to stop herself from laughing out loud, but Reverend Fisher, however, was busy chuckling away to himself, repeating the inappropriate word over and over in his mind; he almost wished they *had* kept the name Church Organisation Committee.

A few hours later, with the discussions complete, the ladies began to disband and head off home, each armed with a list of action points they had to check off. They'd finally agreed upon a suitable date, and Reverend Fisher had undertaken the responsibility for advertising the event around the villages, although he was actually intending to delegate this activity to his wife Cathy, who arrived home just as the ladies were leaving.

'I'm so sorry I wasn't here for the meeting today, ladies,' she said to the group. 'I trust it all went well?'

Poppy liked Cathy. She was stick thin, with a mop of dark, unruly hair that seemed to be crying out to be brushed and tamed. She was always so bright and jolly and just oozed positivity into even the most morose soul. The perfect Reverend's wife.

Poppy began clearing away the teacups, giving her the chance to have a brief chat with the departing group.

'Oh bless you, Poppy,' Cathy said once she'd returned from seeing the others off to find her stacking cups and saucers onto a tray. 'Don't worry; I can take care of this.' Smiling, she lifted the tray from her.

'I don't know how you manage to run this huge house, Cathy, let alone support the Reverend, the church, and the village in all the various ways you do.'

'It's all part of being a vicar's wife.' Cathy stood tall, looking back at Poppy proudly. 'The devil finds work for idle hands, my dear.'

*

After bidding the Fishers goodbye, Poppy headed towards the Maide of Honour. She was glad it wasn't actually opening time yet as she didn't want people to think she was nipping in for a swift drink at this time of the morning.

She chuckled to herself as the thought flitted through her mind, and as she looked up again, her smile suddenly dried up. Surely her eyes must be playing tricks on her?

For just a brief moment she thought she was seeing things, but then the man did a double take too, no doubt having similar thoughts running through his own mind. No, it was definitely him.

She realised that she had no option other than to come face to face with the person now striding quickly towards her. Well, unless she made a run for it, of course, and she didn't think she could manage that; her legs had just about turned to jelly.

'Poppy?' He studied her incredulously, as if he'd uncovered a long-lost treasure. 'Surely not! Is it really you?'

She'd instantly recognised him, of course, even before he spoke, but now she was completely sure – his voice was as gentle and velvety as ever. *And how I've missed that voice!* Her heart was hammering hard against her chest and her stomach churned anxiously as realisation set in.

Of all the people, in all the places.

Despite their little chat about the area – that felt like it had happened a whole lifetime ago – she never in a million years would ever have imagined bumping into him.

Here.

Now.

Like this.

She took a deep breath, trying to steady herself before speaking.

'Hello Anthony,' she uttered, a tad breathlessly. She couldn't, however, hide the cold edge to her voice. It was difficult to stop the feeling of resentment that was beginning to build up inside her as she began to recall the way in which she'd been so cruelly dismissed when she'd tried to reach out to him and Martha after Oliver had died.

He appeared oblivious to all this, however, and just continued to enthuse genuine delight at this synchronous meeting. 'What are you doing here? Are you here visiting family?'

The last thing she wanted was for Anthony – or indeed, Martha, for that matter – to know anything about her reasons for being in the Hamptons and she certainly was not about to discuss Lily. No, that boat had sailed many years ago.

'I could ask you the same thing,' she responded, just as surprised but not *quite* as delighted.

'Me? I'm living here now, Poppy, in Hampton Waters. Just over there actually, at Channing House.' He gestured behind him towards a very grand, Tudor-looking property that was set right back off the church green and to the left of the Maide of Honour.

She simply could not disguise her utter shock at hearing this, and her voice rose to a shrill as she asked, 'You live here?' She started jabbing downwards with her finger. 'In Hampton Waters?'

Her reaction amused him, yet he could not quite distinguish whether her surprise was one of pleasure or disappointment. 'Yes, that's right – I moved here about two years ago.'

Hearing this caused Poppy's mouth to drop open even further. She couldn't believe what she was seeing; let alone what she was hearing! Okay, so she'd only lived in the Hamptons for a few weeks, but she'd spent many a weekend here with Lily, visiting her father, Sally, and other friends and family members. How come in all of that time she'd never, ever seen him? *How could that be?* It just boggled the mind.

She closed her mouth and swallowed before viewing him through slitted eyes. She soon decided that she didn't want to be there even a moment longer. She didn't want to be standing there. With him. And God forbid if Martha came out.

'I can see this has taken you by surprise, Poppy,' Anthony said eventually. 'Why don't you come inside the house and I'll make us some coffee? Then we can have a proper catch up.'

She quickly shook her head. 'No! Er, I mean no, thank you. I, er, I have to be somewhere actually, I'm meeting someone.' She barefaced lied to him as tears threatened to spill out at any moment.

'Hey, are you okay?' He took a step toward her, reaching his arm out to comfort her. 'How have you been? We, I...' He stumbled over his words. 'I never got the chance to see you after; to speak, you know...' He paused for a moment, clearly pained, before looking straight into her eyes. 'I've thought about you often, Poppy, wondering how you've been getting on. I always hoped I'd bump into you one day as I remembered you visited your family home sometimes and used to come to the Hamptons with Oliver before...' He trailed off, staring down at the ground awkwardly.

She was trying to control herself, her body – first the thumping of her heart, then her churning stomach, both of which were made a hundred times worse when he looked directly at her. Being an older version of Oliver, he was still just as handsome and charming as she'd ever remembered him to be. The years had done nothing to change that.

She was struggling to keep a lid on her emotions, but she just about managed it. 'I have to go, really,' she finally blurted out. 'I'm terribly late!' she lied again.

Of course, she didn't want him to know that she now *also* lived in the Hamptons. She needed to get away from him. She needed to take some time to think through how on earth she was going to deal with all this.

'Oh, that's such a shame,' he replied, sounding genuinely disappointed. 'Never mind, I perfectly understand. Perhaps another time?'

She eyed him curiously, wondering why he was being so nice to her. She assumed it was just to compensate for the guilt he surely felt.

'I'd better let you get on then,' he muttered reluctantly, when she didn't say anything. 'It really would be good to catch up at some point, even if it's just to bring some closure.'

His words piqued her curiosity; she thought again of the many times over the past six years when she'd wondered how on earth he and Martha could ever have dismissed her so cruelly, and without at least having taken the time to have really thought through the consequences of their actions. Times not just when Lily was born, but when she first smiled... when she started to crawl and sit up... her first tooth... her first steps... and, of course, her first words. But there was so much more than that, more than her thoughts could express right at that moment.

Of course, Poppy had often harboured secret thoughts that perhaps Martha had acted alone and that, in actual fact, Anthony had been totally unaware of the letter she'd written and therefore, totally unaware he was even a grandfather. As all of these thoughts raced through her mind, she conceded then that he really couldn't have a clue.

She looked at him again, this time smiling fondly back; if he knew, he would have asked about the child, she was certain of it. Or at least alluded to her situation. But right now she needed time to think. She needed an opportunity to take all this in, to think about how his presence in the village was going to impact upon her; more importantly, she needed to think about Lily.

'I really do have to go, I'm afraid. It's been good seeing you, Anthony.' She turned to walk away.

'Wait!' He touched her arm, making her jump. 'Please, take my card, here.' He pulled out a small white card from the wallet he'd retrieved from his back pocket. 'Call me next time you're back in the village at least – and then we'll do lunch,' he added brightly, as though this would be more likely to make her agree.

'I'll think about it.' She met his gaze as he smiled.

'I'll look forward to that.' He took her hand and gently kissed the back of it.

The gesture caught her off guard, and snatching her hand away, she turned on her heel. As she headed off towards home, she raced along in an attempt to put as much distance as possible between them – and as quickly as possible too.

Thank goodness I live in the other half of the village.

She marched along the road, fearful that it wouldn't be long before Anthony would realise that fact, and with this came the added realisation that he would then eventually find out about Lily.

The day that had started out so positively was now looking somewhat bleak, and even more frustrating, Poppy then remembered that she was supposed to have popped into the Maide of Honour. She wasn't even certain she wanted to celebrate anything anymore, deciding instead to think things over once she'd got safely home again.

*

'Good morning,' Reverend Fisher greeted Anthony as he made his way towards St. Michael's.

Anthony – who was still amused at seeing Poppy depart so suddenly – was watching her march off in the direction of King's Oak Road, wondering where she was going.

'Hello, Reverend,' he said eventually, turning his focus to the man in front of him.

'And how is your Lady today?' Reverend Fisher quipped with a wink. It was a regular joke the locals enjoyed, and Anthony didn't mind – in fact, he found it quite amusing. He loved living in the Hamptons and had certainly become well-established in the village.

'As lovely as ever,' he responded charmingly. 'Actually Peter, I couldn't help noticing Poppy Jackson just leaving the rectory…'

Reverend Fisher was the font of all knowledge and loved nothing better than a good gossip; it was widely known that it didn't usually take too much to get him to *spill the beans*, as it were.

'Oh, such an adorable young thing, isn't she?' he enthused, causing Anthony to smile as a glassy look of admiration swept across

Reverend Fisher's face. Anthony was completely unsurprised she'd had this effect, given that she really was such a joy to be around.

'It is such a blessing from the good Lord that she has now become a member of our flock,' he carried on, speaking with genuine fondness. 'So willing to help out for someone so young – a good example to us all.' He wagged his finger in Anthony's direction.

'What do you mean? Has she moved back home with her father?' He wondered if perhaps her father had become ill or was too frail to cope on his own. He didn't know much about her family but he knew that was the sort of thing Poppy would do in such circumstances.

'Oh no, Poppy has her own home along King's Oak Road. They only moved in a few weeks ago, in fact, into the new build on the land that Barney Henderson sold.'

Anthony took in this news like someone who'd just had a dagger thrust into his heart.

Reverend Fisher carried on; he was one of the good Lord's messengers, after all. 'She's been through quite a lot in her short life, what with losing her mother when she was young and then...' He paused, shaking his head dramatically. 'Well, as I'm sure you know, it's such a terrible business. Her dear father thought she'd never get over it, you know, but she seems to have done so – and of course, being left with the baby surely must have helped her come through all the grief.' He raised his hands up in the air, as dramatic as ever. 'Praise be to the Lord! For though he worketh in mysterious ways, it all happens for a very good reason.' He smiled at Anthony whilst pushing his glasses back up onto his nose, his protruding teeth glistening in the late morning sunshine.

This time it was Anthony's turn to stand with his mouth open, trying to make sense of what Reverend Fisher was actually saying. 'I'm not sure I quite understand you, Peter?'

'Well...' Reverend Fisher leaned closer, toning down his voice slightly. 'She was engaged to be married, you know; absolutely adored him, she did. Well, we all did, actually.' He rocked back and forth on his heels, his hands clasped together, a smile playing on his lips as he recalled the events of Sally's wedding and the many impromptu lock-ins at the Maide of Honour. 'My goodness, we had some fun,' he chuckled, before quickly becoming sombre again upon realising where his story was headed. 'Sadly, dear Oliver passed away not long after that; such a devastating loss.' He cast his gaze downwards for a moment before looking back up to Anthony. 'And it was Poppy, you know, who found him.' He shook his head. 'Terrible business.'

Anthony closed his eyes for a brief second, drawing a breath; he didn't need to be reminded of that. Even after all these years, the pain of losing Oliver was as raw as ever.

'As you can imagine, discovering she was with child was a blessing in disguise,' he finished, rolling his eyes upwards.

By now Anthony was utterly speechless. A child? Poppy had had a child with Oliver? That meant the child was his granddaughter and he her grandfather! Why on earth hadn't Poppy told them?

'Of course, Lily was christened here, you know,' Reverend Fisher went on, gesturing to the church behind them. 'And now they've made their home here, which is where they truly belong.'

Lily had been Anthony's mother's name, and Oliver's favourite grandmother. He wondered if Poppy had known that when she named their daughter.

'Which house is it again, Peter?' he asked, a tad impatiently. He needed to see her now. Clearly there were things that had to be discussed.

'Er... it's Honeycombe Lodge, just a couple of houses on from the cottages along the King's Oak Road,' Reverend Fisher confirmed brightly. 'I had no idea you knew Poppy so well, Anthony?'

'Oliver was my son, Peter.'

For the first time in many a year, Reverend Peter Fisher closed his mouth completely shut, having been rendered completely and utterly speechless.

Anthony bid goodbye to the dumbstruck Reverend and went back inside Channing House, whilst Peter scurried into St. Michael's Church to pray for them all, including himself – he never ceased to be amazed at how the good Lord did indeed work in such mysterious ways.

When Poppy finally got inside her house she slammed the front door shut, leaning up against it just to make certain it was tightly closed. She was shaking – partly from the overzealous walking she'd just done and partly from the shock at running into Anthony like that.

Had that really just happened?

She entered the kitchen and clicked on the kettle, the encounter with Anthony racing through her mind while the water boiled. It was certainly an encounter that raised more than a few questions.

She was shell-shocked. She never ever believed she'd see or hear from either Anthony or Martha again. After all, it had been made quite clear to her that she wasn't to contact them again; she assumed that worked both ways. But now, not only had she bumped into Anthony, but she'd also learnt he was living here too; here, in *her* village. Words failed her.

She wondered about Martha, suddenly remembering that Anthony had referred to himself as 'I' rather than 'we'. Did that mean he was here on his own? She supposed it was possible.

I'm not going to be able to avoid him forever.

Groaning, she placed her head into her hands just as the sound of the doorbell jolted her back to the present. She assumed it to be announcing the arrival of Rosie, as she'd promised to catch up with her after the meeting at the vicarage.

Pulling herself together she opened the front door, her smile swiftly disappearing as she quickly slammed it shut again, gasping in horror. She found herself leaning up against it for the second time that morning. Her heart was pounding, she felt sick, and now her head hurt too. *What was he doing here?*

Trying to compose herself, she turned around and opened the door again, but this time only halfway. Her eyes met Anthony's, who was looking at her with amusement; whilst he wanted to have things out with her, he didn't think there was any need for any unpleasantness.

'Hello again, Poppy.'

She glared back, her usually bright green eyes flashing dark as her cheeks flushed red. 'Are you stalking me?' she demanded, which caused him to laugh out loud. She looked down at the floor then, wondering when the hole she was praying for was going to appear and swallow her up.

'Look, I just want to talk to you,' he explained.

'What?' She rounded on him angrily, unable to stop herself. 'And have you throw it back in my face again? I don't think so, Anthony, I've had enough humiliation to last me a lifetime.'

He stared wide-eyed at her sudden outburst, without a clue as to what she was talking about.

'Look.' He held up his hands in front of him, hopeful that the gesture would calm her. 'I came here with purely good intentions, I promise you. Clearly there's more to this situation than perhaps we both realise.'

She looked at him properly then, for the first time that day. He certainly seemed genuine so she supposed there could be no harm in hearing him out. She knew she'd have to speak to him sooner or later anyway. What she didn't know, however, was that he now *did* know Lily existed. That would be tough to bring up.

'Okay,' she relented. 'I'm happy to talk, but not here.'

Disappointment engulfed him, something that was very much visible on his face.

Poppy, however, didn't want him entering their home as it was littered with pictures of Lily – not until she'd heard what he had to say first.

'What about later today then? We could go for a drink if you like?'

She had to think quickly; it needed to be a time when Lily was at school or she'd have to organise a sitter.

'I can't today, and I'm busy this weekend… how about Monday? We could have a coffee somewhere?'

'Really? Not until then?'

Poppy stared back defiantly and Anthony knew better than to push her further.

'Alright, let's meet up at my house then. You know where I live now. I'll look forward to seeing you.' He turned, though he was reluctant to leave.

'What about Martha?' Poppy blurted out nervously. She couldn't bear to take another tongue lashing, not under these circumstances – if Martha was going to be there, she simply wouldn't show up.

'Martha and I are divorced, Poppy.'

Poppy couldn't help but feel hugely relieved.

'Look, if you change your mind and want to meet sooner, just give me a call or come to the house.' He looked at her kindly, smiling. 'You're very welcome anytime.'

*

'Oh!' Poppy groaned as she cradled her head, which was thumping loudly. She glanced at the bedside clock, the ominous green numbers displaying 5.43 a.m.

She'd been awake for just over an hour, unable to switch off the thoughts whirring and whirring around her head. Since bumping into Anthony yesterday, the stress and drama of it all was literally doing her head in.

Carefully, she prised herself out of bed and padded downstairs to the kitchen, in search of Paracetamol. She was feeling quite nauseous, as it happened, and dizzy too. She smiled wryly as she thought to herself, *well at least I can be sure I'm not pregnant this time,* before quietly making her way back to bed, trying not to disturb Lily in the process.

'Mummy, Mummy, wake up!' Poppy tried to open her eyes as a very excited Lily bounced up and down on the bed. 'It's the weekend, Mummy!' she squealed delightedly.

Poppy lifted a hand to her head, which was still thumping. She really didn't feel well at all; she tried to swallow but her throat was so sore this was easier said than done.

'Lily, please,' she croaked, 'calm down, darling – Mummy has a headache.'

Lily stopped bouncing and peered closely at Poppy's face, before proceeding to place a sticky hand onto her forehead.

'It's hot.' She re-enacted a concerned face as she'd seen her mother do on many occasions. 'I think you're ill, Mummy' she added, placing a hand on her hip.

Poppy smiled, watching as Lily jumped off the bed and rushed off out the room, returning moments later with a picture she'd drawn for her.

'This will make you feel better,' she announced delightedly. 'See, this is you, Mummy, and your lovely long hair. And that's me with my hair, that's nearly as long as yours.' She looked up and smiled. 'And that's the sun shining on us.'

Poppy hugged her tightly. 'That's lovely, Lily, thank you. Tell you what, as it's the weekend, how about I let you have a bowl of cereal in front of the TV as a special treat?'

This made Lily bounce up and down with excitement again, shouting, 'Yaaay!' before she slipped off the bed and ran downstairs;

Poppy usually didn't allow the TV on in the mornings but she really needed a distraction today.

Having settled Lily with a bowl of cereal, she took herself off to lay on the sofa, drifting off to the sound of Scooby-Doo and his sidekick, Shaggy, who'd apparently got trapped in an old haunted mansion.

She was woken an hour or so later by the ringing of the phone, which Lily was now answering.

'Hello?' Lily shouted loudly into the receiver. 'My mummy is ill and can't come to the phone and I can't take a message as I'm only nearly five.'

Poppy shuddered, quickly retrieving the phone before Lily could say anymore, and was relieved to hear Sally's comforting voice on the line. She really wanted to tell her all about Anthony and the shock at having bumped into him, as well as discovering he was now living here, in the Hamptons, where she and Lily had just made their home. She wanted to offload her fears, her worries, and her many anxieties, knowing that her dear friend would fully support her and help to make sense of all the thoughts and feelings that were currently racing around inside her head.

But, she couldn't. She couldn't because Lily was bounding around the room, pretending to be a cat, and she couldn't because if she didn't lie down again soon, she was probably going to pass out anyhow.

'I got your message, Pops; sorry you're not feeling well. Do you want me to take Lily for a while?'

Poppy sighed. 'The last thing you need is to pick this up from me, Sally – not with starting your own business where you'll be handling all that food – and besides, don't you want to get yourself all dressed up for tonight?'

Sally had decided to go ahead with the planned celebrations.

'I suppose, but you know I'm always happy to help. Let me know if you need me then, or if you want anything from the shop.'

'Thanks Sally.'

Saying their goodbyes, they rang off, and thankfully, the rest of the day passed relatively quietly. Once she'd put Lily to bed, Poppy took some more Paracetamol and went off to bed herself, unable to stay up any longer.

During the night, she tossed and turned, battling nightmares where either Anthony or Martha arrived to snatch Lily away; she watched in horror as Martha drove away with Lily in the back of the car, screaming hysterically after them as they disappeared into the night.

She woke with a jolt, covered in a film of sweat as her heart raced wildly in her chest. The bright green digits of the clock displayed 3.33 a.m., and a sob rose in her throat as she remembered this being the very time she'd woken up on the morning she'd found Oliver.

Perhaps he's trying to tell me that everything's going to be okay.

But deep down, she had reservations. Big ones.

Realising that it was well over eight hours since she'd last taken some medicine, she padded solemnly downstairs to get some more, in the hope it would ease the thumping in her head and also the aches and pains that had since developed all over her body.

Afterwards she crept quietly back to bed and soon drifted off into another troubled sleep.

TWENTY-TWO

'Are you okay, darling?' whispered Ianthe.

Anthony turned to face her, 'Sorry, did I disturb you?'

'No,' she reassured him, 'I'm just worried about you.'

Bumping into Poppy had given him quite a shock, and she knew it was playing on his mind; thereby troubling her too.

'I'm just a bit worried now.' He rolled over onto his back, placing his hands behind his head. 'You heard them talking in the pub last night – that girl said Poppy sounded dreadful on the phone.'

'Yes, but Anthony, she probably just picked up a cold or something; I'm sure it's nothing serious, darling,' she said, trying to comfort him. 'You know full well what it's like with young children – they're always picking up this and that from school. I was forever taking Richard to our GP with one thing or another, and I imagine that if Lily is at school by now, she's no doubt picking up every cold and virus going; you know how quickly these minor ailments spread.'

'I guess that means Monday's out,' he said miserably.

'Not necessarily,' she tried to reassure him, 'she's bound to be feeling better by then; I'm sure you're worrying over nothing.'

Whilst he was keen to discuss matters with Poppy, Ianthe didn't want him rushing into anything; she didn't want him to get hurt. After all, it wasn't as though they didn't have issues of their own to iron out. He'd already had two restless nights, and she dreaded to think what would happen if things didn't go well on Monday.

'Anyway, Richard's coming for lunch today,' she reminded him brightly.

He scowled at her. 'Yes, another situation that needs to be dealt with.'

She remained quiet. She knew he was right, of course, but perhaps now really wasn't the right time to discuss it, and anyway, she was rather more hopeful that Richard would be ready to talk business today.

'You're right, darling,' she agreed, patting his hand affectionately, 'but let's tackle one problem at a time, shall we?'

*

At 61, Lady Ianthe Hambly-Jones was still a very attractive woman, and immaculately presented. She'd just turned 22 when she started out in her career as a journalist for a women's fashion magazine, and she encountered Lord Roderick having been dispatched by her editor to interview him for an eight-page special they were featuring in celebration of the Hambly-Jones department store's 25th anniversary year – as well as the launch of a new range of luxury goods.

Hambly-Jones was renowned for its up to the minute designer fashions, luxurious home furnishings, and vast range of opulent gifts and accessories. Indeed, it was quite a gem in the Swinford St. George village crown, the locals would say.

Lord Roderick had not long taken over the running of the family business following the death of his father, and whilst considerably older than her at 39, they'd hit it off immediately, the age gap being of no significance whatsoever. In no time at all it seemed Lord Roderick was a regular visitor to her then modest home on the outskirts of Midford County, but it wasn't for a further two years that he plucked up the courage to ask her to marry him; having no confidence that such a young beauty could possibly wish to spend the rest of her life with someone like him.

Ianthe, however, was deeply in love with him by this time, and felt as though she were the luckiest woman alive as she walked down the aisle – not only as his wife but also as the new Lady Hambly-Jones.

In the early days, their marriage had been idyllic, but as the success of the family business went from strength to strength, their relationship was put under immense strain, and the time they spent together became less and less.

It was during this time that Lord Roderick employed the services of Anthony Sullivan as his financial adviser.

*

Anthony looked at his watch for the umpteenth time that morning. It was twenty-two minutes past ten.

She's not coming. Disappointment flooded through him, though he sat there for a few more moments before getting up.

'If the mountain won't come to Mohammed...' Grabbing his keys, he set off on the short journey to Honeycombe Lodge.

TWENTY-THREE

By now Poppy's cold had really taken hold, and Lily was suffering too, having developed symptoms herself the previous day. Poppy phoned the school before settling Lily on the sofa and then tried to tidy up and get some breakfast together. She'd attempted to eat something herself yesterday but had promptly thrown it back up again. She made some toast for Lily, cut it into strips, and placed it on a small coffee table for her along with a cup of milk. Hopefully Lily would have more luck keeping it down than she'd had.

'Hey Lily,' she said gently, trying to coax her daughter who was snuggled up under her beloved *Hello Kitty* blanket, sucking her thumb, 'try and eat something, my darling, and have a drink of milk; it'll make you feel better.' Lily just stared back at her mum – she wasn't convinced of that right now.

Poppy wandered back to the kitchen, shivering at the sight of the cups and plates that were piling up in and around the sink – she just hadn't had the strength to clear anything away over the past couple of days. Percy had offered to help during each of the many calls he'd made over the weekend, but now that Lily was ill too she insisted he stay away until they were better, not wishing to pass the virus onto him. Soon she had filled up the dishwasher and had decided to go and make the beds.

'Back in a minute!' she called out to Lily on her way upstairs, 'I'm just going to make the beds!' but Lily just carried on sucking her thumb. She was watching *Shaun the Sheep* and was worried about little Timmy who was stuck on the roof again.

*

Having stopped off at *Candy's* – the village florist – on the way and requesting a monstrous bouquet of their most colourful flowers, Anthony swallowed nervously as he approached the front door of Honeycombe Lodge.

He lifted his hand to ring the bell, but then he paused, reconsidering. After a couple of moments, however, he took a deep breath and pressed the shiny gold button, which immediately emitted an array of musical bells. As he waited for Poppy to answer, he mentally prepared himself to face her. He knew she wouldn't be happy to see him here, but then, she didn't know that he *did* know about Lily, and if that's what was keeping her away from him, it needed to be out in the open.

A moment later the door swung open, but instead of meeting Poppy's glaring eyes as he'd expected, Anthony had to drop his gaze until it fell upon a head full of soft curls and the cutest face he'd seen in a long time, her eyes blinking up at him inquisitively. He was quite taken aback for a moment – he'd imagined her to be the spitting image of her mother, when in fact his assumptions couldn't have been further from the truth. She was undeniably a Sullivan, that was for sure.

He knelt down until he was at the same eye-level as the little girl. 'Hello,' he said brightly, his voice shaking a little with emotion, 'you must be Lily.' He cleared his throat, waiting nervously for her reply.

'Hello, I'm not at all well,' she announced before turning around and walking off, leaving him there on the doorstep.

Standing back up again, Anthony wondered where Poppy was, and tentatively peered inside the house. After a second or so of hesitation he decided to hedge his bets and be brave, so he stepped inside the hallway. He could see into the lounge from the front doorway, noticing that Lily had settled onto the sofa and was sucking her thumb.

His heart swelled with pride, and when she looked over at him – taking him slightly by surprise – she pulled out her thumb and said, 'Mummy's upstairs, you can go up if you like.'

Anthony hesitated again – he didn't think he ought to. After all, what if Poppy was lying in bed, seriously ill?

Looking towards the stairs, he started considering his options.

*

Poppy stepped out of the shower, glad to have made the effort to have one in the first place. She was still feeling rough, but the heat of the shower had at least helped to ease the aches and pains in her head, back, and neck.

As she dried herself, she thought she heard the front door close, and then realised with horror that Lily was speaking to someone. Grabbing her dressing gown, she headed downstairs apprehensively, and then − as his face slowly came into view − she saw him. She gazed into his eyes, the same blue eyes of her beloved Oliver.

His arrival − combined with the events of the past few days − suddenly proved too much, and collapsing in a heap on the stairs, she started sobbing her heart out.

Anthony placed the bouquet he'd brought on the floor before rushing over, gathering Poppy up and pulling her tightly against him as he stroked her hair and allowed her to cry. He couldn't stop the tear that escaped down his own cheek as the complete emotion of the situation took hold of him too.

'Mummy, Mummy!' An extremely anxious Lily came running out to comfort her, throwing herself against her mother's legs and wrapping her arms around them. 'What's wrong, mummy? Are you feeling ill again?'

After taking a few deep breaths Poppy started to feel much calmer, so Anthony guided her towards the lounge whilst Lily comforted her mother from the other side.

'My mummy doesn't cry much, you know,' she informed Anthony, clearly concerned to have witnessed her mother in the very scenario that Poppy had tried her utmost to avoid. 'Mummy says it's good to cry, though. Do you cry?' She looked up at him, without a clue as to who he was.

'Sometimes,' he replied. In all honesty, he was lost for words; this was all so incredibly surreal. The situation hadn't gone at all how he'd planned, and now he was deeply regretting having come at all.

'Who are you?' she suddenly asked then, full of her father's boldness. 'Are you staying for lunch?'

He smiled, not wanting to say too much; he didn't want to upset Poppy any further.

'My head hurts,' Lily added, placing her head down on Poppy's lap.

Anthony took a handkerchief out of his pocket and handed it to Poppy, who accepted it gratefully, blowing her nose on it noisily. This made her smile slightly, and also helped to lift some of the heaviness that had been lurking in the air. Poppy was such a funny, quirky little thing at times and Anthony felt a rush of paternal love towards her.

'Feeling better?' he asked, praying that he wouldn't set her off again.

She nodded, her eyes all red and puffy.

'Shall I make us some tea?' he suggested, not sure what else to do. Tea always made things better, anyway.

She nodded again, watching him go off in the direction of the kitchen and glad to have made the earlier effort to clear away the dirty dishes.

'Feeling better, Mummy?' Lily lifted her head up, full of concern.

'Yes, darling, I'm sorry about that. Anthony – the man in the kitchen – is a very old friend and Mummy was just shocked to see him, that's all.'

Lily seemed to consider this for a second or two before agreeing, 'Yes, he *does* look old, Mummy.'

This made Poppy smile. She knew that in Lily's eyes he seemed old, but then anyone over 30 was old to Lily. In reality, she thought that Anthony may have been 64 or 65, but he could easily pass for a man in his fifties.

Getting up, she settled Lily back onto the sofa with her blanket. 'It's time for some more medicine, Lily; I'll just go and get it for you, alright, darling?'

Lily nodded then pulled her thumb out of her mouth to speak. 'You're not going to cry again, are you, Mummy?'

Poppy smiled at her reassuringly. 'No darling; I'm feeling much better now.'

She entered the kitchen just as Anthony was pouring the tea, and he immediately stopped what he was doing. 'I didn't mean to upset you, Poppy. I'm sorry for turning up like this.' He hugged her again, though a little hesitantly this time.

'It's okay… I'm okay… I know we need to talk, and even more so now, obviously.' She gestured back at Lily. 'But we have to be careful not to upset her, Anthony.'

He readily agreed.

'I'll just get Lily some medicine, then I'll get dressed and we can talk.'

As he waited for her to return, he admired the many pictures she'd placed around the house of Oliver. Many had been taken with her, while some were of him alone, and he was pleased to see several pictures of Lily too, at various stages of her young life. It was quite clear that Poppy was doing her best to keep Oliver's memory alive – presumably for Lily's sake – and he had nothing but the utmost respect for her in doing so.

By the time Poppy returned, Lily had fallen asleep, so she gently closed the door to the kitchen – not wanting to disturb her – and went to join Anthony at the kitchen table. He handed her a cup of tea, which she gratefully accepted.

Then, slowly, he reached across the table, covering her hand with his. 'It really is good to see you, Poppy,' he said, with genuine warmth and sincerity in his voice, 'it's been a long time.'

'Six years in November,' she murmured, *and the pain in my heart has yet to ease* – though she declined to say that part out loud.

'When you didn't arrive today as we'd arranged, I assumed you'd changed your mind.'

She shook her head whilst swallowing a mouthful of tea. 'As you can see I'm not at my best, and of course with Lily not being well either, I couldn't very well bring her with me, could I? I had intended to call you later though.'

There was a brief awkward silence, neither of them knowing how to address the elephant in the room.

Eventually, Anthony decided to take the plunge, and taking a deep breath, he asked, 'What happened? Tell me, what caused you to disappear from our lives?'

Poppy eyed him cautiously. She needed to be sure this wasn't just him now conveniently deciding he wanted a relationship with his granddaughter; she had to be certain he was genuine. 'It's what you asked of me,' she said simply.

He slowly retracted his hand. 'I'm not sure I understand…'

She stood up. 'I think that rather than try to explain, it's better to just show you.' She didn't have to look far, of course; she kept everything together in a wooden chest at the bottom of her wardrobe, which was where she headed next. She opened it up, took out the letters, and then returned to the kitchen, handing them both out to Anthony.

'This is a copy of the letter I wrote to you and Martha, and this,' she explained as she handed him a second letter, 'is your reply.'

She sat back down and sipped her tea, giving him time to take in all the information he'd just been given. She watched his face carefully as he read; it was clear by his reaction that both letters were news to him, and judging by the way his face changed when he read the reply sent by Martha, it was obvious that he was less than impressed with it too.

'Oh my Lord,' he whispered, placing the letters on the table before him whilst still keeping them in focus. 'I can't quite take all this in.' He looked up, his face almost white. 'Poppy, you have to believe I had no idea about any of this!'

She said nothing.

'I mean, I knew Martha was distressed when you threw your engagement ring back at her like that, but...'

'What?' she hissed through clenched teeth, setting her cup down and slowly rising out of her seat. She placed her hands on the table, as though it would somehow infuse her with the strength she needed to tackle this shocking revelation.

Anthony saw her green eyes flash dark and he leaned back in his seat, confused.

'You *are* joking?' she exclaimed, whilst still trying to keep her voice down so as not to disturb Lily. 'Honestly, you've absolutely *no* idea, have you, Anthony?'

Recalling how Martha had demanded the return of her engagement ring in such an unnecessarily vociferous manner unearthed emotions Poppy thought were long buried; her voice cracked and her bottom lip trembled as she relayed the details of Martha's disgraceful behaviour, whilst Anthony sat there quietly, listening to every word.

He'd always suspected that Martha's version of events had been rather dramatically overstated, but she had presented him with the ring at the time, therefore leading him to believe that some unpleasant altercation had occurred. He hung his head as realisation set in; all those wasted years, and all because of Martha!

'It seems we're both the victims of a terrible injustice,' he said, before pausing for a moment. 'What a dreadful business.'

Whilst grateful for his support, it was a bit late coming, and Poppy couldn't hold back the tears that were now trailing down her cheeks.

'I can only give you my deepest and heartfelt apologies,' Anthony went on, 'but even that's not good enough, really. Martha can be unbearable once she sets herself against someone, a behaviour I abhor, and one of the many reasons our relationship deteriorated... although to be fair it was mostly of my own doing, but I'm not going to get into that now.' He sighed, suddenly looking extremely tired.

His words piqued her curiosity, and she raised her eyebrows at him, willing him to go on.

'It's no surprise we finally divorced – it was finalised about three years ago. Now I have Ianthe, who's been an important part of my life for some time; I'd love you and Lily to meet her, when you feel ready, of course... I mean, if that's acceptable to you?' he added quickly. 'I'd really like us all to get to know each other better and to try and make up for lost time.'

They talked a while longer, discussing how best to approach the matter with Lily, with them both agreeing to wait until she was feeling better. More importantly, though, Poppy needed to speak to Percy first, and she made it quite clear to Anthony that she certainly didn't want her father to feel pushed out in any way whatsoever, which he readily agreed with. Percy had been a complete rock for her and Lily and she wasn't about to push him aside now just because there was a new grandfather in town.

That said, they agreed to arrange for everyone to meet up for tea the following Saturday.

'Just out of interest,' she asked as they hugged each other goodbye, both of them now exhausted and emotionally wrung out, 'how did you find me so quickly?'

Anthony was relieved to see that she looked a bit brighter now, and he smiled as he replied, 'Reverend Fisher.'

They both laughed.

'I suspected your presence here was rather more than a visit; I just needed someone to confirm it,' Anthony explained. 'The news about Lily, though, really was a complete surprise – and a very welcome one too.'

They said their goodbyes, and as Poppy watched him drive away, she felt as if a huge weight had been lifted off her. It seemed as though – finally – she was able to move on from the past and look forward to the future, a future that looked a lot brighter than it had done just a few days ago.

TWENTY-FOUR

'I'm so glad you're here, Dad,' Poppy said, 'what do you think of this? Look, here, the one I've highlighted.' She waited patiently whilst Percy read through the job advert she'd just pointed out in the Midford County Gazette.

'PART-TIME PA REQUIRED
Local entrepreneur seeks a Personal Assistant on a part-time basis. Must have a minimum of three years working at a senior level, together with suitable qualifications and experience.'

Her father placed the paper down on the table and went to fill up the kettle.

'Well? What do you think?' Poppy asked, impatient.

'What are you looking for a job for?' He had his back to her whilst he poured water into the teapot. 'You've got a full-time job already, looking after Lily – and me.'

He winked at her cheekily but she wasn't amused. Her face fell and disappointment surged through her; she'd really hoped he would at least have shown some interest.

'The thing is, Dad, now that Lily's at school, I've got too much time on my hands and – well... I'm bored! Besides, my savings aren't going to last forever.'

'If it's money you need, love,' he started, turning around and showing the concern sweeping across his face.

'No, Dad,' Poppy interrupted, 'it's not that I need money.' She sighed, going over to him and giving him a hug and a kiss on the cheek. 'Look, thanks for thinking of me – I know you'd never see us short – but really, we're okay, honestly.'

He nodded in acknowledgment. Percy was very proud of how Poppy was both managing her life and bringing up Lily. Indeed, his own life had been greatly enriched since they'd moved to the Hamptons, and with Anthony in the village too he loved having more family around him. In fact, life had really become enjoyable again, for the first time in a long time. He and Anthony got on famously and had even played a couple of rounds of golf together. And then there was Rosie, who lived just across the road from Poppy – he so enjoyed having a bit of female company with someone nearer his own age. Why on earth would Poppy want to go back to work with so much going on? He shook his head, trying to make sense of it.

'It's only part-time, Dad.'

'But what about the school holidays?' he asked, trying to make her see sense.

'Oh goodness, listen to us. We're talking as if I've got the job already and I don't even know what's involved yet.' She laughed, and Percy couldn't help but laugh too. 'Listen, I'm going to give this guy a call to see what it's all about and we'll take it from there.'

With that she headed off to the study to make the call, and Percy watched her go, sighing; he knew there was no use trying to reason with her once she'd made her mind up, so instead he sat down at the kitchen table with his tea, and helping himself to a few biscuits, he looked through the morning paper.

'Richard Jones,' the voice trilled smoothly down the line, sounding oddly familiar.

'Good morning, Mr. Jones,' Poppy began brightly. 'I'm calling about the part-time PA position that's being advertised in the Midford County Gazette. I wonder if you could please give me a few more details regarding what the position involves and what you're looking for?'

Placing his pen down on the table, Richard relaxed into his chair. He liked the sound of this caller; it was a remarkable change from the many others he'd received so far that morning.

'I'd be happy to,' he enthused. 'May I ask who's calling?'

'My name's Poppy Jackson.'

Poppy Jackson. He ran the name through his head several times. He liked it.

'Well hello, Poppy, I'm Richard. Thanks for your interest in the vacancy. Basically, I'm looking for someone to work with me on a part-time basis. I've been working on my own now for just over a year, and have managed to build up quite a decent client base, but now that I'm travelling quite a lot I really need someone to support me from here. As a guide I imagine the position would be about 70 percent from home and 30 percent office-based.'

She thought that sounded perfect, and they chatted a while more, with Poppy outlining her career history and experience and explaining what she could bring to the role. She certainly piqued his interest at the mention of Hawkins, Monroe & Sable, although he didn't mention it. He knew the organisation very well and was aware that Greg had now left the company. In fact, he'd been at university with Dominic Hawkins's eldest son, Robert, and still maintained a friendship with him. He fancied he might give Dom a call later for a catch up.

'I think it might be a good idea for us to meet up, Poppy, what do you think?'

'I think that would be great,' Poppy replied, with the two of them going on to organise a time and place for her interview.

Pinching herself with excitement, she skipped off to the kitchen to tell Percy, who – realising how happy she seemed – thought that maybe a job was just what she needed after all. Perhaps it might give her a chance to meet someone new too; after all, as much as they'd both dearly loved Oliver, she was still young enough to find love again and maybe enrich her own life further.

The following day, Poppy made her way nervously to the offices of 'Richard Jones Consultancy' based in Midford County. Courtenay Place had been converted from a former hotel into several contemporary office suites, just perfect for small businesses, and arriving at the fifth floor, she stopped for a moment to admire the company name proudly emblazoned in gold lettering on the door. She could hear a man's voice as she opened the door, and as he worked alone, she presumed it belonged to Richard Jones himself. Once inside she allowed the door to close slowly behind her.

He looked up, gesturing for her to sit down, then once he'd finished his call, he stood up to greet her, a welcoming smile on his face. 'Poppy?' She stood up and smiled back at him, accepting his proffered hand and returning the firm handshake.

'Yes, hello, you must be Richard Jones.' He noted how her whole face lit up as she smiled, and he was immediately drawn to her bright, sparkling eyes.

The office consisted of two rooms; one for work and one for meetings or relaxing in, and Poppy looked around as he led her through to the other room, which housed a conference table and a small kitchen. To the far side there were a couple of sofas, which he walked towards before gesturing for her to take a seat, whilst he chose to sit opposite. His friendly smile caused her stomach to flutter. *Just nerves.*

He kicked off the interview by telling her a bit about himself and what his work involved, explaining that he'd started the consultancy some eighteen months ago, and that ever since, the business had quickly gone from strength to strength.

'As I explained on the phone,' he went on, 'I've started to establish clients throughout the whole of Europe, and as I'm now travelling so much, I really need an assistant to support me here. I'm looking for all the usual support you'd expect from a PA – you know, answering the phone, booking appointments, making travel arrangements, etc. – but I'd also like someone to take a more active role in the financial part of the business. Someone who can work on their own initiative and not have to ask me about every little decision that needs to be made. Do you know what I mean?' He looked directly at her then and she got the weirdest feeling that she'd seen him somewhere before, though that seemed unlikely. 'I'm so sorry,' he said, suddenly getting up. 'I haven't even offered you any refreshment; can I get you a coffee or something?'

'Water would be great, thanks.' She watched as he strolled over to the kitchen area, retrieving two bottles of water from a fridge and collecting two glasses from a nearby shelf, her eyes following his every move.

When he handed her one of the bottles she caught the faint aroma of his aftershave as he leant forward, and she took a gulp from her water before placing her glass down on the table.

'Of course, it makes complete sense seeing as you're away so much; you can't have eyes everywhere so there will be certain aspects of your business that you just have to delegate.' Poppy nodded, showing she understood.

'Exactly,' he enthused, liking what he was hearing. 'That is exactly what's currently missing. I just want to be able to focus on what business I currently have as well as getting more new business in.' He crossed his legs, placing his hands in his lap and leaning towards her expectantly. 'Now, tell me all about you.'

She swallowed, cursing herself for feeling so nervous as she passed him a copy of her CV.

'As you can see, after leaving Midford County College, I joined Schofield Brothers, whose offices aren't too far from here, actually.' She gestured vaguely outside. 'I worked as PA to the director of marketing. I then left to pursue a career in London and was very fortunate to secure a position with Hawkins, Monroe & Sable as PA to Greg Sable.' Of course, Richard already knew all this and more since his discussion with Dom, who was more than a little pissed that this meant they would never get Poppy back.

For fuck's sake, Richard; I don't know why we're even having this discussion – you'd be a fool not to snap her up, even if she is far too good to work for you,' Dom had joked, and Richard knew that Dom and Alfie would take her back at a moment's notice. What Dom hadn't told him, however – and what he hadn't expected at all – was just how beautiful she was.

'I see you live in Hampton Ash?' He only asked because he wondered if she knew his mother, although he wasn't going to discuss that today.

'Yes, we moved there a couple of months ago.'

'Oh, does your husband work locally?'

'I don't have a husband,' she replied, and judging by the look on her face, Richard wished he hadn't asked.

'Well,' he continued, attempting to divert the attention away from the awkwardness he'd briefly created, 'the idea I have so far is to set you up with a full home office, as you see here.' He stood up as he spoke and she followed him back to the other room, which housed a plethora of office equipment.

He stood aside, allowing her to pass, when suddenly she lost her footing, wobbling and almost falling. She had no other option than to brush up against him, and as she put her hand out to steady herself, she was mortified at finding it coming into direct contact with his chest. She could feel the warmth of his body through the crisp cotton of his shirt.

'Oh good God, I'm so sorry.' She retracted her hand almost as quickly as it had fallen there, her face flushing a very bright shade of beetroot.

He reached out, grasping hold of her arm to steady her. 'My fault, I must have disturbed those cables when I pulled out the router earlier. It's me that should be apologising.'

Their eyes met only briefly, but it was quite long enough for her to experience the thrill that was now coursing through her body. They soon returned to their earlier discussions and she hoped he wouldn't notice her legs quivering beneath her.

'I've no doubt that you're the right person for this job, Poppy, but there is just one thing that concerns me,' he said, frowning.

She groaned inwardly, praying that he wasn't about to say something along the lines of, *'you do keep looking at me with awfully hungry eyes; has it been a while since you've been fed?'*

She bit her lip, and Richard cleared his throat as he continued, 'I want you to be honest – would this position be enough to fulfil you, given your previous experience and certainly your management experience with Greg?'

Poppy paused for a moment, mulling over his words. *Why did he speak Greg's name as if he were a friend?* The only concern she had at that moment was whether she could work with someone as handsome as him, but she quickly pushed those kinds of thoughts out of her mind. The job *was* a great opportunity, and one she'd enjoy in the otherwise empty hours she spent waiting for Lily to come home from school.

'I do miss working with Greg and everyone at Hawkins, Monroe and Sable,' she said after a bit more thought, 'after all, they were a major part of my life for a long time, but for the last five years I worked there, I juggled my career with bringing up my daughter, and I missed out on such a lot.' She paused, straightening up to look at him as if the gesture underlined her seriousness. 'However, now that she's started school I've got too much time on my hands and I'm horrendously bored. I've plenty of skills and experience that I could put to good use and I don't want to waste any of it, so instead of taking a full-time role and going back to hardly seeing my daughter again, a part-time position would fit in just nicely. And besides,' she smiled, 'I need the money.' This made them both laugh.

'That's always a good reason,' he agreed, taking a moment to digest her words. 'In that case, I'd like to give it a go and see how we get on. What do you think?'

Poppy left the offices of Richard Jones Consultancy as if she were walking on air, completely delighted at having secured a position – and one that was so flexible too. She was really looking forward to working with Richard, although she hoped she wouldn't get too distracted by his handsome good looks.

She paused; actually, she'd quite surprised herself for a moment there, as it had been such a long time since she'd been attracted to anyone – certainly not since Oliver.

Hastily, she made her way home to see Lily and Percy so she could deliver her good news.

TWENTY-FIVE

Poppy checked her reflection for the umpteenth time that morning, just as the sound of the doorbell went, causing her heart to thump wildly and her stomach to flutter.

She felt like Christmas had come early with the arrival of all this new IT equipment, and she put her reaction down to her excitement and not at all anything to do with the fact that she was spending the whole morning with Richard. She did her best to walk down the stairs as calmly as possible before opening the front door.

'Good morning,' she trilled breathlessly, greeting Richard who'd arrived to set up her home office.

Almost six weeks had passed since her interview and she'd spent much of that time (during school hours) at his office in Midford County, gleaning an understanding of the business, how Richard liked to work, and what tasks and responsibilities he wanted her to undertake. They'd got on really well so far and had seemed to click almost instantly – they were quite relaxed with each other already.

'Morning!' he responded brightly, 'Glad to see you've cleared the way.' He nodded, indicating the empty desk in her study. 'I'll start bringing things in from the car.'

The next three hours were spent unpacking various bits and pieces of IT equipment and then setting it all up. She pulled up a chair to watch as he set up the laptop, showing her how to link it to the computers in the Midford County office.

'That's it.' He smiled, turning to her. 'You're all good to go.'

'Yaayy!' She waved her arms in the air like an excited child on their birthday, and they both laughed.

'I'll just test it my end when I get back to the office, but it should all work fine,' Richard added. 'Of course, the proof will be in the pudding.' He was referring to the fact that he was just about to set off on an overseas trip, leaving her in full control of the office. She was nervous, but he was completely confident that his business would be perfectly safe in her hands.

He stood up to go at the exact same moment she arose out of her chair, the action unexpectedly bringing the two of them face-to-face, their bodies just inches away from each other and their mouths less. For a brief moment she thought he was going to kiss her, but as quickly as the thought entered her head, he turned briskly away.

He cleared his throat as he picked up his jacket and keys. 'Right, I'm off,' he announced, certain to avoid eye contact. 'Any problems – anything at all – just give me a call. I'll switch the phones over tonight when I leave the office.'

Poppy nodded and then followed him out to the front door.

'I'll see you next week then,' he said brightly, 'good luck!' Then he was gone, and – she noted – he didn't look back.

Poppy went inside and closed the door, resting up against it for a moment or two. Back in her study, she couldn't escape breathing in the aroma of Richard's aftershave that still clung to the air from where he'd been sitting; her stomach churned and she sank into the chair feeling deflated and empty.

'What's wrong with you, Poppy Jackson?' she asked herself. 'Surely you're not getting hooked on the first attractive guy you've met since Oliver?'

But it wasn't just that. She'd seen and met plenty of attractive men since Oliver had died; it's just that she hadn't been interested in any of them. Marnie, Greg, and Sally were always attempting to set her up on blind dates, or inviting her over 'to meet the friend of a friend,' but she hadn't felt ready for any of that, or even the slightest bit interested. Since meeting Richard, though, she felt different – it seemed as if her senses had been reawakened after lying dormant for so long. Perhaps she was just infatuated with him; after all, she'd spent every day of the past few weeks working in close proximity with him – that was bound to create some feelings of attraction, wasn't it? If she was being *really* honest, though, she'd found Richard attractive the very first moment she'd set eyes on him; even hearing his voice on the phone prior to them actually meeting had been enough to pique her interest.

What if he just doesn't find you attractive?

But she wasn't completely convinced of that; thinking back to when they'd stood up together before he left, she felt sure they'd shared a 'moment'. Sighing, she placed her face in her hands, feeling very silly, like a love-struck schoolgirl.

At the end of the day, you're only spending time with him at all because you work for him.

She reflected back on her relationship with Greg; whilst she'd enjoyed a close friendship with him and his family – whom she loved immensely – it was never anything more; she'd never felt attracted to Greg in all the years she'd known him. Richard, however, seemed quite different, and the whole thing felt more, sort of – Oli-ish.

She gasped aloud. 'No, no, I didn't mean that!' No one could ever replace the love she'd had – and *still* had – for Oliver, but whilst that was true, there was no denying that Richard appeared to evoke similar feelings of attraction Oli had when she'd first met him, the same depth of attraction she hadn't felt at all since then.

TWENTY-SIX

Richard drove back to the office, glad of the 15 or so mile journey to clear his head; his heart had just about stopped racing now. Up until today, he hadn't realised the depth of feeling he'd developed and, in all honesty, it unnerved him. Of course, the moment he'd set eyes on her he was hooked, but he met attractive women both in and out of the business circuit all the time and so he'd dismissed it as being no more than that. However, they'd got much closer in the past few weeks than perhaps they should have, and he considered this carefully.

With it just being the two of them in the office they'd spent a lot of time together, getting closer, whilst he introduced her to the workings of his business. On several occasions he'd caught himself thinking about her, and he always looked forward to her arrival, but today? Well, today he'd nearly kissed her.

He swallowed, taking a deep breath. Yes, today he'd nearly lost control, and he couldn't allow that to happen again. He wondered if he'd made a mistake employing her but dismissed the thought as quickly as it had appeared. Of course he hadn't made a mistake; he just hadn't bargained for developing bloody feelings for her.

He banged the steering wheel in frustration as he looked at his phone, wishing she'd find a reason to call, giving him an excuse to go back. Could he really afford to be so reckless? But he was 30 years old, for god's sake! Apart from the string of girlfriends he'd had through university, he'd been pretty much celibate for the past two years and he was sick of it. He'd been so focused on making a success of his business that he just hadn't had time for relationships, not to mention all the distractions that came with them – or so he'd thought. Perhaps the real truth of the matter was that he just hadn't met the right girl yet.

He looked at his phone again, willing it to ring, but it stayed silent.

Had she sensed it too, their 'moment'?

She certainly didn't come across as someone who gave way to her feelings easily, but then again he didn't really know her that well. He did know that she was a single parent, which didn't faze him in the slightest, even though he didn't know much about it. He didn't know where the father was, for instance, but he didn't want to either – that was none of his business.

That made him think of his own situation, causing him to shake his head; once Poppy learned about his background, she'd probably want to run a mile anyway. Even *he* wanted to run away from it, but he was biding his time on that one.

After more reflection, he decided that the best thing to do was to put some distance between them – at least that way any feelings would soon dissipate once they realised it was nothing more than infatuation and lust. But, as he guided his car into Courtenay House, he suspected that in reality, he was just kidding himself.

*

Richard's father had died from a heart attack when he was just 13 – completely unexpected, a full-on total shock. Although he'd never had a particularly close relationship with him – as most of his childhood had been spent at boarding school –he'd nevertheless very much admired, respected, and loved him. There were several occasions when he'd taken Richard to watch cricket at Lord's or to the rugby at Twickenham, but apart from this, he never really got to know his father as much as he'd wanted to.

Upon his father's death, his mother had inherited everything, ensuring that the two of them were well provided for due to his father's clever planning and careful investments. The family business, on the other hand, was to be run by his mother until Richard was old enough to take over. Of course, with him now being 30, his mother considered him more than ready and did little to disguise her frustration at his continued refusal to step up and take the reins.

He recalled how, just a couple of weeks after his father's funeral, he'd arrived home for the summer break, desperate to see her; she'd been so distraught the last time he was home and he was anxious to make sure she was alright. Now that his father was no longer around, he considered it his responsibility to take care of her as best he could. However, he hadn't bargained for the shocking discovery he was to make that day; a discovery that nearly broke him.

The school master had allowed some of the boys to take an earlier train back, and on the journey home Richard had imagined how delighted his mother would be to see him, and how she'd fawn all over him; perhaps even suggesting they go out for dinner to celebrate his homecoming. He practically raced all the way along the drive from the bus stop – as though a huge, ferocious bear was snapping at his heels – but he managed to calm down in time to creep quietly into the vast Victorian property they shared, anticipating her surprise and knowing she'd be thrilled at his unexpected arrival.

Then he saw them – or rather, he heard them first. They were in the drawing room, arguing, and he quickly realised that the argument concerned him. Disappointment surged through him as he hovered and listened, keeping quite out of sight although he doubted they'd have noticed him anyway. He recognised the male voice immediately, of course, with him having been a regular visitor of his parents for some years. It seemed he was trying to reason with his mother.

'Please think about it. Now is just as good a time as any.'

'No. It's far too soon; we need to give him time to adjust.'

'But the sooner he knows, the sooner we can be a family.'

'For God's sake, his father's not even cold in his grave yet!'

'But that's my point; he wasn't even his father, was he?'

The words had stung Richard as much as if he'd been slapped hard across the face, and bravely holding back the tears that were threatening to spill over at any moment, he quietly retreated out of the house and back down the drive, although not with the same gusto that had accompanied his arrival. His bottom lip wobbling, he went off in search of sanctuary; he needed to get away for a while to process this unexpected revelation.

The family home consisted of a huge estate based on the outskirts of Swinford St. George; part of the River Thames ran along the South side, which is where he found himself sitting just a few minutes later.

He sat by the river, staring into the water for hours, trying to make sense of what he'd overheard. He wondered if his father had known the truth, an idea that made him feel very confused and slightly panicky.

So his father hadn't been his father after all. What on earth would become of him? He'd lost a vital part of his identity and he didn't have a clue as to how he could rebuild it. He was only 13. He'd spent more time at boarding school than he had at home, and suddenly he longed for the familiarity of Stanford Hall and dormitory 3b.

Wiping his eyes dry with the back of his hand, Richard slowly made his way back to the house; his heart heavy, his steps slow as if each shoe were filled with concrete. When he got back he was relieved to discover that his mother was now alone. He'd always held a very bright light for his dear mother but on that day, a part of that light dimmed – and it had never really come back since.

TWENTY-SEVEN

'Hi Poppy, it's Richard.'

Her heart skipped a beat as the sound of Richard's voice floated over from the answering machine, filling up the little room.

'I'm sorry to have missed you; I hope all is well and you're managing okay. I just want to let you know that I'm flying onto Munich and then travelling to Frankfurt, so I won't be back until the end of next week.' Her heart sank. 'Do call if you need anything; you're doing a fantastic job, by the way – thanks for sending those referrals over. Speak soon,' and he was gone.

She sighed deeply; he was supposed to have flown in from France at lunchtime and now he was travelling for another week. She'd been so looking forward to his return, eager for him to see how well she was progressing in her work, not to mention showing off some of the new systems she'd introduced. She was really enjoying getting to grips with the business, liaising with all manner of people via the telephone and the internet, but more importantly she was pleased to be working with *him*; it had been just what she'd needed to fill her time whilst Lily was at school.

She also knew that had she *not* been around during the past few weeks, Richard could well have missed some lucrative opportunities, and she was grateful he'd noted as much in his message.

Well, he can't avoid me forever.

In the meantime, she switched her attention to the job in hand.

*

As well as her part-time job, Poppy still kept actively involved in village life, thoroughly enjoying being part of *COG*. Her and Lily had made lots of new friends since moving to the Hamptons, and even more so since reconnecting with Anthony and Ianthe. They always looked forward to catching up with everyone at church on Sunday mornings, followed by lunch at the Maide of Honour with Percy and, as was more usual these days, Rosie too. Poppy was delighted that after all these years her father had found a companion again.

The four of them left church together – having given thanks to Reverend Fisher for yet another fine sermon – and made their way across to the pub, soon being joined by Anthony. It was such a glorious sunny day that they decided to make the most of the good weather and sit outside in the garden; Percy and Rosie took everyone's food order and went off inside, leaving Poppy and Anthony together, happily watching Lily play on the swings with some of her friends from school.

'No Ianthe today?' Poppy had really taken to Ianthe; she was an elegant lady and such a joy to be around – completely different to Martha in every sense. Anthony had explained that she was quite involved in a business she owned, which was why she was often out when Poppy visited.

'Oh, she's off running some errand or other for Richard,' he explained.

Her heart jumped; the very mention of the name immediately evoked an image of her Richard... only he wasn't *her* Richard, was he?

'Who's Richard?' she asked, wondering why the name had never come up before. Perhaps it had and she just hadn't noticed.

'Ianthe's son,' Anthony replied casually, before turning to meet her gaze. As he looked directly into her eyes, she felt a strange chill run through her.

'Her son?' Poppy repeated.

'Yes.'

'I didn't know she had a son?' She looked away then – over towards Lily – wanting to break eye contact; it had started to feel pretty odd.

'Yes.'

She realised Anthony was trying to make his voice sound light, which was strange. It was also strange that he'd never mentioned her son before.

'How old is he?' Poppy asked.

'Er… about thirtyish,' he replied. He knew exactly how old he was.

'Oh, he doesn't live at home, then? That must be why I haven't seen him.'

'He travels quite a lot, actually, with his business and stuff… which reminds me, how's your new job going?' He was glad to have found a way to divert her attention onto a different subject. Or so he thought.

'Yes, very well thanks – I'm really enjoying it.'

'How are you getting on with your boss?'

'Okay, but then he's away quite a lot so I don't see that much of him…' She trailed off, stopping herself from adding, 'or not as much as I'd like to'.

'Hello Poppy!'

She looked up, having immediately recognised the voice of policeman Matt Hudson, who was grinning from ear to ear, clearly delighted to see her.

She smiled back. 'Matt, how are you?'

'Great, thanks! Glad to see you're back in the village.'

'Yes, it's good to be back on home ground. Let me introduce Anthony Sullivan, Lily's grandfather.'

Anthony greeted Matt warmly, smiling as she introduced him.

'Matt's a Sergeant at Midford County Police Station,' Poppy explained.

Anthony winked jokingly at him. 'I imagine this one keeps you busy.'

She gasped in mock horror, making them both laugh.

'We're thinking of expanding the team, actually.'

She gasped again. 'Rude.'

'Why don't you join us, Matt?' interjected Anthony. 'We're just ordering lunch if you're interested?'

Matt nodded. 'Don't mind if I do, Mr. Sullivan, thank you.'

'Oh, call me Anthony, please – we're all friends here.'

Poppy turned to Matt, smiling. 'Dad's at the bar ordering now, do you want me to go and add an extra lunch for you?'

He smiled too. 'I'll go; can I get anyone a drink whilst I'm there?'

As they watched him go back inside the pub, Anthony turned his gaze to Poppy. 'He's keen on you.'

She looked back at him, surprised. 'And?'

Anthony shrugged. 'I'm just saying, that's all. He seems a nice chap.'

'You don't know him.'

'He can't be too bad if he's a policeman, and a Sergeant at that,' he pointed out.

'True.'

'Well?'

'What?'

'He's keen on you...'

Poppy squirmed on the bench. 'But he was our village bobby when I was growing up...'

'So?'

'Well, it's not right, is it?'

Anthony had a hard time not rolling his eyes at her. 'You're what, thirty-two? And he's how old?'

'I'm not sure,' thought Poppy out loud, 'he must be forty at least.'

'You make that sound like it's a bad thing,' laughed Anthony.

'No, it's just... well... that's quite a gap, isn't it?'

'Nonsense. I'm several years older than Ianthe and it makes no difference whatsoever; anyway, do you like him? That's the real question.'

Not as much as I like my Richard.

She mulled Anthony's words over for a few moments. It wasn't that she didn't find Matt attractive – on the contrary, he was quite a dish – it's just that her heart didn't flip at the sound of his voice, and her stomach didn't flutter whenever she thought about him. There just wasn't that... *spark.*

'Well?' Anthony encouraged.

'Well, I guess, but what about Lily?' she asked, knowing it was a lame excuse.

'Oh, come on, isn't it about time you had some fun of your own?' He paused, smiling at her. 'Listen, all I'm saying is if he's as keen on you as I think he is, then he's likely to ask you out on a date, and why not? It would do you good to go out and have some fun.' He hugged her to him, planting a kiss affectionately on top of her head.

Poppy sighed. She knew he only had her best interests at heart, but it wasn't always as easy as all that, was it?

A while later, once the others had re-joined them, she tried to look at Matt in a different light. She also noticed that he kept looking at her every now and then, something that she quite liked. Of course, when Lily re-joined them, she was soon the star of the show, with Matt being clearly delighted to finally meet her. He noted that whilst she had inherited her father's looks, she had indeed inherited her mother's stubbornness – something that made him laugh.

After a hearty lunch – combined with lots of laughter – the group started to make moves towards going home, and as they headed out towards the exit, Matt took the opportunity to take Poppy aside. He asked if he could take her out for a drink some time, which of course she'd been expecting, given her earlier discussion with Anthony.

'Yes I'd like that,' she replied, smiling politely.

Matt looked relieved. 'How about this Thursday? I can pick you up about seven if that suits?'

'Sounds great,' Poppy agreed. 'See you then.'

As she walked out to re-join the others, Anthony winked at her. 'Need a sitter?'

She smiled up at him. 'You're not free this Thursday, are you?'

'As a matter of fact...'

TWENTY-EIGHT

Lily was nervous; it was her first day back at school following the summer holidays and she was moving up from Nursery into Class 1. She was also, however, quite excited, as this meant she had a new teacher, Mrs. Davies. Everyone *loved* Mrs. Davies.

As Poppy and Lily made their way to the Hamptons Primary School, they both tried to still the fluttering inside their tummies.

Poppy was nervous for another reason; it was her first day back in the office and the first time she'd seen Richard in over six weeks – she'd taken the last two weeks of the school holidays off to spend some time with Lily before the autumn term started. She hadn't spoken to Richard at all during this time and, as she drove towards Midford County having dropped Lily safely off at school, she wished she'd had her own mother with her to calm her nerves at the door, and to kiss her reassuringly before she went inside.

As Poppy entered Courtenay House the security guard greeted her brightly, and taking a deep breath, she made her way up to the fifth floor.

*

Richard had been pacing the floor for the past half hour or so, looking out for her car that would signal her arrival. He'd thought about nothing else these past few weeks and he really didn't know how he was going to react at seeing her today; all he *did* know was that he'd really missed her.

Suddenly he caught sight of her car, and he lurched back from the window in case she spotted him. Returning to his desk he tried to look busy, but he was completely unable to concentrate on anything.

He listened out for the sound of the lift, which seemed to be taking an eternity, his throat going dry as he attempted to compose himself ready for her arrival. His heart was thudding madly in his chest.

*

Here goes.

Taking a deep breath she pushed open the heavy door to their office, her stomach fluttering like crazy. She tried to put on her best 'oh fancy seeing you here' expression as she stepped inside – she wanted to keep things casual yet professional.

'Poppy!' Richard stood up and welcomed her enthusiastically, clearly pleased to see her. He looked amazing – quite tanned – and she wondered if he'd been on holiday too.

'Hello Richard,' she just about managed to say, hoping her knees weren't visibly shaking as much as it felt like they were.

He immediately noticed that there were dark smudges beneath her eyes and that she looked a little drawn. 'Coffee?' he asked as he walked towards the kitchen, seeking a distraction whilst she placed her bag and jacket onto her chair before following behind.

'How was your holiday?' He deliberately kept his back to her as he made them both a drink.

'Lovely thanks, how about you? Did you go away?' It was her best attempt at sounding detached.

'I spent a couple of weeks at my mother's villa, actually,' he said, turning and passing a cup to her, 'she has a property in the South of France and I often go there during the summer.'

She smiled; Anthony had just come back from the South of France and also had an amazing tan. She looked up at Richard again, looking at his own tan, to find he'd been watching her. He quickly reverted his gaze as she drew her eyes in line with his own.

He cleared his throat. 'Right, shall we go through a few things? I imagine there's a lot to catch up on,' he said, setting off in the direction of his desk.

She inwardly sighed before walking over to sit down at her own desk.

I might have fallen for him, but I'm not going to fail him.

So, trying to concentrate on her job rather than her boss, she listened to her instructions for the day.

*

'You're quiet tonight. Is everything okay?'

She didn't just look tired; she seemed distracted too. It had been over two weeks since they'd first gone out and Matt hadn't been able to think about anything – or anyone – else since. He'd really been looking forward to seeing her again tonight, but she wasn't herself. It concerned him.

Poppy knew that she had to pull herself together – it wasn't fair on Matt – but how on earth could she tell him that 'Actually, I think I'm in love with a guy who doesn't love me back, and I'm out with a guy who *might* love me but I actually want to be somewhere else'?

Instead, she shrugged and said, 'I'm sorry, Matt. It's just it's my first day back at the office today and I think it's taken its toll on me.' She looked into his eyes – he had green eyes, framed by long lashes – and shook her head. 'I'm sorry, I should have suggested we meet at the weekend; I've had so much going on today with Lily starting a new school year and me going back to work...'

'It's okay, really.' Matt placed his hand affectionately over hers. 'Why don't we do just that then? Let's get together on Saturday night.' As soon as he said it, an even better thought crossed his mind. 'Actually, I'm off from Friday, and you don't work on a Saturday, do you?'

'No, I don't work at weekends.'

'What about taking Lily over to that petting zoo outside Swinford St. George? We could always get a takeaway afterwards or something?'

She liked the sound of that. She liked the sound of that a lot. 'That would be lovely, Matt. Thanks.'

So, with that decided, they left the pub and walked back towards his car.

'I'm really enjoying spending time with you, Poppy, and getting to know you better.'

She smiled. 'I know, Matt, it's just... well... you're the first person I've dated since Oliver, and...'

Matt placed a finger gently on her lips. 'It's okay, I know. There's no pressure, Poppy, none at all. Let's just take things one step at a time shall we?'

Smiling, Poppy agreed.

*

The following day, life at the office didn't start out quite as enthusiastically as the previous one had. After the initial 'good morning' greetings they both settled into their work, but it soon became apparent that Poppy was struggling to concentrate; her many restless nights were beginning to take their toll, something that hadn't gone unnoticed by Richard.

He'd been glancing at her throughout the morning, keeping an eye on her as she'd started to get quite clumsy, losing two calls and dropping things. The atmosphere was becoming a bit strained and he was growing concerned.

He knew the responsibility for this lay at his door – and if he was honest, he was struggling too – but he was so unexpectedly close now. Never had his goal seemed more achievable than at that very moment, the goal that was causing him to fight the feelings he'd clearly developed towards Poppy, even though it was making him quite miserable – not to mention his suspicion that it was also affecting her.

He couldn't wait for the weekend when he could take some time out, although his mother had been on at him again; well, she'd just have to wait, wouldn't she? He'd far more pressing matters to deal with first.

*

Poppy welcomed the arrival of the weekend like a long-lost friend; she was hopeful that a day out in the fresh air would be just what the doctor ordered to aid a good night's sleep and to provide a much needed distraction.

She busied herself making a picnic lunch for their jaunt to Elderberry Zoo, including some healthy stuff but also some treats as well. It was quite a pleasant day for the second weekend in September – although not as warm as it had been recently – and the sun was shining, promising to be a clear day. Lily was particularly excited as they'd invited her new best friend, Anna-Maria, to come along; the two girls were happily dancing around the lounge, waiting for Matt to arrive. Poppy had just finished packing up their lunch when he knocked on the door.

'Morning all,' he greeted them brightly before being quickly swamped by two excited five-year-olds who were jumping up and down in front of him, causing him to laugh out loud.

Poppy helped load everything into the car and then off they went; the zoo was only about 15 miles away from the Hamptons so they didn't have too far to travel. As they drove along the girls excitedly asked question after question: what were they going to see? What were they going to do? When were they going to get there? And they weren't giving anyone much of a chance to reply either, much to Matt's amusement. The atmosphere in the car was bursting with excitement, happiness, and positivity, and as she took a moment to take a couple of deep breaths, Poppy just knew it was going to be a great day.

*

Richard was not amused. His mother's call had woken him up early – well, he hadn't *actually* been asleep, but that wasn't the point. They'd rowed, of course, about the wretched business – *again* – and then she'd demanded that he meet her that morning as a matter of urgency.

He wasn't usually one to give in to any of her demands, but her constant pursuit of him over the past few weeks was beginning to interfere with his ability to make sense of anything, and now he'd had enough.

He agreed to meet her at Swinford St. George – hoping that the journey over there would calm the anger and frustration that was threatening to boil over inside of him – but along the way he decided to go via the Hamptons, causing him to drive past Poppy's house. As he did so, his mood lifted slightly.

He slowed down a little as he passed by, noting her car on the driveway, and considered stopping for a moment to see if she was in… but then what would he say? He'd love to take her and Lily out for the day – especially as it was quite a sunny morning – and on a whim he decided to call in on the way back from meeting his mother.

He wondered then why they hadn't arranged to meet at Channing House, but after thinking about it for a while longer he realised it was probably for the best, given that *he*'d be there; he wasn't sure how much longer he could restrain himself.

He cursed with frustration as he pulled up at yet another set of traffic lights, which appeared to be permanently stuck on red. *Why is it that whenever I'm in a hurry the fucking lights are always against me?*

His attention was suddenly drawn towards a car pulling up beside him, causing him to do a double take; in fact, he did a *quadruple* take, as he couldn't quite believe his eyes. There in the car next to him was Poppy, laughing and joking with some bloke and two children. He quickly recognised Lily, and he guessed that the other child must belong to the bloke who was driving.

Oh very fucking cosy, he silently fumed. *Well, it hasn't taken her long to move onto someone else, has it?* He was then reminded just how clumsy and absent-minded she'd been in the office the past couple of days, his mind going into overdrive as he wrongly assumed it must have all been due to one too many late nights with the new guy.

Just then the lights changed, and as the car next to him drove forward he quickly changed lanes, deciding to follow them instead; much to the disgust of the other frustrated Saturday motorists behind him. Richard didn't even notice – he was much too focused on the car ahead. *Just who the hell was this guy anyway?*

He stayed on their trail for a couple of miles – ensuring that he kept just far back enough not to be noticed – and then watched as their car pulled into Elderberry Zoo. Driving up to the next roundabout, he turned around and drove back up towards the zoo; this way he could drive in unnoticed by Poppy.

From a few vehicles away he watched them get out of the car, jealousy surging through him as the 'new guy' held Poppy steady while she changed her shoes for wellington boots. He felt sick – how dare he fucking touch her!

Having seen enough, he slammed the car into gear and drove off, heading back towards Midford County. Fuck his mother! Right at that moment, she could go to hell as far as he was concerned.

*

Poppy flopped to the ground, glad to finally have an opportunity to sit down, and proceeded to spread out the picnic blanket she'd brought along on top of the grass; Matt had taken the girls off to wash their hands as they'd just been feeding the goats and sheep.

They'd had a lovely morning so far and, surprised at how hungry she felt, Poppy imagined the girls would be ravenous too. After unpacking the lunch she waited for them to join her, thinking about Richard and wondering what he was doing.

Probably working, she guessed, although he'd mentioned that he was looking forward to a relaxing weekend. He'd crept into her thoughts several times that morning, especially when she thought she'd seen his car earlier, but she knew that was just wishful thinking; honestly, what on earth would he be doing at Elderberry Zoo? She dismissed the thought, of course, but still she couldn't help wishing he was here with her and the girls.

She stopped those thoughts in their tracks. This really wasn't being fair to Matt. She needed to stop thinking about Richard if she was ever going to have any sort of relationship with him.

*

Richard paced the floor. He sat down, he got up again. He wanted to scream yet he felt sick. His stomach definitely hurt, but not as much as his heart did.

He tried to reason with himself. *Maybe he's just a friend or a cousin or something. Just because she's out with someone doesn't automatically mean they're in a relationship, does it?*

He was still wondering who the man could possibly be when he was distracted by the ringing of his mobile; the umpteenth call he'd received that day. He was filled with a strong desire to smash the phone against the wall – as if it would evoke a deep sense of satisfaction – but he knew that was just being foolish. He wasn't certain it would actually make him feel any better anyway. He knew exactly who the caller was, of course, and she would just have to wait.

Sitting down, he ran his fingers through his hair as he looked at the clock: it was almost seven. He decided to drive over and speak to her; he was certain Lily would be in bed by this time and he desperately needed to see Poppy, to tell her before it was too late.

His mind made up, he got in his car and, as calmly as he possibly could, drove towards Hampton Ash.

*

She pushed her plate aside, sated. 'I cannot eat another mouthful.'

Matt smiled; the meal they'd had delivered from the local Chinese was delicious.

Poppy put on some music and lit a few candles before re-joining him on the sofa, and as they chatted over the day's events it wasn't long before she sensed a change in the atmosphere.

It was a natural progression in their relationship, wasn't it?

After only a brief hesitation she leaned towards him, allowing him to take her in his arms. She sensed his nerves just before he brought his mouth down to meet hers, but it was only a sweet, gentle kiss. A nice kiss. They kissed some more, Poppy slowly allowing his kisses to move from her mouth to her neck. But it was just no use; she couldn't continue.

She pulled away as sensitively as she could, though there was no escaping the disappointed look in his eyes. 'I'm so sorry, Matt, I...'

Ever the gentleman, he played the situation down. 'I guess it's been a long day, Poppy; it's me who should be apologising.'

'No, Matt, it's not you,' Poppy replied quickly, desperate to explain herself.

Her words, however, dissipated as he looked deep into her eyes, and after holding her gaze for several moments Matt said, 'the thing is, Poppy, I've started to develop feelings for you.'

She swallowed as she gazed downwards, too ashamed to look up at him. 'I *do* like you, Matt, really I do – it's just that I need to be certain of what I'm feeling.' She paused for a moment, shrugging. 'I don't want anyone to get hurt.'

Matt stood up then, silently berating himself for misreading the situation. 'Look, it's been a long day and we're all tired; call me when you've had time to think things through, okay?'

Poppy followed him out to the door, where he turned and held her for just a brief moment, making her sigh. She knew she could do far worse that build a relationship with Matt, but she also knew that she needed to be over Richard in order to do so.

And the only way *that* could happen was by confronting him with her feelings once and for all.

*

As Richard drove along he ran various scripts through his mind – what he was going to say, why he was there, and just who the fuck was the mystery guy, anyway? Maybe he should just come out and ask her if she was seeing someone. Or maybe he should just start by telling her how he felt… he really didn't know anymore. He didn't want her to think he was angry and jealous – he wasn't that guy at all. Usually. Poppy just seemed to do things to him. In all honesty, she drove him crazy – in a good way.

He drove along King's Oak Road towards Honeycombe Lodge, feeling like a knife had ripped into him as his eyes took in the now familiar sight of the car that Poppy and Lily had been travelling in earlier. Whoever he was, it seemed he was making a night of it.

He raced off in disgust. For a brief moment he considered driving over to Channing House and venting all his anger and frustration out on his mother; after all, if she hadn't insisted on meeting in Swinford St. George that morning he'd never have seen Poppy and would not be experiencing the despair and heartache he was feeling now.

Realising, however, that this wasn't entirely fair to his mother, he retreated back to his cottage in Midford County to lick his wounds.

TWENTY-NINE

Lady Ianthe Hambly-Jones was feeling quite pleased with herself. She basked in the shards of sunshine filtering in through the window, enjoying the warmth of the rays on her face and neck. She really hoped she'd finally worn her son down and made him see sense; the very fact that he'd agreed to meet her that morning was certainly a good sign, anyway.

At 61, she was tired of running the show and wanted to hand everything over to him, leaving her and Anthony free to marry. Thinking of Anthony evoked a warmth all of its own; she loved him deeply and longed for the day they would be united in marriage, allowing them to finally shake off the 'illicitness' of their affair. Seeking a diversion whilst she waited for her son to arrive, she used the time to think back to when they'd first met.

After seven years of marriage, Roderick seemed to enjoy spending more time at the office than with her. She had, of course, become genuinely interested in the business —mainly as a potential way of strengthening their relationship – but later, much to her delight, she discovered that she really enjoyed it, and was actually good at it too.

However, be that as it may, whilst Roderick was more than happy for her to be as involved as she wanted to be, it remained his responsibility to grow the business and get the best out of it, which was easier to do when she wasn't around to distract him. He soon became so focused on profit and growth that he failed to appreciate just how little time they were spending together.

It was around this time that he decided to employ the services of Anthony Sullivan. Initially, this was just to manage his own share portfolio but later, as their friendship grew and trusts deepened, he came to highly respect him and his advice, which never seemed to let him down. The more Anthony taught him about investments, the more involved he became in taking his businesses investments and interests further, and over the years, their meetings soon developed into a regular routine.

At first, Anthony travelled from London one a day a month. They would have their meeting and then dinner at Roderick's private club, after which Anthony would travel back. Later on, he was invited to stay overnight at the estate – giving them more time to discuss business – and it wasn't long, of course, before that arrangement became a regular event too.

During those early days, Ianthe only met Anthony briefly maybe on one or two occasions, but when he began staying at the estate regularly, they would all dine together before taking part in long discussions that usually carried on into the early hours.

The first time Roderick didn't show up, Ianthe didn't think anything of it. Her husband left instructions for her to dine with Anthony, citing some urgent business matter for his delay and promising to join them later. But the second time he didn't show up, her concerns began to grow; he was becoming more distant towards her of late and it hadn't gone unnoticed. She knew he was desperate for an heir to continue the family name – and, of course, to keep the business going – but it just didn't seem to be happening. He refused point blank to discuss the matter with her and said he would rather die than consider seeking medical advice.

It's easy to say that I was desperately lonely.

But that's exactly what she was: desperate and lonely. Having not long turned 30 she felt she was living the life of a much older woman, and one who was never going to experience anything fun ever again.

Anthony, of course, should have known better; he too was married and had a young child, but his wife Martha had become cold and distant towards him since Oliver's birth, causing him to feel pushed out. At times he even found himself vying for her affections against his own son. It was totally ludicrous. He wasn't completely without empathy, of course, and tried a million different ways to talk through his feelings with Martha, trying to unearth her own anxieties, but she always maintained that everything was fine. Soon he knew he was fighting a losing battle.

When Roderick first contacted him during this time he hadn't realised what a lifeline this relationship would present, and as their friendship developed, Anthony welcomed the opportunity to get away from his own troubles for a while. Whenever Roderick needed him, he'd be there.

The first time Anthony and Ianthe made love it was almost animalistic; having both been starved of such intimate affection for so long, their connection was wild and passionate. At times Ianthe feared her husband would arrive home before they'd finished, but she was quite unable to fight against the strong feelings of desire and attraction that had been building up inside her towards Anthony.

Before long, both she and Anthony longed for his weekend visits, each of them praying that Roderick would not be joining them. More often than not, their wish was granted, and life was wonderful again – delightfully wonderful – until, that was, she fell pregnant.

Whilst there was never any option other than going ahead and having the baby, the real problem, of course, was telling her husband. She'd wrestled and wrestled with finding the right time, the right words, and Anthony had even offered to take care of the matter, but she knew that this was something she had to deal with alone. She still loved her husband, but now she loved Anthony far more.

Neither of them, however, had been prepared for his reaction – you really couldn't make it up.

She'd waited until Roderick had arrived back from the office late one evening and, having prepared drinks, she'd asked to speak to him. They sat in the drawing room; him in his favourite armchair, her on the sofa opposite. There was no sound in the room other than the softness of her voice as she laid bare the sordid details of her and Anthony's illicit affair, and what it had now resulted in.

Once she'd finished, she waited anxiously for him to speak, wringing her hands nervously in her lap and expecting him to banish her from his life and the family estate forever. After a few moments he calmly placed his glass down on the occasional table, and after crouching down in front of her, he lifted up her face with his hand so he could look into her eyes. She felt sick with nerves as she met his gaze, and in doing so was stunned to see that tears were beginning to fill his eyes.

'You have no idea,' he began, 'just how happy you have made me, my darling. I promise you that you and our child shall not want for anything.' He took her hand and kissed it before returning to his chair, and his drink. She watched as a tear slid down his face.

'But Roderick...'

He held up his hand. 'This is *our* child, Ianthe; we are husband and wife and this child will be heir.'

The matter was simply never referred to again. Anthony's visits continued as usual – which was an odd set-up, some might say – but it worked for them and it appeared to harm no one, at least not at the time. Roderick had been delighted when Richard was born, choosing to name him and making great provisions for his son's future, a future that Ianthe very much hoped Richard would now take responsibility of.

THIRTY

Monday morning seemed to take forever to arrive, and it certainly didn't bring any better a mood than Richard had harboured all weekend, ever since seeing her Saturday morning.

He was still angry.

He was still frustrated.

He was still very much in love.

But he wouldn't be admitting that anytime soon, oh no – that ship was currently moored. He tried his utmost to find something to distract him but it was no use; all he could think about was Poppy.

He walked over to the window for the umpteenth time that morning, keeping watch for her car whilst his stomach did a strange fluttery thing, making him feel sick. He'd never experienced this kind of feeling before, and he didn't at all know how to handle it.

*

Poppy drove to the office feeling emotionally lighter than she'd felt in a long time. She hadn't been up for joining the others for Sunday lunch the day before and had been relieved when Percy and Rosie offered to take Lily for the day, giving her a chance to catch up on some housework – putting her home in order as well as her thoughts.

She hadn't yet decided how she was going to broach matters with Richard this morning, but one way or another, she wasn't leaving until she'd placed all her cards on the table – or so she thought.

She pulled into the car park at Courtenay House, her stomach churning in anticipation of seeing him, and as she approached the office door she paused, taking a moment to steady herself before going inside.

She could feel the tension in the air as soon as she entered, and when she caught Richard glaring at her angrily, she almost turned around and went out again. Later on, she'd wish she'd done exactly that.

'Good morning, Richard,' she began tentatively, 'good weekend?'

'Not as good as some it would seem,' he growled back, catching her off guard.

Unsure what to make of that remark, she made her way over to her desk. 'Coffee?' she trilled brightly, trying to ignore his obvious mood.

'No, thank you.'

Looks like grumpy goose is in the office today.

The morning progressed relatively smoothly, and Poppy was just getting engrossed in a rather lengthy email when Richard approached her, making her jump – she hadn't noticed him coming over.

'So, good weekend then?' he asked, after a few seconds of silence.

She looked up at him, confused. *What's he up to?* 'Er, yeah... not bad, thanks. You?'

'Do anything special, did you?' He was staring at her in a strange way, and Poppy immediately put her guard up, furrowing her brow as she tried to establish what he was getting at.

'Not anything in particular,' she replied eventually, 'what about you?'

She met his gaze then, and while she could see he was angry, she was dumbfounded as to why. After glaring at her for a moment he stomped off moodily back to his desk whilst she returned her focus back to the email, having decided that sooner or later he would spit out whatever was troubling him.

As predicted, it wasn't long before he returned, this time literally throwing a document towards her, which landed squarely on her keyboard.

'I think you need to take a look at this; it's not right,' he seethed.

She gripped the edge of her desk, trying to keep her cool. This wasn't like Richard at all – usually he was so polite and professional at work. Friendly, even. 'What seems to be the problem exactly, Richard?'

'Well, for a start the costings don't add up, the flow charts aren't in the order I requested, and you've left out one of the appendices.'

She paused, taking a deep breath before replying, 'That surprises me —the costings added up each time I checked them, which was at least three times, and that's without taking into consideration the fact that the spreadsheet contains automated formulae, so they're therefore calculated automatically.' She paused again, and she could have sworn she saw his eye twitch. 'Interestingly, the flow charts are in the order you specified them to be, as are the appendices.'

'The costings do not reflect the changes I made,' he barked at her. 'I switched page 6 for page 2, and where is the additional appendix I added?'

'What changes, Richard?' she raged back. 'You didn't make any changes!' She was getting annoyed now, and she didn't care if he knew it.

'On Friday, I gave these to you on Friday!' he yelled, before adding, 'Oh wait. Hang on a moment, that's right, you weren't exactly with it on Friday, were you? A little absent-minded and clumsy as I recall; another late night, was it?' He was sneering at her, though there seemed to be something else hiding under his angry expression – sadness, perhaps. Or disappointment.

Slowly, Poppy stood up to face him. Despite the strange expression on his face, it had been quite some time since she felt so very angry. Not since the incident with the idiot Head of IT when she'd worked for Greg; not since the rejection letter she'd received from Martha.

'I have never,' she began with a deathly calm voice, '*ever* had my work questioned, or indeed criticised in such an abhorrent and vociferous manner, and let me tell you – I am not about to allow that to happen now.' Her chin jutted out as she spoke and it took every inch of effort she had to stop her hands from shaking as she gathered together her belongings.

Realising that he'd gone too far – *way* too far – Richard attempted to stop her, but she was having none of it.

'It's quite clear that something's rattled your cage this morning, and quite frankly, I've got better things to do than humour your childish tantrums.'

Her words resounded around the room like a lion's roar and he watched, opened-mouthed, as she walked out. She didn't bother waiting for the lift, preferring to race down the stairs instead, and was in her car in what seemed like no time at all.

She waited until she was safely on the road to King's Oak before pulling into a lay-by and sobbing her heart out.

*

He'd never seen her so angry; in fact, he didn't think he'd ever seen *anyone* that angry, and he'd certainly not been spoken to like that before. While she was leaving he'd tried to say something – anything – to stop her, but he'd found himself completely dumbstruck.

He ran to the window just in time to watch her race out of the car park, silently praying that she'd slow down as anger writhed around inside him. It wasn't anger at Poppy, though – he was angry at himself.

Sinking into his chair, he placed his head in his hands. What had he done? What on earth had he been thinking? He knew the answer to that already, of course, he just didn't like it.

Just then his mobile rang and he made a grab for it, hoping it was her. It wasn't; frustration surged through him like water through a dry desert when he recognised his mother's number flash up on the screen.

'What the hell do you want?' he raged. 'I'm trying to work!'

There was a slight pause before she answered. 'Well, if you were to take my calls, Richard, or at least reply to one of the many messages I've left, I wouldn't have to keep calling, would I?'

'I can't cope with you right now,' he said, his voice now completely void of emotion. 'Please just leave me alone.'

*

Poppy managed to get home in one piece, no longer angry but desperately hurting. She supposed it was the wake-up call she'd long needed to make her realise the truth: that she meant nothing more to him than being the hired help.

She almost crawled inside her house before heading upstairs and throwing herself on the bed, sobbing her heart out all over again. She felt like a silly little schoolgirl with a crush on a teacher who she knew deep down would never look twice at her; let alone take her seriously.

Her thoughts turned briefly to Matt, but the reality of it was that even if Richard wasn't in the picture – which he clearly wasn't, she now knew – there was no future for them either. She never thought she'd find love again after Oliver – and oh how she had mourned his loss – and then she'd met Richard. She doubted anyone would come close to either of them ever again. It was a sad thought.

The sound of doorbell echoed up the stairs, making Poppy sit up. For a fleeting moment she hoped it was Richard, coming to apologise, and she rushed downstairs to fling the door open in anticipation.

It was Anthony.

'Oh,' he said, taking in her tear-stained face and dishevelled look, concern gripping him, 'what's happened? Have I come at a bad time?'

She bit her lip, fresh tears threatening to spill over as she slowly nodded.

He guided her back inside, closing the door behind them. 'What's happened, Poppy?' he urged again.

She collapsed in tears against his shoulder whilst he held onto her tightly, an action that made her cry even more; it had been such a long time since anyone had held her like this.

Anthony did his best to soothe her, unable to imagine what on earth was causing her such distress. 'I only popped in because I saw your car and wanted to make sure everything was alright; I thought you were supposed to be at the office today?'

The mention of work brought fresh tears to her eyes, and slowly but painfully, Poppy managed to explain the earlier events of that morning.

'What a complete idiot,' Anthony exclaimed, surprised that a run-in with her boss would cause this much upset. 'I really wouldn't take any notice to be honest, Poppy; it sounds like there's a lot more to his mood than just the sodding proposal. You really shouldn't let it get to you like this.' He paused, wanting to change the subject to something more positive. 'Anyway, how are things going with Matt?'

She looked up at him, biting her lip again.

'Not good, eh?' He felt a rush of disappointment at her response but tried not to show it. 'I'm surprised to hear that; I'm certain he's keen on you, my darling.'

'He is.'

He stared at her with utter confusion.

'It's me. *I'm* not keen on *Matt*, that's all.'

He looked at her closely. He'd heard what she'd been saying but it just didn't seem to make sense. Then the penny dropped. 'Oh. You're in love with him, aren't you? With your boss?'

The fresh new tears beginning to slide down her face confirmed his suspicions.

'Who even is this chap, anyway?' Anthony was irked at seeing her so upset. 'What's he called? For that matter, what's the business called?'

'Richard Jones,' Poppy whispered.

His expression turned to one of alarm. 'What did you say?'

'Richard Jones,' she repeated, more than a little confused.

Now it was his turn to be silent.

It really couldn't be… no, that would be too weird; far too much of a coincidence. It just couldn't be.

'Are you okay, Anthony?' she asked after a while.

'Yes. Yes, my darling, I am, but I'm afraid I've just remembered that I'm supposed to be meeting Ianthe for lunch. She'll have my guts for garters if I'm late!' He paused, hesitating. 'I don't want to leave you, not like this… I'm so sorry.'

'I'm okay. Honestly, you go. Anyway, it's easier now I know how he feels,' Poppy said, trying to convince herself of that.

But Anthony wasn't listening anymore. If *her* Richard Jones was *his* Richard Jones, he very much doubted that he had the slightest clue as to how he felt about anything right now.

'How about I call you later tonight? See how you're feeling?' he said after what felt like an eternity of silence.

She nodded, blowing her nose noisily on a tissue she'd snapped up from a box off the coffee table. The gesture always made him smile. He kissed her on the cheek and left; he was now a man on a mission.

*

For the second time that morning Richard felt as if he'd been thumped in the stomach, the breath being taken out of him. He'd just received one of the most exciting phone calls of his career to date, and yet there was no one to share it with. No mother, no father, but more importantly, there was no Poppy.

To make matters worse, instead of being on his way to her house to apologise – as he should have been doing – he was now on his way to Germany.

If this meeting turned out as he dared hoped, it could be the answer to a lot of people's problems.

THIRTY-ONE

Poppy pulled her collar up against the bitter cold morning as she made her way to the car. She had just deposited a very excited Lily, who was having a sleepover with her best friend Anna-Maria; Lily had stayed with the Davies' before and had had so much fun that she was thrilled to be asked back again. Thinking that she really should reciprocate the invitation at some point, Poppy made a mental note to seek out a suitable date. This made her think of Christmas, which – now being the last day in November – was just 25 days away.

Driving towards Midford County, she considered calling Sally to see if she fancied meeting up at the Maide of Honour for a drink later on. She hadn't caught up with her friend in ages, although she no doubt would have her hands full with *Sally's Deli*, which was doing a roaring trade and was sure to get busier as the Christmas season approached.

Poppy arrived at the office to discover Richard on the phone, and as he had his back to the door she slipped off her coat unnoticed and went to make coffee for them both. She hadn't seen that much of him over the past few weeks as he'd been in Germany, negotiating what she understood to be a rather lucrative deal. There were apparently some complexities that needed to be ironed out and agreed on if his bid were to be completely successful.

Following their angry exchange he'd made several attempts at rebuilding their relationship, but she remained cautious; she wasn't prepared to risk being humiliated again. She did appreciate, however, the huge bouquet of flowers he'd sent her along with a card that read: *There's no easy way to say sorry, except I'm truly sorry. Will call later, Richard.*

He'd tried to call her too but she'd ignored it, letting it go to answerphone instead. She'd kicked herself later though, when she replayed the message informing her he was in Germany; she hadn't expected that. However, the distance had certainly helped to smooth things over between them, and slowly their working life was returning to normal – well, as normal as two people trying to suppress strong feelings for one another can be anyway.

She was just pouring hot water into cups when he came up behind her.

'Guess what?' he half whispered.

She turned, eyeing him curiously. 'What?'

'That was Markus.' A big smile spread across his face. 'We've only gone and won the Sonne Tragen job!'

She gasped in delighted amazement. 'That's brilliant, Richard! Well done.'

Without thinking, they hugged each other – understandably ecstatic at the good news – and then, realising what they were doing, they quickly pulled apart again. Poppy returned to making the coffee, her heart thumping in her chest as she listened to him ranting on excitedly, clearly not quite so affected by their contact as she was.

'They were so impressed with the documentation you produced, together with my presentation too,' he explained, still beaming.

She smiled as she handed him his coffee; she'd never seen him like this before and she liked it. His remarks regarding the paperwork hadn't gone unnoticed either.

'This is a big moment for me, Poppy – for both of us, actually,' he added, before pausing briefly. 'This is what I've been working towards; this is a major, major achievement for me.'

She watched him carefully, suddenly aware that there was much more of a personal angle to this contract than she'd fully realised. She didn't have a clue what it all meant, but seeing how happy it made him was enough for her to know it couldn't be anything but good.

'We have to celebrate!' he announced dramatically. 'You know, I couldn't have secured this deal without your assistance.'

She very much doubted that. 'I'm not sure that's true, Richard,' she said gently.

He looked at her, surprised. 'Well, I've certainly never put a proposal like that together before. It was you who suggested adding in those graphs, together with the detailed projections and project plans…' He placed his hands at the top of her arms, causing a thrill to surge through her entire body. 'All of our hard work has paid off;

you've every right to take some of the credit.'

She smiled; it was hard to resist picking up on his excitement. 'Well, when you put it like that... thanks.'

'So, how about dinner? Tonight?' Then, thinking about Lily, he added awkwardly, 'Er... that's if you can get a sitter?'

'I don't need to as it happens; Lily's having a sleepover.'

This news seemed to surprise him. 'Isn't she a bit young for a sleepover?'

Poppy laughed at his sudden concern. 'It's good for children to get used to the odd night or two away from home, and besides, her best friend's mother is also their class teacher, so I think she'll be pretty safe.'

Richard smiled. 'Good. Then it's settled.'

THIRTY-TWO

oppy was nervous yet excited, even though she had no right to be nervous – dinner was nothing more than a reward for winning the Sonne Tragen deal.

She added a few drops of Patchouli oil to the bath water, forgetting it was more of a stimulating oil than a relaxing one. After enjoying a good long soak she dressed simply in a long-sleeved black dress with a sweetheart neckline, and she'd just finished getting ready when the doorbell rang, signalling Richard's arrival. Her stomach shimmered nervously as she went to open the door.

They exchanged pleasantries whilst she grabbed her coat and bag, and then she followed him out to the car, impressed when he held the door open for her. As she waited for him to join her, she wondered how on earth she was going to cope being in such close proximity with him, but then mentally told herself to get a grip.

'Gosh, it's cold,' he shivered as he connected the seatbelt, accidently brushing against her hand as it clicked into place.

She froze in her seat, though he didn't seem to notice.

Initially, they drove in silence. Richard was trying to focus on the road ahead, but the aroma of her perfume – combined with actually having her right next to him – was proving to be a little distracting. Perhaps this really wasn't such a good idea after all?

'I've booked a table at a popular bistro in Swinford St. George,' he enthused, trying to break the silence and distract his thoughts at the same time.

She smiled encouragingly. 'Oh yes?'

'It has a Michelin star, apparently. I don't know if you've been there before – it's called the *Angel*.'

Poppy gasped, the weirdest feeling suddenly blossoming in the pit of her stomach.

'Are you okay?' he asked, glancing sideways with concern.

'Yes, I'm fine, and no... no, I haven't been there,' Poppy stammered.

She felt quite emotional as memories of when Oliver had taken her out in Chelsea on the night he'd proposed came flooding back to her. The newly opened restaurant had been called *l'ange*; the French word for Angel. She shuddered. Was this merely a coincidence or was it some kind of warning?

The restaurant seemed pleasant enough, and the two of them soon picked up on the relaxing atmosphere as they followed the Maître d' to their table. He helped relieve Poppy of her coat, revealing her dress, which Richard silently admired – it emphasised her figure beautifully. She'd drawn her hair back with braids, in a style that made it flow loosely down her back.

She looked stunning. Richard inwardly groaned.

Having ordered their food they began to relax, allowing the rich undertones of the Rioja that Richard had selected to soothe their nerves. He gazed at her, his heart swelling, and at that very moment he knew there was no point in trying to deny his feelings any longer – and nor did he want to, either. These past few months had been hell and he'd finally had enough. Here he was, having dinner with the most beautiful, caring, and giving woman he'd ever met, and yet he'd been continually pushing her away. He knew he couldn't keep it up any longer. He also knew that now he'd secured the Sonne Tragen deal, everything had changed.

'I'm glad you asked me here, Richard,' Poppy said, breaking the silence.

He loved her voice, so soft and light, and when he allowed his gaze to meet hers, it just confirmed what he'd already realised.

'It wouldn't be as enjoyable without you, Poppy,' he replied, before surprising her by lifting her hand to his mouth and gently kissing it, just like Oliver used to.

She mentally berated herself for continually comparing them, but it was hard not to – they were so similar in so many ways.

The food arrived soon after but despite their best efforts, they knew it was just prolonging the inevitable.

Spurning dessert, Richard settled the bill and then retrieved Poppy's coat from the approaching waiter, managing to resist the temptation to put his arms around her as he slipped it onto her shoulders. They headed out of the restaurant and towards his car, both trying not to allow their hands to drift anywhere near to the others'.

Once inside, they sat in silence for a few moments, each thinking similar thoughts but neither certain whether to express them or not.

'Home?' Richard asked eventually.

She nodded, her eyes wide and full of confusion.

He gripped the steering wheel, fearing he'd misread things, but then – deciding to throw caution to the wind – he turned to face her, breathing the word, 'Mine?'

For a moment Poppy was uncertain as to whether she'd heard him correctly, then she nodded again.

Finally he did what he'd been desperate to do for such a long time; he leaned across and kissed her. She kissed him back passionately.

Afterwards he held her tightly, stroking her hair and then gently tilting her face towards him, his eyes scanning hers. 'I love you, Poppy,' he murmured as tears filled her eyes, finally relieved that she hadn't acted alone with her feelings. 'I love you and I've tried not to, but I just can't fight it anymore. I'm truly sorry for what I put you through, but I've realised that I simply have to have you in my life, you and Lily.'

Poppy nodded again; she didn't trust herself to speak, she had so longed for this moment.

'It's going to be okay,' he whispered, bringing her in closer to him, 'I promise you everything is going to be just fine.'

Having arrived at Orchard Cottage, they were soon snuggled up together on the sofa in front of a roaring fire as Richard poured them each a glass of wine.

'You've absolutely no idea, Richard, how much I've dreamt of this,' Poppy gushed. 'From the moment I first saw you, I haven't been able to get you out of my mind, and the more time we spent together the more my feelings seemed to develop further, and then...' She trailed off, a pained expression on her face. 'When you went away for so long and I didn't see you, I suspected it was because you were avoiding me. It hurt so much.'

He kissed her hands. 'I wasn't trying to hurt you, Poppy. Believe me.'

She continued, relieved at finally being able to express herself. 'I mean, there I was projecting all these feelings towards you, but you didn't seem interested and then, when I walked back into the office today, I knew.' She paused. 'I knew my feelings were real and that I'd fallen deeply in love with you.'

'You weren't alone, my darling; it's not as though I wasn't battling feelings of my own, I promise you. I've been so focused on achieving a particular goal it caused me to almost lose out on something far more important.' Richard sighed. 'Still, we'll talk about that another time. That was why I'd been blocking all other distractions and practically working 24/7… well, until you bounded into my life, that is.' He smiled and kissed her. 'I've tried every damn thing to get you out of my mind,' he continued, 'but every time you're in the same room as me I can't concentrate on anything except wanting to take you in my arms and kiss you, and make love to you like neither of us have ever experienced before.'

She closed her eyes as he spoke those words, desire searing through her entire body. It had been a long time since she'd been intimate with anyone; too long, in fact.

'Even when I talk to you on the phone I can't get you out of my mind,' Richard continued, smiling. 'Today, I was blindsided for a while by the Sonne Tragen news, but once I set eyes on you this evening I knew there was no turning back; I love you, Poppy Jackson, and I'll never try to push you out of my life again.'

He took her in his arms then and kissed her gently on the mouth, holding her tightly while also trying to keep a hold on the intensity of the emotions building up inside him.

After a while they lay down side by side on the vast sofa, which threatened to engulf them with its huge overstuffed cushions, but which also provided a comfortable place to lie. They stroked and kissed each other, Richard slowly moving his mouth down her neck, enjoying her gentle gasps of pleasure. She arched, pushing herself into him.

'Are you sure this is what you want?' he asked.

'Yes,' she whispered, returning his gaze and leaving him in no doubt.

Later, they lay in each other's arms as they waited for their breathing to return to normal and their passions to subside – at least for the time being – having sealed the start of a promising future together.

Tuning into the music that was playing in the background, Poppy recognised one of her and Oliver's favourite songs – *Stars* by Simply Red – and she smiled, taking it as a positive sign; it was time for her to begin a new chapter in her life, and one she felt sure was right to include Richard.

THIRTY-THREE

T he following weeks leading up to Christmas were quite hectic whilst Richard was commencing the Sonne Tragen project. Poppy perfectly understood the necessity for Richard to stay overnight in Munich from Monday to Thursday and very much looked forward to him flying back each Friday, when he'd spend the weekend with his girls, them all getting to know each other better.

They'd decided to keep their relationship between themselves for now, intending to tell their respective families the good news over the Christmas period, when they hoped to bring everyone together to meet. Richard had been reticent about divulging further information about his family other than saying, 'it's complicated,' whilst she had yet to mention Anthony. She was worried that having her ex-fiancé's father in their lives might be slightly off-putting at such an early stage in their relationship, and had therefore decided to brush such apprehensions aside for now, preferring to take things one step at a time.

With today being the end of term it was, of course, the traditional Christmas Party, and all the children were invited to wear fancy dress for the day; Lily had chosen to dress as Cinderella.

Having settled her into school, Poppy drove towards Midford County, intending to collect Richard's post from the office before carrying on into town to complete her Christmas shopping. She wanted to get something really special for Richard, and she pondered on this as she collected the post from the Courtenay House reception before making her way up to the fifth floor.

The office felt cold so Poppy turned up the thermostat, though she kept her coat on while the room warmed up. After sifting through the assortment of white and brown envelopes, she began opening them up. There was nothing too exciting: a few invoices, a late payment she'd been chasing, a few Christmas cards, and a letter from the local Chamber of Commerce inviting Richard to speak at one of their forthcoming seminars. Thinking he'd like that, she placed the letter to one side whilst picking up the next one.

Mr Richard Hambly-Jones. She mused on this for a moment before heading back to reception. 'Hi Clive,' she greeted the security guard, 'we seem to have got someone else's post again.' She handed the stray letter over to him and turned to walk away.

'It's for Mr. Jones,' Clive responded curtly, sick and tired of being moaned at for mismanaging the post.

She turned back. 'No, look again, it's for a Mr. *Hambly*-Jones,' she confirmed, pointing out the name with her finger.

'Yeah,' he retorted belligerently, 'and it's Mr. *Hambly*-Jones that you work for.'

She looked at him again, taken aback. 'What on earth are you talking about?'

'Mr. Richard Jones is Mr. Richard Hambly-Jones; he just doesn't use the Hambly on account of who his family are,' he informed her, rather cockily, 'even though everyone around here knows who he is anyway.' Or apparently not *everyone*, he thought to himself.

'What family, Clive? What are you talking about?' Poppy was beginning to get a strange feeling deep down in her gut.

'Where have you been, Missy? Asleep? His mother is Lady Hambly-Jones, proprietor of Hambly-Jones department store in Swinford St. George,' he smugly informed her.

Poppy's hand flew to her mouth; she couldn't believe what she'd just heard. It couldn't be true, could it?

She rushed back upstairs without uttering another word and placed the letter onto Richard's desk, trying to avoid looking at the name on the front. Then, grabbing her bag, she hurried back out of the building without so much as a glance at Clive on her way past who, whilst somewhat perplexed, also seemed quite amused by her reaction.

No wonder Richard wasn't keen on telling me about his family!

It hadn't sunk in initially, but when Clive had started to explain, she recalled the time Oliver had taken her to Stone House to meet his parents.

'Do you know the Hambly-Jones'?' Anthony asked her, after

214

they'd discussed her hometown.

The only Hambly-Jones I know is the one that Anthony lives with.

She was devastated. As the realisation set in, she wondered then if it was in fact Anthony who'd talked Richard into giving her a job in the first place, no doubt taking pity on her. Had he also warned Richard against divulging any family secrets? What with her being such a gold digger and all! She felt utterly betrayed by them both.

Then another thought hit her. Was this actually the real reason Richard had been so reluctant to start a relationship with her? After all, it had to be said, if he knew Anthony – which he certainly must – then surely he also knew that Anthony's son Oliver was Lily's father, and therefore Poppy's deceased fiancé. Otherwise, why had neither of them mentioned anything to her before?

She remembered the angry exchange they'd had in the summer before Richard went to Germany and how – rather *too* conveniently, it now seemed – Anthony had suddenly appeared at her house, somewhat unexpectedly, to find her sobbing her heart out. He'd kept up his apparent act by even questioning her about who she was working for before suddenly leaving, feigning lunch with Ianthe; what a joke! Perhaps it all really *was* some sort of sick joke? Maybe Anthony *did* secretly blame her for Oliver's death all along, and this was some sort of elaborate revenge attack against her?

That seemed unlikely – she had to admit – but honestly, right now she didn't know *what* to think.

She didn't recall the journey home at all; she was hurting, really hurting. She'd fallen deeply for Richard, alright, and she couldn't simply sweep such feelings aside, no matter what she'd just found out.

All manner of thoughts began to flood into her head then, and she didn't know how to analyse any of them. She needed to think. No, she needed to go somewhere to think. Somewhere she could collect her thoughts and try to make sense of it all.

She really needed Percy, suddenly yearning for the security she knew he'd give, but he and Rosie were away on a pre-Christmas 'Turkey and Tinsel' weekend with the local over '60s club and weren't due back until the 22nd. There was Sally, of course, but she was up to her elbows running the deli and coffee shop, so now wasn't the best time to go and see her either.

She took a deep breath. As everyone else was seemingly busy, no one would notice if she went away for a few days, just her and Lily. After all, what else was she meant to do?

Filled with renewed enthusiasm, Poppy slipped off her coat, kicked off her shoes, and went upstairs to wash her face. She glanced in the mirror but looked quickly away again, not liking how red and blotchy her reflection was from all the crying she'd done in the car.

Once she was finished she returned downstairs, and switching on her laptop she began to search online for a cottage to rent for a few days. She'd taken Lily away on several cottage holidays in the past, so had a good understanding of how to find what she was looking for.

After 40 or so minutes of browsing she managed to find the perfect place; a secluded cottage on the outskirts of Bodmin, which was available until the 23rd. She left the booking confirmation to print out whilst heading upstairs to fetch a few items for her and Lily, and soon she had both of their bags packed into the car.

Lily was tired and grouchy. She'd had such a great day dancing, playing games, and eating lots of sugary snacks she wasn't used to, and now she was clearly suffering the after-effects of them. Poppy secured her into the car seat, doing her best to explain where they were going, but Lily was far too exhausted to take anything in. In the end she just placed one of Lily's favourite CDs into the player and set off, deciding it would be better to explain things when Lily was more rested.

As she drove, Poppy continued to wrestle with all manner of thoughts flying back and forth through her mind, doing her utmost to push them aside for now in order to focus on the road ahead.

The journey to Bude was quite straightforward and was one she'd made many times before; finding the cottage once they arrived, though, wasn't quite so easy. However, after putting the postcode into the satnav, they finally arrived just after seven thirty, stopping at the first house along Maer Lane to collect the keys before driving further along to their destination.

Poppy pulled up outside Little Pippins just as Lily was stirring.

'Where are we, Mummy?' she mumbled groggily, trying to focus.

'It's alright, Lily, we've just come on a little holiday. Remember? I told you all about it earlier when I collected you from school. It's just you and me getting away for a few days.'

Lily looked at her thoughtfully, then her eyes widened in a mixture of surprise and horror. 'But what about Father Christmas, Mummy? What if he doesn't know we're here? How we will get our presents?' she babbled anxiously.

Poppy smoothed her hand over Lily's hair and cheek. 'It's okay, my darling,' she reassured her, 'we'll be back in plenty of time for Father Christmas, I promise.'

Hearing this prompted Lily to exude a huge smile of relief and she flung her arms around Poppy as she helped her out of the car.

Once inside the cottage, they soon got a roaring fire going before exploring what was to be their home for the next few days. There were two bedrooms – one upstairs with twin beds and one downstairs that housed a large, double bed – with each room having its own en-suite bathroom. There was also a cosy – and very comfortable – lounge and a reasonable-sized kitchen; basically, the cottage contained all of the home comforts they could want.

Poppy busied herself unpacking the shopping she'd brought earlier and then made a plate of sandwiches for them to share.

'Where's Richard?' Lily queried as realisation set in.

Poppy swallowed. 'He's away, darling, in Germany.'

This wasn't entirely the truth, but it wasn't exactly a lie either; it was just that right now he was probably on his way to their house, having landed at Heathrow that afternoon and... well... she didn't really want to think about that anymore.

Not right then, anyway.

THIRTY-FOUR

Richard couldn't wait to see Poppy; he kept patting his inside breast pocket that housed the two carat diamond ring he'd bought a few days earlier from one of the finest jewellers in Munich.

He was intending to propose this weekend, rather than wait until Christmas – why did they need to wait a moment longer anyway? His progress on the Sonne Tragen project meant he was well ahead of schedule and therefore didn't need to return until early January, so he could look forward to spending a relaxing time with Poppy and Lily, planning their new life together.

Driving towards Midford County, he made a quick pit stop at the office to pick up any last minute things that might need his attention, thus leaving them both free to wind down for the holiday season. As Richard entered the reception area of Courtenay House he greeted Clive, who was shrugging into his overcoat, getting himself ready to go off shift.

'Evening Sir,' Clive greeted him. 'I trust your assistant's a bit happier now,' he muttered smugly, causing Richard to stop in his tracks.

He stepped back and eyed Clive curiously. 'I'm not sure what you mean, Clive?' irritated that he was referring to Poppy as his 'assistant', let alone referring to her at all.

'The mix up earlier,' Clive started to explain, 'y'know, the confusion over your name. Quite upset she was, went storming off too like she'd seen a ghost.'

He stiffened, not in the least amused by Clive's obvious enjoyment at relaying the details of the situation. He gazed coldly at him. 'What do you mean my name?' Perhaps you could explain?'

Clive – who was now pretty rattled by the furious look on Richard's face – was beginning to wish he'd kept his mouth shut.

However, it was too late now so he relayed his earlier conversation with Poppy. He didn't do himself any more favours, though, by embellishing her reaction far more than was really necessarily.

Richard listened to what he had to say, threw him a look of sheer disgust, and swept past him to the lift, his heart thumping wildly in his chest. He wondered if this explained why he hadn't been able to get hold of Poppy on either her mobile or landline, but he brushed such concerns aside. That would be ridiculous, surely?

He unlocked the office and was met by a cloud of heat, causing him to smile wryly as he walked over and turned down the thermostat. He knew that Poppy felt the cold and had no doubt forgotten to turn it down again in her obvious haste to leave, which appeared to substantiate Clive's story.

Richard could feel his heart starting to thud again as his stomach lurched; he suddenly felt quite panicky.

Looking around, he took in the opened mail on her desk, quickly flicking through it. There didn't appear to be anything out of the ordinary here. A quick glance over his own desk soon provided the answer, though; the familiar white envelope was just underneath his keyboard, taunting him. He snatched it up, glancing at the typewritten envelope addressed to him in his full name. He knew only too well who it was from even before he angrily tore it apart.

'Mother!' he gasped aloud before turning on his heel, locking the door behind him.

He took a few deep breaths, trying hard to suppress the anger that was currently boiling up inside him and threatening to explode. She'd been pestering him for months now, but her desperation was becoming beyond reasonable. But, more than that, she'd upset Poppy – and he *definitely* wasn't having that. She'd had her day; now it was time for his, and he wasn't about to let her spoil it.

If only he hadn't tried to shield Poppy from his family and all the trials, tribulations, and responsibilities that came with it! He really should have just been honest from the start. The truth was, he'd wanted her to get to know the *real* Richard Jones – the kind, considerate, loving guy who'd worked his way up from nothing. Not Richard Hambly-Jones, who'd had everything handed to him on a plate. He'd wanted her to get to know *him*, not the persona of a rich person from an extremely wealthy family, who appeared to have nothing else going for them other than having an enormous inheritance – and one he didn't feel he truly deserved, at that.

'Anyway!' he shouted into the night, thumping his hands angrily on the steering wheel, 'I was going to tell her everything this weekend; if only my mother wasn't so fucking persistent!'

Aiming his anger back towards his mother, he drove towards Hampton Waters, deciding to deal first with her and then with Poppy, who he would explain everything to.

Having pulled up outside Channing House he almost ran down the driveway, and by the time he rang the doorbell, his heart was racing again.

Anthony came to the door, pleasantly surprised to see him. He greeted him warmly. 'Richard, I've been trying to get hold of you for weeks; where on earth have you been?'

Richard threw him a look of pure anger, marching straight past him. 'Well, I'm here now, aren't I?'

Anthony wondered if this was it; time for everything to be out in the open. *Better late than never.* Closing the door, he followed Richard, who had by now discovered his mother in the dining room.

She looked up and paused, halting her spoon midway between her mouth and the bowl on the table. Placing the spoon down, she lifted her napkin to her mouth, ready to talk. He was angry – she could see that – yet she didn't seem surprised he was there.

'Sit down, Richard,' she ordered calmly.

Anthony – who'd by then returned to his seat at the table – maintained a dignified silence, waiting to hear what Richard had to say.

'You've done it again,' he hissed through clenched teeth.

She sat upright. 'What are you talking about, Richard?' she asked, remaining quite still and calm.

He threw the letter onto the table. 'This!' he spat, making her glance at it, not that she needed to. She knew exactly what this was all about.

'Oh, for goodness' sake, Richard, why must you overreact so?' she asked, trying to reason with him. 'You're being unnecessarily dramatic.' She let out a gasp of frustration.

'I've told you before – don't send mail to my office address! Why can't you listen?' he shouted.

'I really don't know why you're so upset about it.' She stared ahead, refusing to meet his gaze. Anthony rested his elbows on the table, clasping his hands in front of him as if to steady himself; he was still uncertain as to where this was going.

'You knew she'd see it.' Richard had tears of frustration in his eyes now. 'That's why you sent it.'

His mother recoiled slightly, confusion crossing her face. Now she *really* didn't know what he was talking about.

Anthony, however, thought *he* did. 'Are you talking about Poppy, son?' The words were out before he realised exactly what he was saying.

Richard's eyes widened. 'Oh yes, that's right,' he began with mock delight, 'decide to play the father now, why don't you? For God's sake, you both make me so fucking sick! Didn't you think I already knew?' He sat down at the table as tears of anger and frustration slid down his face; this wasn't the way he wanted to handle this.

Ianthe and Anthony exchanged shocked glances; this was certainly not the way in which they'd intended to discuss the matter either.

'Richard, I can explain...' his mother began, but he cut her short.

'Save it. The only person I'm interested in right now is Poppy.'

They looked at him and then at each other.

Finally, Anthony cleared his throat, speaking cautiously as he said, 'I've been trying to get hold of you, Richard, to discuss Poppy.'

'What the fuck has Poppy got to do with you?' he questioned incredulously.

Anthony held his hands up, before continuing calmly, 'There's something you need to know, Richard; it's important.'

He turned angrily to face him. 'Oh, come on, don't tell me. Are you secretly Poppy's father too?'

'No, Richard, that's not what I'm saying!' Anthony's loud words rang angrily around the room, causing all of them to pause for a moment. The situation was in danger of getting completely out of control.

After a moment Anthony tried again, somewhat calmer this time. 'My dear boy, as if we haven't had quite enough surprises, you'd better ready yourself for this one.'

Richard listened as Anthony explained about Oliver and Poppy –

and of course the fact that Anthony was actually Lily's grandfather – and when he'd finished, Richard turned to look at him. He was much calmer now and he took a few moments to process the information.

'We had absolutely no idea it was you that Poppy was working for; and as you never discuss your business interests – or much else, for that matter – with us, we had no idea that you'd taken her on as your PA.'

'But all that's no reason why Poppy and I can't be together.' Richard stood up, beginning to get agitated again. 'Okay, so Oliver and I were half-brothers, as I now know.' He threw a withering look over in the direction of his mother, who was still calmly watching the two most important men in her life, choosing to say nothing. She was more than relieved that the truth was finally out and she didn't quite know what to say.

'There's nothing to stop us being happy together; being a family.' He looked at Anthony in exasperation. 'She means everything to me! She's the woman I've fallen in love with; the woman I want to marry and spend the rest of my life with, and who has no doubt now been frightened off because of what this fucking family represents!' he screamed. He was angry, sure, but more than anything else he was terrified – terrified that he'd lost Poppy for good.

Anthony Sullivan wanted to hug his son, as he'd wanted to infinite times over the years, but he made no move to do so. He so wished Richard had told Poppy all about his family sooner, then perhaps none of this would have happened. However, now was not the time to play the blame game. 'I visited Poppy after your showdown with her several weeks ago,' he said eventually.

Richard winced; he wasn't proud of how he'd acted then and he didn't want to discuss it with him either.

'Look at me, Richard,' Anthony continued. 'I've no doubt you recall what I'm talking about. When I found her, she was devastated. Do you hear me? Simply *devastated* at having realised she was deeply in love with you, and then you behaving so terribly towards her. I can tell you it took me ages to console her, and when I finally got it all out of her, I was staggered to realise she was talking about you.'

Richard kept his gaze low.

'I didn't say anything; I should have, but I wanted to speak to you first to check I had my facts right. Of course, I haven't been able to get hold of you, Richard.'

'Well, I've been working so hard, haven't I?' Richard responded defensively. 'You know, to reach my goal so I can take over the sodding family business that I'm not so sure I want now anyway.'

'Richard, listen to me. I've seen how much Poppy loves you, believe me; go to her, explain everything, and clear up this misunderstanding once and for all. If you love her as much as you say you do, you'll find a way to work through this, together.'

Richard smiled at them wryly. 'Do you know the ironic thing about all this? I was going to tell her everything tonight.' He took the ring box from his inside jacket pocket and placed it, opened, onto the table. 'I was going to propose to her and then tell her everything; I was even going to tell her I knew you were my father.'

Anthony nodded, a little sadly. 'Then it would all have come out anyway.'

'Yes, but it would have come out *my* fucking way, wouldn't it? But instead my mother had to ruin everything because she only thinks of herself.' He knew as he said the words that they weren't fair, but once they were out there, he couldn't take them back. And he was still just *so* angry!

'Richard, please,' begged Anthony. 'You've got to stop blaming your mother in this way; it's not fair. If you want to put the blame on anyone, it's me you need to look to.'

Although he knew he'd said some things he shouldn't, just then all Richard could think of was getting out of that house. So, running out, he got into his car and drove straight over to Poppy's – he was desperate to see her, desperate to explain himself.

His heart sank, however, once he got there to find her car missing. There were no lights on in the house either. Picking up his mobile he tried calling her, but he just kept getting her answerphone.

'Fuck!' he screamed into the night, angry at his mother, angry at Anthony, angry at the world. Of course, he was most angry at himself, but that was something he didn't want to admit.

Unsure where to go or what to do next, he sat outside for several minutes before grabbing his mobile again, only this time he punched in the number for Channing House. Anthony answered.

'It's Richard,' he said dejectedly. 'She's not here, and the house is in complete darkness.'

Anthony thought for a moment. Percy was away, so she wouldn't be there with him, he knew. He paused, searching for the right words before starting his explanation. 'My ex-wife Martha wrongly accused Poppy of being a gold digger, not long after Oliver's death. It may well be that Poppy has tried to put two and two together and come up with five, assuming your reluctance to tell her about your background was because you didn't trust her. At the very least she's no doubt made the connection between your mother and me, and is probably feeling she's been set up in some way.'

Richard listened, deep in thought. He reckoned Anthony had hit the nail on the head; now it was beginning to make a whole lot more sense to him. Poppy was indeed a proud woman, and a very stubborn one at that. It was one of the things he loved about her, and he knew she'd be devastated if she thought that was why he'd had been reluctant to talk about his family.

'Do you have any idea where she might be, though?' he asked desperately, all of his anger now gone. 'Where would she go? I've tried calling but I just keep getting the answerphone.'

Anthony thought again. Apart from her father, the only other person was Sally… but knowing Poppy, she'd probably decided to get away somewhere for a while, to go somewhere she could think. He shared his thoughts with Richard.

'For God's sake, that's like looking for a needle in a haystack,' he exclaimed, thumping the steering wheel again.

'Just give her time to think things through, Richard. It's a lot to take in – after all, she's been through an awful lot already.' He decided against adding, 'and wait until she finds out I'm your father'; things were bad enough as it was.

Richard expelled air out through his teeth in frustration. 'Fine. Look, if you hear or think of anything, please call me.'

Not knowing what else to do, Richard drove home to Orchard Cottage, racking his brain for ideas on where she might be, even though he felt it was a pointless exercise. His only hope was that maybe she'd gone off for the night – or even just a few hours – and would soon be back, refreshed and ready to talk things through with him. Well, that's what he hoped anyway.

For once, the cottage didn't offer its usual comforting welcome. He didn't bother to switch on the lights; he just slumped down on the sofa, noting that his head was beginning to thump.

He lay there, staring into space, until his attention was caught by the sight of the large, full moon in the sky, shining in through the window and illuminating the whole room. He could still smell the faint aroma of Poppy's perfume, the fabric of the sofa having soaked up her presence, and his stomach flipped; he so wished she was here with him now. Of course, he couldn't blame her for going off like this, and he imagined she'd been totally freaked out by the events of the past day, but he just needed a chance to explain. Regret flooded through him; he should have just told her everything from the start.

He glanced up at the moon again; so full of life, so full of hope.

Richard had never felt so hopeless in his entire life.

He sat bolt upright. He had an idea.

Getting up, he went through to the hall to retrieve his laptop. Noting the nip of the cold night air, he rubbed his arms to warm them as he waited for the computer to start, mentally cursing himself for not thinking of it sooner.

Because of the way in which he'd set up the network, Poppy had full access to his email account – and vice versa. There just might be a clue there.

He wasted no time in loading her email account and was immediately rewarded for his efforts, having found the booking confirmation for Little Pippins. *Bingo.* He retrieved his mobile from his pocket and redialled the last number.

'I think I've found her.'

Anthony took a swig from his whiskey glass as he listened; he didn't know whether he was more relieved that Richard might have found Poppy, or that he'd called him not once but twice in as many hours. Either way, he was inwardly delighted. Surely this was progress. 'Where?' he asked.

'It looks like she's rented a cottage for a few days, in Bude of all places. Can you believe it?'

The news didn't totally surprise him. 'She's taken Lily, then?'

'Well, it's got two bedrooms so I guess so, although I doubt she'd have gone anywhere without her; you know Poppy.'

Anthony did. 'What's your plan?'

'I'm going to drive there. I have to see her and explain everything before she reads too much into all this. There's no need really...'

'Tonight?'

'Of course. Why wouldn't I go tonight?'

Anthony chose his words carefully – he'd already lost one son, he didn't want to lose another. 'It's late, Richard, and you've just travelled back from Germany. If you go now, you won't be thinking straight. Leave it until the morning; it'll be more productive to tackle things when you're both fresh. When you've both had a good night's sleep.'

Richard knew he was right, but he didn't for one moment believe he'd get any sleep anyway.

'Do you want me to come with you?' added Anthony.

He appreciated the offer, but this was something he needed to do alone. 'I'll be fine, I'll call you.' He paused before adding, 'Thanks.'

Richard looked at his watch: it was almost eight o'clock. If he set off straight away, he just might get there by midnight.

THIRTY-FIVE

Poppy was worn out. Lily had fallen asleep earlier and she'd carried her up to bed, but she didn't feel quite ready to retire herself just yet. So, she snuggled further into the cosy sofa, hugging her knees towards her whilst allowing the heat from the flames of the open fire to warm her face.

She thought of Richard and then of Oliver; she thought of Anthony and Ianthe and then of Martha. Her heart ached, her stomach ached, and overall she felt emotionally destroyed. Why hadn't Richard ever mentioned who his mother was? How come he'd never even told her the family home was in Hampton Waters? Surely, he must have thought there was a strong chance she might even know Ianthe? How on earth had she not made the connection sooner?

She recalled Anthony mentioning Ianthe's son, Richard, but she never imagined it was *her* Richard – after all, it was such a common name. She recalled another time when she'd told Anthony with great excitement about finding a part-time job, and how he'd reacted oddly, now she came to think of it. Was it because he thought she was out to bag herself a rich suitor? After all, she'd just missed out on Oli; if only he'd lived a few months more she'd have been financially set up for life once Lily had come along. She inwardly shuddered, knowing full well this was not the case.

Anthony has no idea of the lengths Greg and I went to in order to protect Oliver's name.

Well... she wasn't even going to go there; that was something no one needed to know, ever. She stretched out, exhausted by the barrage of thoughts continually circling around her mind, deciding it was time to rest. She really couldn't think clearly anymore.

She woke with a start, her heart racing and her senses on full alert. It

227

was pitch black – save the glow from the embers in the grate where the roaring fire of a few hours ago had almost died out – and she shivered, feeling the chill in the air.

There it was again.

She sat upright, keeping still as she listened, trying to work out if she'd dreamt the noise or perhaps imagined it. Glancing upstairs to see a shard of light escaping through the bedroom door where Lily was sleeping, Poppy breathed a sigh of relief; everything seemed in order.

'Tap, tap, tap.'

She swallowed, her heart thudding madly in her chest. Struck by the sudden realisation that they were deep in the countryside, and alone, she was quick to wish she had not ventured out so far.

If only Richard were here.

'Tap, tap, tap.'

There it was again.

She put a hand nervously to her throat, proper frightened now. After all, who the hell would be knocking on the door at this time of night? She was in the middle of nowhere, for Christ's sake.

'Poppy. Can you hear me?'

She recoiled, startled by the sound of her name. She gingerly crept over to the door; perhaps it was someone from the cottage in Maer Lane where she'd collected the keys earlier; after all, no-one else knew they were here.

She cleared her throat. 'Who is it?'

'Oh, thank God. It's me, Poppy, it's Richard.'

She gasped. 'What the hell?' What on earth was he doing here? And how had he found her? 'Richard, what are you doing here?'

'Well, I've hardly driven all this way at this time of night for a spot of sightseeing, have I?' he retorted, though there was a hint of humour in his voice. 'Can you let me in, please? I need to talk to you, and it's bloody freezing out here.'

Only because she knew just how low the temperature was outside did she let him in. After all, he was the reason she'd taken off in the first place, and oh boy, did he have some explaining to do.

Slowly, she pulled back the front door bolts so the noise wouldn't wake up Lily and stepped aside to let him in. To be fair, he did look pretty cold too. His hands were huddled underneath his arms, and when he tried to release them to hug her, she stepped back quickly, though not before catching the hurt expression on his face.

'Poppy, please.'

'Ssssh,' she pressed a finger to her lips, 'Lily's asleep.' She pointed upstairs, indicating the illuminated doorway where her daughter was sleeping.

After a moment of hesitation she walked over to the fireplace, starting to rebuild the fire and indicating for him to follow, still quite unable to believe he'd tracked her down to Bodmin. He came over and sat down, glad of the warmth from the renewed fire.

'How did you know where to find me?' She kept her voice low, mindful of Lily.

He smiled, quite proud at his method of deduction. 'Your email.'

'Ah.'

'Why did you rush off so suddenly, anyway? And why here?' he asked, glancing around the room.

She looked at him in amazement; *she* should be asking the questions of *him*, not the other way around. Instead of replying, she reached for a blanket from the armchair. 'Here, wrap this around you whilst you warm through. I'll go and fetch us both a drink; I've a feeling we're going to need it.'

Richard watched her go off to the kitchen and return with a bottle of wine and two glasses. He was worried how she would react to the news that he was, in fact, Oliver's half-brother, but he decided to take it one step at a time. After all, she had let him in, which surely was a good sign? He watched her pour the wine as he silently tapped his jacket to make sure the box was still there, finding its presence reassuring.

She handed him a glass and then crouched down in front of the fire, adding more logs to keep it going. He thought she looked so beautiful, with her hair all dishevelled from where she'd been sleeping.

He patted the space next to him. 'Come and sit here. Let's talk about this properly, shall we?'

She snuggled next to him, all bundled up in the thick woolly blanket, and immediately felt an enormous rush of love towards him. Surely there must be a glimmer of hope if he'd bothered to track her all the way down here?

Now feeling a bit more hopeful, she decided to get her questions in first. 'I'm finding it difficult to understand why you never told me about your mother, and why did you never mention Anthony? Why is your family such a big secret?'

He paused before answering; he didn't know how much she knew and how much she'd worked out for herself.

So, he started at the beginning. He told her all about Lord Roderick, his mother, and the Hambly-Jones Empire. She did, of course, already know that Anthony and his mother were a couple, and he in turn now realised that Poppy, Lily, and Anthony were related. What she didn't yet know was why he was so reluctant to take over control of the family business.

'I discovered quite by chance that Roderick was not my actual birth father,' Richard explained. 'Being quite young at the time, it was an enormous shock – as you can imagine – and one that I felt no longer gave me the automatic right to inherit the family business, even though Roderick left provisions otherwise. In my mind I had to – no, I *wanted* to – earn the right to my inheritance, which is why I set myself a personal goal; a goal that my mother has long been aware of.' Richard sighed. 'If she'd only waited a few more days instead of being so damn impatient, she'd have realised that I've finally achieved what I've been working so long to attain, and that I'm now more or less in a position to take over from her.'

Poppy frowned. 'But that means...'

'That I'm unofficially the CEO of Hambly-Jones department store?'

She looked up at him, shaking her head from side to side. 'No, something much worse; it means I'm out of a job.'

This made them both laugh, and Richard was relieved to see she had seemingly taken the news well. So far, anyhow.

'I can't imagine how you must feel,' Poppy went on, 'finding out about your father like that, and at such a young age too, but I still don't understand why you didn't just tell me all about it sooner? I've been imagining all sorts; I can't begin to tell you...' Her voice trailed off as she noted the concern etched on his face. 'Surely there's not more?' *And she thought things only happened to her.*

'It's about Anthony.'

She furrowed her brow. 'I know he's going to marry your mother, if that's what you're worried about. And believe me, I couldn't be happier for the two of them.'

He unearthed his hands from the blanket he'd swaddled himself in and reached to take her hands in his, concerned at how she would take the news.

'The thing is, Poppy, at the same time as discovering Roderick wasn't my biological father, I also discovered who *is*.' He took a deep breath before adding, 'It's Anthony.'

She gasped in disbelief as her eyes widened in horror. 'But... we've...'

He put out his arms to soothe her. 'All this means is that Oliver and I are half-brothers. There's nothing untoward about our relationship, I assure you.'

Poppy tried to process this information for a moment. 'You mean, we can still be together?'

'Of course we can!' He reached out towards her again, this time gathering her into his arms and bringing his mouth down to meet hers. 'I love you so much,' he said, his voice husky and thick with emotion. 'Please don't ever run off like that again. Promise me?'

She looked first to the floor and then back up to meet his gaze. 'I am sorry for rushing off like that, really I am. I just needed to take time out to think this whole situation through; sadly, I feared the worst.'

Richard nodded. 'All perfectly understandable, given what Anthony's told me. Anyway, I should have told you all about my family from the start. I'm sorry.' He picked up her hand to kiss it, holding it against his mouth for far longer than was really necessary. 'This isn't quite the way I'd planned it,' he began nervously, 'but I guess that this way we'll at least remember this night for more than one reason.'

She looked at him, perplexed. 'What are you talking about now, Richard?'

Slipping his hand into his inside pocket, he pulled out the ring box he'd been safely incubating inside. He then quickly flipped it open, revealing the stunning two carat diamond engagement ring, causing Poppy to gasp with delighted surprise. She'd never dared imagine this scenario in her wildest dreams.

Richard slipped off the sofa, getting down on one knee whilst still keeping hold of her hand. 'I know we've not had the perfect start to our relationship, and I also know that I haven't necessarily handled things as well as I perhaps should have, but one thing is certain, my darling, and that is my love for you. Will you marry me? Will you do me the honour of becoming my wife?'

She sat bolt upright, her heart pounding wildly in her chest. 'Are you serious?'

'I can assure you, my darling, that I've never been more serious about anything in my entire life.'

A big grin spread across her face, mixed with utter disbelief. 'Yes, Richard,' she responded breathlessly, 'absolutely yes!'

He enfolded his now bride-to-be in his arms and kissed her; a kiss so gentle and tender that it could only ever be given out of pure, deep love.

As they parted, he looked deep and longingly into her eyes. 'I love you more than anything, and I will do my utmost to ensure that you, me, and Lily have the best life ever.'

They fell into each other's arms again, and he stopped kissing her just long enough to place the ring on her finger; he wasn't going to risk her changing her mind now that he'd finally got his girl.

Poppy couldn't stop smiling. 'It's been a rough ride, Richard, but we made it. All these challenges we've faced have strengthened our relationship, and any future challenges that come our way we'll tackle together. I love you so much; I'm going to be the best wife ever.'

As he took her in his arms and kissed her, he never doubted for one moment she'd be anything else.

THIRTY-SIX

The villagers of Hampton Ash and Hampton Waters were awash with excitement at the impending nuptials of Miss Poppy Jackson to Mr Richard Hambly-Jones being held at St. Michaels Church at 2.30 p.m. that afternoon.

A marquee had already been erected at the rear of Channing House for the wedding feast, which was being organised by Marcus and Piers, the landlords of The Maide of Honour public house situated just next door. They were particularly excited at having secured such a prestigious event; having recently undergone a civil ceremony themselves, they'd been telling just about anyone and everyone all about it.

They busied themselves with an abundance of deliveries whilst waiting for the ladies from COG to arrive, who were yet to decorate the church and tables.

Having presided over numerous marriages, Reverend Fisher had never yet managed a society wedding before and was busy practising his speech and flouncing around in his new robes; he felt like a million dollars and kept pausing every now and then to give his thanks to the Lord.

Having spent the night at Channing House, Richard was up and about, fussing over his wedding clothes – ensuring they were all in order – and constantly checking that he had the rings; he couldn't wait to become Poppy's husband and for her to become his wife, and he wanted the whole day to be perfect.

His relationship with Anthony had blossomed since last Christmas, both of them feeling much more comfortable around each other now that everything was out in the open, and Richard had delighted Anthony by asking him to be best man.

There was improvement in his relationship with his mother too, although they still had a long way to go. Nevertheless, he was making more of an effort, which was easier now that she'd been able to step away from the family business; finally leaving him to get on with his life. The future looked bright for them all.

*

Poppy was at Honeycombe Lodge with Lily and Rosie, eagerly awaiting the arrival of Sally, Marnie, Louisa, and Lottie. Greg, Marnie, and their children had flown in from Canada just a week ago and were also staying with Anthony and Ianthe at Channing House. Poppy was ecstatic to see them all; it was so good to finally have the chance of a proper catch up with her dear friend, and of course, for them to meet Richard too.

'Oh, I think I'm going to be sick again,' Poppy moaned. Nerves seemed to be getting the better of her.

'For goodness' sake, Poppy, stop fretting – it's all going to be okay.'

She was glad that Rosie was with her, being the closest person she had to a mother figure; everyone needed one of those on their wedding day. Rosie bustled off to answer the door whilst Poppy dashed to the bathroom again.

Lily was sitting on the sofa watching *Dick and Dom* on Saturday morning television. Normally, even Poppy found these two amusing, but today she was too nervous to find anything funny.

She returned downstairs to discover Claire in the kitchen; Claire was the owner of the Hamptons Health and Beauty salon and had arrived to attend to everyone's hair and make-up.

'Right, let's start by giving you a facial, shall we? Then you can rest for a couple of hours until we start your make-up.'

Poppy made herself comfortable on the therapy couch Claire had set up and then really started to relax for the first time that day. She heard the doorbell chiming out every now and then – the musical chords echoing throughout the house – but knew she didn't need to worry as, thankfully, Rosie was on hand to take care of it. By the time Marnie and the girls arrived, Claire had finished.

'Poppy!' Marnie gasped excitedly, 'I can't believe you're getting married today!'

'Oh Marnie, I'm so nervous,' Poppy admitted.

'You've no need to be, sweetheart. You're marrying a wonderful, kind, handsome, and not badly off guy who practically worships the ground you walk on. Take it from someone that had to sit across the table from him at dinner last night and listened to him going on and on about how fabulous you are and how much he's looking forward to you all becoming a family. Oh per-lease!' She rolled her eyes, making Poppy laugh.

Sally arrived next, producing a couple of bottles of chilled champagne. 'Let's drink a toast to Poppy and Richard!'

Everyone cheered and joined in, clanking their glasses loudly.

'Now, Poppy,' Sally announced earnestly, grasping everyone's attention. 'The best advice my mum gave to me on my wedding day was this: *Now listen, Sally, if you want to keep your Dave happy you need to be a chef in the kitchen and a whore in the bedroom.*' Sally paused, ensuring she still had everyone's full attention, which she did. 'Well, it's seems that my Dave must've overheard my dear old mum and somehow misunderstood her.'

Poppy, Marnie, and Rosie all exchanged confused glances before giving their attention back to Sally in eager anticipation as to what she would say next.

'Well, my Dave didn't just have a chef in the kitchen, oh no. Seems he had a right old whore in our bed from what I've heard, and if Mavis from the Post Office is to be believed, he also had that bitch of a barmaid from The Dog House too; quite apt that, really.'

The four of them collapsed in hysterical laughter, knowing full well that Sally's anecdotes were just another way of dealing with what had actually been a rather traumatic experience.

'Seriously though, Poppy,' Sally continued. 'That's something you've got no worries about. If I ever find me a bloke that looks at me even half the way your Ricky does at you, I'll consider myself blessed.'

Struck by Sally's heartfelt words, the four women came together in a group hug.

*

'Goodness, you do look handsome, Richard.'

He scowled at his mother as she fiddled with his cravat.

'Very smart; Poppy's a lucky girl.'

'I'm the lucky one,' he insisted.

'Ah. There you both are.'

They turned as Anthony entered the room, going over to kiss his wife. 'You look amazing, darling.'

'Thank you. Would you like me to help you with your cravat too?'

'Yes please. All set?' He looked over at Richard as Ianthe expertly fixed his cravat in place; the soft, smoky rose-coloured fabric matching perfectly with the bridesmaid gowns Poppy had chosen.

'I think so,' Richard said, tapping his inside pocket again.

'I can't tell you how proud we are, Richard; today not only brings you and Poppy together as husband and wife, but it's also an opportunity for us all to begin our lives as a family unit.' Anthony felt his heart thudding in his chest, concerned he might have chosen the wrong day to push his luck, but Richard smiled, and much to his surprise, hugged him.

'I'd really like that.'

Anthony swallowed back a rush of emotion. 'Come on then, son, let's go and get you married.'

*

Poppy was so nervous she wasn't sure her legs would hold out long enough for her to walk down the aisle. She came out of the bathroom again, finally ready to put on her dress, which Rosie helped her into. Claire fussed around, touching up her make-up and helping put her veil and tiara into place. The finished effect was stunning.

Rosie stepped back and admired her. She was wearing an antique silk and lace cream wedding gown with a hand-embroidered veil that flowed like waves down her back. She looked amazing. Rosie dabbed at her eyes.

'Oh Poppy, you look so beautiful, my lovely – I'm so proud of you.'

Poppy blinked back tears; it was as though her words had been spoken by her very own mother, causing an intense rush of emotion to well up inside her.

'Oh no you don't, Poppy Jackson.' Claire swiftly dabbed at her eyes before the tears started sliding down her face, causing enough of a distraction to make Poppy and Rosie laugh and swallow back their tears of joy.

Rosie and Claire made their way downstairs to join the others as all eyes were on the staircase, waiting patiently for Poppy to descend. Slowly she came into view, taking one step at a time, evoking gasps of admiration and tears of joy.

Percy, who'd not long arrived – as he didn't want to be amongst a group of 'scantily clad women being all emotional' – had tears of joy in his eyes as his daughter took his arm. He led her outside to the waiting car, feeling like the proudest man on the planet.

Quite a few of the neighbours and local villagers had come out to watch the bridal party descend, and Anthony had even organised a local Chimney Sweep to greet Poppy as she came out as a gesture of good luck.

*

There was one person on the periphery who no one noticed but who also had tears in his eyes; but for a very different reason.

*

Reverend Fisher clasped his hands together excitedly as the bridal cars arrived at St. Michael's, a big grin fixed firmly on his face. He couldn't be happier, really. Not only was he presiding over the marriage of two of the loveliest people he knew, but he could also eat and drink all he wanted for the rest of the day. 'The good Lord thanketh me for all my hard work,' he muttered as he helped the bridesmaids descend from their car.

There seemed to be photographers everywhere and he kept smoothing his hair down every now and then, wanting to ensure he looked his absolute best. He stepped forward as Poppy's car came to a halt and greeted her warmly as Percy assisted her. There were many pictures to be taken before the marriage service could actually commence but all she wanted to do was to get inside as soon as possible and be with her beloved Richard.

She caught sight of Lily, Louisa, and little Lottie dancing round and round, allowing their dresses to billow out behind them. Marnie was handing them each a basket of rose petals and trying to stop them spinning around so there would be at least some petals left to scatter on the aisle.

Finally, everyone was ready.

Poppy took a deep breath.

'Okay, my dears. I shall now go inside and instruct the organist to start playing.' There were a few giggles then for as was usual, Reverend Fisher uttered his words with immense drama. 'As soon as you hear the Wedding March, the ushers will open the church doors and you should begin walking down the aisle.' He scuttled inside, ensuring everyone was in position.

Poppy's heart thudded madly and her stomach was doing all sorts; she just prayed she wasn't going to be sick again.

*

He looked over his shoulder as soon as he heard the church door open to see Reverend Fisher come into view. *This is it.* Anthony smiled and patted his arm reassuringly, then they both leaned forward as Reverend Fisher bent down to whisper to them, 'She's here. Looks completely stunning too,' before giving Richard a huge thumbs-up. Anthony stifled a laugh while Richard just looked on in amazement, muttering under his breath, *'Just get on with it.'*

'Dearly beloved,' Reverend Fisher began, ever dramatic; he was going to enjoy every second of this wedding and make the most of his part in it too. 'We are now ready to receive the bridal party. Would everyone please stand?' A ripple of laughter went around the congregation as they watched him give another thumbs-up sign, this time to the organist.

Richard and Anthony stood up. They both kept looking over their shoulders and they both gasped when she came into view. Richard could see she was nervous and, when she finally came and stood next to him, he grasped her shaking hand comfortingly in his.

He wanted to hold her and kiss her, but he knew he couldn't just at that moment so instead he mouthed, 'I love you', which made her smile.

Reverend Fisher conducted the marriage ceremony perfectly. Whilst sticking to the tradition of the marriage service, he made space for a brief sermon where he spoke of how the two of them had overcome difficulties in their individual lives and were now coming together as a family, in more ways than one.

There wasn't a dry eye in the house as they exchanged their marriage vows and when Reverend Fisher pronounced them man and wife, the congregation cheered and clapped, and Richard finally got to do what he had long been waiting for – kiss his wife.

*

'Richard, Poppy, many congratulations. I hope you'll be very happy together.'

Richard shook Dr. Anderson's proffered hand. 'Thanks Jon, it's great to see you.'

The speeches had just finished and their guests were moving into the bar area so the room could be refreshed, ready for the evening's festivities.

'Any plans for a honeymoon?'

Poppy smiled excitedly; it had been years since she'd been abroad.

'We're off to St Lucia for two weeks,' Richard enthused.

'Lovely. You'll really enjoy it, believe me. We were there just last year actually, such a beautiful place; it'll do you good, Poppy – you do look a bit peaky.'

She looked up, grinning from ear to ear, which didn't go unnoticed by her husband. He looked from her back to Dr. Anderson, who was now looking back at Poppy, an expectant eyebrow raised.

'Actually, I've been meaning to call you; I was hoping to see you just before we leave, only, I've not been feeling too well over the past few weeks. I'm getting this awful sickness and I keep experiencing dizzy spells.' Her grin widened. 'I don't suppose you know what it could be?'

THE END

ABOUT THE AUTHOR

Tina-Marie Miller is a UK based author and writer of women's fiction. Having previously enjoyed a successful career working for a number of blue chip organisations based in London and the Home Counties, Tina-Marie now lives in a small village in South Cornwall where she spends her time reading, writing, meditating and walking along the idyllic Cornwall coasts.

She enjoys nothing more than curling up with a good book and a cup of tea (or a glass of red!), and losing herself in tales of love, life and laughter.

For more information please visit www.tinamariemiller.co.uk or connect with her on social media:

https://www.facebook.com/tinseymiller

https://twitter.com/tinseymiller

NEW RELEASE

Available Now

THE CURIOUS MISS FORTUNE

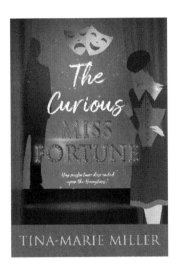

Welcome back to the Hamptons! This is the second book in the series where we meet a number of new characters as well as keeping up to date with some of the favourites we got to know in Book 1.

There's great excitement as the Hampton Players gather to begin rehearsals on their annual am dram. However, it's not long before the cast begin to make a connection between the fictional storylines and coincidental occurrences in their villages leaving them fearful that a murder is about to take place!

Tiggy Lawrence is devastated to learn her father is terminally ill. As she returns to the family home after a nine year absence she's fearful of a run in not just with step monster Bobbie but also ex fiancé Patrick.

Aster Maxwell is a successful maxillofacial surgeon who is hungry for success. Desperate to maximise his specialisation by opening his own private clinic, will he stop at nothing to get what he wants?

Diana Fortune's forgotten past could be her strength when she auditions for the Hampton Players. Only it's a dark and stormy night as she makes her entrance. Has Miss Fortune finally arrived?

Drama finds itself back in the Hamptons as Poppy and Richard Hambly-Jones make an appearance as they prepare to host the annual Autumn Ball. Expect the unexpected!

Enjoyed this story?

Please visit my author page and leave a review

www.amazon.co.uk